August Moon and the Gold-Laced Secret

M.P. Heller

In Bloom Press

Published by In Bloom Press in the United States of America

To contact the author or publisher, please email at:

mpheller@inbloompress.com

info@inbloompress.com

Paperback edition:

ISBN-13: 978-1-957016-02-3

ISBN: 1-957016-02-7

www.inbloompress.com

Contents

Dedication   V

1. One   1

2. Two   16

3. Three   25

4. Four   38

5. Five   46

6. Six   52

7. Seven   68

8. Eight   77

9. Nine   93

10. Ten   97

11. Eleven   112

12. Twelve   122

13. Thirteen   132

14. Fourteen   144

15. Fifteen   157

16. Sixteen   166

17. Seventeen   174

18. Eighteen   189

19. Nineteen   198

20. Twenty   208

21. Twenty-One   214

22. Twenty-Two   220

23. Twenty-Three   233

24. Twenty-Four   246

25. Twenty-Five   250

Acknowledgments   258

About Author   260

Alternate Ending   261

Dedication

To Alec Landon
My best friend
♥

ONE

The days leading up to summer are ones for the biggest, grandest ideas. The taste of freedom looms with a tantalizing closeness that makes it nearly impossible not to scheme for the summer of a lifetime. This desire is mischievous, borderline chaotic, like you'd do anything for a little adventure. For me, my big, grand plans usually fade after the first day by the pool and its subsequent sunburn.

Now, though, I'm seventeen and wrapping up my junior year. The seniors are leaving. Their freedom is real. Mine, not so much. Watching them finally reach that place of liberation from school and legal childhood caused something to stir in me. Time was dwindling, and I needed to do something about it. It was almost an itch. Like I needed to seize *something*, anything. After yet another full year of dedicated studies, shouldn't I seize *some* opportunity?

During the last minutes of the school year, I gazed on at the seniors scattered in the hall. There was a certain lightness about them. The burdening weight of twelve years of public school education had actually lifted. The smiles were easy. The shoulders were upright. The conversations were sprinkled with relief.

While many look forward to summer, part of me did kind of dread it. I have no car, no siblings, and my parents often work more than full time, leaving me rather isolated in our rural home. It also made a lot of my grand plans entirely unattainable, and any opportunities to seize the day nearly impossible. How can you take your summer by the horns if you're stuck at home all day?

As I traversed through the growing crowd of students emptying their backpacks and lockers, I didn't know how to feel. I was caught in between a desire to grow up and prove myself to the great big world, and also a fear of that very thing.

Thankfully, a distraction saved me from tumbling down the rabbit hole of late high school existentialism. A flurry of binder paper shot into air like fireworks and fell to the ground onto the big "S" in the middle of the hall. It was a moment premature, since the bell rang *after* the cast of papers erupted into the air, but it was a joyous occasion nonetheless.

"Ooow!" a guy in a Wolves letterman jacket howled, meeting a fellow student with a loud high five. He flexed like he had just won a boxing match. I recognized him as a senior, obviously celebrating the final bell of his high school career.

"Is it summer or is it summer?" My best friend thudded against the lockers next to mine. She is my saving grace every day, but especially in the summer when I need the company the most. As I fiddled with my lock, she slumped. "Seriously, August? I trekked all the way here from the English building, and you *still* don't have all of your stuff together?"

"Sorry, I was busy." *And distracted.* Knowing me since preschool, Isabell Trudeau saw through my meaningless apology in a heartbeat. It became especially obvious when I turned to look down the hallway, just as Landon Jones rounded the corner at the opposite end.

"Mm-hmm," Isabell clicked her lips. "That's what I thought. You were with him in the stairwell, weren't you?"

"Izzie," I whisper-yelled, knowing my face was turning red. As a matter of fact, I had not been with Landon in the stairwell prior to the bell ringing. I did not care for her insinuation, and wished she would not make such vocal assumptions about this forever-doomed-crush of mine.

"Relax, I'm just teasing." Isabell laughed, running a hand through her blond waves to free the back of her neck. "For crying out loud, it's only June 9th and it's already 105 degrees out. Why, Redding? Why do you insist on scorching us with your heat?" She addressed the town with her arms extending up to the skies before facing me head on. "Are you almost done? I need A/C."

"One second," I told her while grabbing the last of my belongings. My head was stuffed in my locker when Isabell cleared her throat. Startled, I jumped. Standing beside my locker was none other than Landon Jones.

Tall, dark, handsome.

"Oh, Landon, hi."

"Hey Auger. Isabell." He nodded in her direction. "My ride's about to dip, but before I go, I wanted to make my case one last time. Come to Tyler's tonight."

There was no time for me to deny this offer. Isabell interjected and beat me to the punch. The mention of her own object of infatuation sparked her immediate response. "What's at Tyler's?"

"A party," he said, smiling a bit devilishly. "A grad party. August here refuses to attend, but with your help, we can get her on board."

"Why not, Auggie?"

"Yeah, why not?" Landon's grin only grew with Isabell's support.

I resisted a gruff groan. "I just . . ."

"Landon, let's go!" a male voice hollered from down the hall.

"That's me. I'll see you tonight."

I opened my mouth to contradict him, but snapped it shut in annoyance. There was no point now. He wouldn't hear even if he wanted to, over the celebrations and chaos. Isabell snickered beside me, but her laughter soon faded. "Oh no. HBIC. Incoming."

She was pointing subtly in Landon's direction. He was with a crew of a few friends, ready to take off, when a girl approached him.

Stacey Higgins. Or as Isabell calls her, HBIC: Head Bitch in Charge.

She's not exactly known for her kind and bubbly nature, but for striking fear in the hearts of all she passes. With her ripped shorts and black tank top, she swayed right over to Landon and put her hand on his back. Classic HBIC move: touchy-feely with whoever she pleases. I didn't really mind when it was anyone else. But when she flirted with Landon, it ground my gears.

"Ugh." Isabell frowned at Stacey and Landon before grabbing my elbow. "Let's go, this is gross." Once she dragged me down the hall and outside, I let out a dragon breath in the heat. It was the type of weather that makes you wish it were possible to melt into a puddle and seep into the pores of the earth.

After climbing into Isabell's car, I cried out, "Cool air, blast me please!"

Isabell grabbed my shoulders before turning on the car. "We are going to that party tonight, August."

I fanned myself dramatically. "Is this some kind of torture?"

"Landon clearly likes you. I maintain he has ever since science class last year. The will-they-or-won't-they thing you guys have going is just mind-boggling. Let's just clear it up once and for all: obviously he likes you, and you still like him. The party is the best way to get things rolling!"

"Izzie," I warned. She was treading in dangerous waters. I've already spent the last two years swooning over Landon, rather embarrassingly, might I add. And nothing had happened to date. I was simply the girl who helped him with his homework, that's all. It hardly mattered at this precise moment, as I drowned in my sweat on Isabell's black leather interior.

"Auggie! Aside from the Landon thing, we are seniors now, officially. Let's celebrate."

"We don't party," I said through my sweat mustache.

"So? There's a first for everything. Tonight is our night."

"But—"

"No buts! You always talk about seizing things, now is your chance. I will not turn on this car until you agree to go tonight." Isabell's steely blue eyes were determined, and a little frightening. I was baffled, and dripping with salty excretion, so I consented.

"If it means you'll turn on the freaking air conditioner, then fine, we can go."

Isabell cheered, shifting gears to excitement and forgetting that I was forced into this endeavor. I spent the entire school year avoiding all these people. Why would I go to a party with them right after school was out? Reluctant as I was, maybe this was just what I needed to get my summer off on the right foot.

As soon as she turned the key, I beat her hand to the controllers and cranked up the air to high, lifting my arms to dry off my wet armpits. "You are such a dork." Isabell laughed, though she was also facing her armpits to the fan.

"At least I'm not alone," I retorted as she put the car in reverse and backed us out.

The Shasta High School parking lot was flooded with cars and students, all making plans for summer and saying their goodbyes. Some were swapping yearbooks for the signatures they had been too shy to ask for, or too lazy to get done. Just as we were about to exit the lot, Landon came into our view once again and he was still walking with HBIC.

I frowned, festering at the sight of them together. They were so engrossed in their dumb little world that they failed to notice they passed right in front of where our car was waiting to exit.

HOOOOOOOONK!

Isabell startled even me when she laid on the horn. I was about to snap about the lack of warning she gave me, but then I caught a glance of Landon and HBIC's faces. Then turning to Isabell, we busted up laughing into one of those deep belly laughter fits, while Landon and Stacey shuffled out of the way in alarm. Landon at least seemed like he thought it was funny, and I could hear him outside yelling at us.

"I'll get you back for that one!"

That was our signal to get a move on, and we sped out of the lot. I stole a final peek at Landon Jones. He was still shaking his head, looking on at us.

Facing the front, Isabell was the one who spoke up. "Alright, Auggie. Tonight. Tonight is *our* night."

Little did I know, this night would be the one to spur the wildest, most topsy-turvy Northern California summer of my entire life.

And it was just getting started.

"This was a huge mistake. Let's turn around and head back to your place. We can watch all the casino heist movies we can keep our eyes open for? That sounds much better. With some popcorn and—"

"August," Isabell cut me off. "You're fine. You look hot. This is going to be fun! Just relax."

I sighed down at my outfit. Since we spent all afternoon at her house, lounging by the pool with our pink lemonade, Isabell had let me borrow some of her clothes. 'Let' is a strong word. She had been insistent on picking out clothes for me, and what she chose was not exactly my style.

The outfit was a pink t-shirt dress, which fell several inches above my knees. Pink is not really my color of choice aside from lemonade, but Isabell can be cunning in her persuasion. She wove my dark brown hair into two long braids, and I had reluctantly compromised to let her put the smallest touch of mascara on me.

"Turn left here, Brett," Isabell instructed her older brother. He was twenty-two, and visiting for the week from Seattle. Since he was meeting friends tonight, he agreed to drive and pick us up later. Tyler's house was only a few minutes down the road from Isabell's, anyway.

We all lived on the outskirts of Redding, where everything outside of town felt like the boonies. Folks lived on decent plots of land, surrounded by oak and pine trees. Great for privacy, and even better for parties when your parents are out of town, which Tyler's were for the night.

"Izzie, it is a mistake. There's going to be so many people here and —"

"Stop here. Thanks, Brett!"

"Call me when you need a ride back and be sure to keep an eye out on your drinks. Equally important, make sure you keep an eye out for each other and call me if—"

"We're fine, I promise," Isabell insisted. Brett opened his mouth to continue, but she intuitively answered for him. "Yes, yes, I heard you before. Don't you think you'll be the one I call if things go south? It won't be mom and dad," she tsked him as she applied more lip gloss. She had this natural way about her, where she could make anything seem effortless. I envied it in times like these when I was overcome with social dread.

"Be safe," Brett cautioned in his parting words.

"Izzie," I whispered as I rushed to her side of the car. We were walking up the driveway to Tyler's house, and my stress was only building. Isabell flipped her blond hair to reveal the spaghetti strap of her hot pink tank top, which was tucked into her black-belted jean skirt in a look she called "very Britney." As always, she was breezily beautiful.

"Izzie," I started again. "What am I supposed to do here? I don't want to talk to all these people."

"Mm-hmm," she hummed. "You just want to talk to Landon."

"Everyone here knows you, and you'll float around from person to person while I follow you like a little lost puppy."

She tossed her arm around my shoulder and laughed. "Oh, silly! That's not true. You're my best friend. We are a package deal. You know all these people, too." When I groaned, she stopped.

"Look, if you are hating the social atmosphere, you just feign illness and get Landon to take you outside for some fresh air. Then you get him alone, and you get to be away from people. Besides, this is the very last time you'll have to deal with all these people until senior year starts. Think of it like that."

"Alright, fine. That helps a little," I mumbled, knowing I didn't have much of a choice as we walked up to the front door of the house. It was a pretty classic home for the area: built of wood, a shade of light blue, two stories. All the lights were on, illuminating the high-vaulted ceilings. A few cars filed in behind us, and the house appeared to be already full of people and a bumping bass.

The moment we entered, that place was chaos. It was only nine at night, and it had still erupted into a full-blown party. Truthfully, I hadn't realized that these types of parties actually existed outside of the movie world. One senior—everyone calls him Nuke—yelled something from the top of the coffee table. He proceeded to lift two red solo cups to his mouth at once, chugging and then smashing them both on his forehead.

Yeah. I'm out of my element here. I sure wish I had worn close-toed shoes instead of my flip-flops. Now my toes will be sticky.

"Hey! You guys made it," a warm voice greeted. It was Tyler, in his khaki shorts and a blue Santa Cruz t-shirt. He was smiling, the beaming one that earned him Best Smile in the yearbook.

"Hi Tyler," Isabell grinned, her cheeks faintly red. "Did we miss anything?"

There was a scream from behind him, and we turned to see Nuke pounding back another solo cup. Tyler laughed and gestured with his thumb. "That sums it up. Come on in. I'll show you guys where the drinks are."

Thankfully, Isabell linked arms with me as we weaved through the house. The farther we went, I worried we were entering layers of hell that would be inescapable. Tyler was so soft-spoken and sweet, it surprised me he could throw a party this crazy.

A moment later, Tyler's best friend flew into the kitchen, tying my stomach in a small web of knots. It was Landon, diving for a hacky-sack like his life depended on it.

Tyler shook his head and chuckled. "I don't know what I'm going to do with that guy." Landon was oblivious to where the three of us stood in the kitchen, and jumped right back in to the other room. "Can I get you guys a drink?"

Isabell and I looked at each other for confirmation. Our experimentation with alcohol had been very limited so far. Isabell drank at a party before, but this was a first for me. As we had a mini-conversation with our eyes, Isabell whispered, "It might take off the nerves." Right then, Landon whooshed back through the room with a group of people, including Stacey. It was the push I needed to accept Tyler's offer.

"Sure," we said in unison.

"Coming right up!" he said, and a half minute later, we both had a can of beer in our hands.

"Ty! Where you at?" Of course, it was Landon, calling out from beyond a small crowd. He emerged with Stacey, but came to a halt when he saw me and Isabell. "Oh, August. You made it!"

"By some miracle," was all I could retort.

Tyler nodded, "What's up, Lanno?"

I seized my moment to pull Isabell away, and we retreated from the kitchen. Once we were out of both view and earshot, I shuddered. "Why am I even here?"

"Stop that! We are here to have a good time. Who cares about the boys? Landon seemed excited to see you, I thought."

I noted she used a plural, to refer to Tyler as well, but decided not to comment on it. If I didn't interrogate her, she wouldn't interrogate me.

"Agreed! Agreed." I nodded. Panning around the room, and taking in all the chaos, I was ready to resign for the night. Since I'm here, I might as well stop fighting the party. "Maybe we should drink these really quick and grab another one.

My best friend approved, and we drank our cups as fast as we could. It didn't taste as bad as I expected—it was kind of watery.

"Not bad." I shrugged. "Not great, but not bad."

Isabell coughed. "That was *terrible!* What are you talking about?"

I wrinkled my nose, thinking I wasn't a huge fan of the aftertaste. Despite not liking it that much, we went back for round two. Entering the kitchen, Landon and Tyler were nowhere to be seen, so we helped ourselves to another can from the cooler. Once we cracked open, we clinked them together.

"Cheers." I raised my can and took a sip, fighting off a frown.

"Bleh," Isabell shuddered. "Do you want to step outside?"

"Definitely."

We wandered on to the back deck. From there, I heard *his* voice. Moderately loud, but smooth like velvet, Landon's was easily recognizable. It could charm a legion of loyal followers, I was sure of it. As we joined the small mob around the fire pit, it was clear he had done just that.

"Landon, tell us the story of the Ruggles brothers!" someone yelled, and the crowd egged him on.

"Come on, you guys. I just told it a few months ago!" Landon teased.

"Not *everyone* heard it. What's the point of this campfire if we don't have any stories?" someone else chimed in.

"Alright, alright. I'll tell you." Landon raised his hands as if surrendering, and the group crowded closer. Isabell and I exchanged a confused look and slowly approached circle.

"Once upon a time," Landon joked, and a few people chortled. "This story takes place in the lawless, wild, wild, west. You know, the dirt beneath our feet. Seriously, it was just a few miles down the road from here. All over a little gold . . ."

My attention was fixated on Landon. I tried to shake off the feeling, figuring it was just me. Then I looked around, and noticed that everyone was equally entranced. When the guy spoke, people hung on his every word. It was a little maddening, especially the way Stacey was smiling coyly at him from a few seats away.

Tyler approached, standing next to me and Isabell. Then his face lit up in recognition. "Ah, the Ruggles brothers story?"

"Yep," Isabell confirmed.

"You've probably heard this one, August. Either from Landon or your dad. Have you heard it, Izzie?"

"I've heard it enough to know it gets more dramatic each time." Isabell rolled her eyes, making Tyler laugh.

"Amen."

"Hey, Ty, is it okay that we grabbed another beer?"

"Of course! Help yourself. I usually keep one in my pocket for easy drinking," he joked. "But I finished my back up. I was just going to get another."

"I'll come with," Isabell invited herself, and Tyler accepted her offer.

For a moment, I dreaded she would leave me alone out here. But she grabbed my arm and tugged me along behind her. With a final look back at Landon, I sighed, figuring it was better to let him be with his adoring fans. I hated feeling like I was just another person looking on and admiring him. So stupid.

The group laughed at something he said, and I fought another urge to steal a peek at him.

"So anyway, a few days later, another stagecoach breaks around the corner. Along with it, the worst kind of trouble they could find themselves in ..."

Once we broke away from the crowd that was huddled around Landon, I was ready to put him out of my mind. It was foolish to hold on to any hope with my dumb crush. He was graduating tomorrow anyway. Of course, Isabell was not ready to put the topic to rest. She *had* to dig a little deeper.

"Tyler, what's the situation with Landon?" Isabell asked.

He chuckled. "The situation?"

"Isabell," I snapped at her.

"Relax, it has nothing to do with you!" She waved me off. It was a blatant lie, as she then cupped her hand over Tyler's ear to whisper to him. I rolled my eyes and pretended it wasn't happening.

"He's definitely not with Stacey, nor does he want to be," Tyler said loud enough for me to hear. I cringed, and then groaned before passing by them into the kitchen. I wanted another drink, even though I still had half of my second beer left. Well, what I *really* wanted was to go home, but my annoyance began to push me toward rebellion. Against what, I don't know.

With impeccable timing, Nuke grabbed me by the elbow and said, "August! We need a fourth to take a shot with us. Come on!"

What else was there to do? I seized my shot. Probably not my best move. It was the first one offered to me in my life.

The shot hurt way more than the beer. It burned my throat and sent me in to a coughing fit, like I was a tuberculosis patient on my last leg. Isabell and Tyler found me, probably by following the sound of my heinous hacks.

Turning to face them, my flip-flop caught on something on the floor and I tumbled down.

"Auggie," Isabell said as she rushed to help me up.

"You good?" Tyler asked as Isabell pulled a few pieces of confetti out of my hair.

"It's chaos in here," I told them, flailing my arms wildly.

"Yeah, geez. Let's go back outside." Isabell looped her arm with mine.

"I'll grab the beers and meet you out there," Tyler told us. We shoved through the crowd to the back door, a cool evening breeze drying the sweat on my face. Trekking across the back lawn, we rejoined the circle by the fire.

"So they hung the Ruggles brothers in the middle of town: a physical warning to robbers and looters that we don't take too kindly to that around here. Nothing really happened after that, either, proof that California was truly the wild, wild west."

"What happened to the gold? I thought you said that John hid it?" someone asked from the group.

I resisted an eye roll. Of *course*, everyone was even more enthralled with his story.

"Ah, a keen ear." Landon nearly smirked. "That's just the thing. It's been 120 years, and the gold still hasn't been found. Rumor has it that John offered to disclose the treasure to save his brother, but others say that he spit on the shoes of the mob men when they demanded he lead them to the treasure. And that, my friends, is the tale of the Ruggles brothers."

A few people applauded, and I crossed my arms as Stacey stood up from her seat and sat herself on Landon's lap. He shifted, and perhaps it was my imagination, but he looked like he was trying not to touch her. And, dare I say, he was frowning just a smidge. Refusing to appear frustrated, I uncrossed my arms and held my head up, despite how it was spinning a wee bit now from the shot and the beer.

"Desperate." Isabell coughed under her breath so only I could hear.

"Whatever," I tried to brush off casually. In hindsight, there was absolutely nothing casual about the way I downed the last half of my beer. Isabell looked at me with eyes about to bulge out of her head, while Tyler thought nothing of it. In response, he handed me a new can.

"August," Isabell started in shock, covering her mouth as she giggled. "You are a rebel on a mission, aren't you?" Ever since we were kids, whenever we got annoyed, that was our phrase. We were never the type to get in any real trouble, but we would act out in these small ways or make believe that we were bank robbers. On our good days, we pretended to be CIA agents.

"Don't you know it," I grinned. "We are going to rob some banks tonight."

"What?" Tyler asked, blinking back and forth between us. I could hardly blame his confusion. Isabell and I have enough inside jokes to last a dozen people a lifetime.

"It means, we drink!" Isabell cried, raising her cup dramatically to the sky before chugging it herself. I watched on like you do when your favorite player steals the ball and drives it down court for an uncontested slam dunk. She finished the cup and we high-fived, laughing.

I stole a glance at Landon, and my stomach about ate itself when I saw him staring right back at me. Was it really as intense of a look as it felt? Even from twenty feet away, I swore the fire illuminated his eyes. They were blazing gold. I turned back to Isabell and Tyler, fighting Landon's pull. *Trust* me, it was harder than it sounds.

Only a moment later, he walked up behind me. "Hey, Auger. You like the story?" he asked with a beer in hand.

"Loved it. So was it ounces or hundreds of pounds of gold that they stole this time?"

Tyler snickered alongside Isabell. Landon played along and raised his eyebrows all-knowingly. "It was actually hundreds of thousands of pounds. Check your facts."

"Don't you know who you're talking to? August is a history fiend," Isabell smirked.

"Ah, yes. The information mogul. Tell me then, August, where do you think the treasure is?"

"Well, obviously it's in the north state," I said with a hiccup.

"*Obviously*," Landon mocked, his voice dancing around me.

"He supposedly attached it to some type of floatie in Middle Creek, but when the cops went to check, it wasn't there. My theory is that it didn't get too far. It either *sank* because he had a shoddy floatie, or he *stashed* it in the hills," I reasoned. My voice moved at twice its normal speed, but I couldn't stop it.

"Floatie," Isabell muttered with another giggle.

Landon tilted his chin up, challenging me. "Why wouldn't he have taken it with him? They found him closer to Sacramento."

With all the buzz hitting my brain, I was too easily baited by his provoking. "True," I shrugged, "but if the stagecoach got away, he would have had a limited time to flee before the cops were on his heels. Shedding the weight of the treasure let him be faster on foot, so he could escape with more ease. Plus, it's a little suspicious to be carting around a fat old chest. It wasn't long until the authorities came and grabbed Charles. John knew you can't return for your precious hidden treasure if you're in jail." As I spoke, I was aware of my raising volume, but I was just getting started.

Isabell snorted a horse-like sound, snapping me out of my history mode. Did I even breathe at all while I was talking? I was vaguely aware of my panting—and Landon's eyes watching me—and grew a bit nervous. To keep in on his toes, I flashed him the smallest of glares.

He was clearly amused, pointing at himself and looking over his shoulder.

"Stop that." I laughed, giving him a mini shove, which caused him to drop his beer. "Oops," I mumbled awkwardly, having committed the biggest party foul. Even in this intoxicated state, -I dreaded the social retribution.

Landon's expression didn't change. He instead pulled out a flask from his back pocket. "It's okay, Auger. It wasn't the liquid gold," he said as he tapped the side of his metal bottle.

"What's in it?" Isabell asked this time.

"Whiskey. Jack Daniels."

With that, he took a swig and held it out to her. "Want some?"

Generously, he let it pass around the four of us. When the flask got to me, I paused and smelled it. Landon coughed to cover a laugh.

"Bottoms up, Auger," he said with a smirk.

I took a good long sip, just like the others had. After, I stared directly into Landon's golden-brown eyes and was all too quickly absorbed. My head was fuzzy, and I worried I might just say or do something of the utmost humiliation. How do I get out of these eyes, again?

"Cheers," I tried for.

After that, the night became a blur.

Two

If I wake to the sound of birds chirping, or an acorn woodpecker knocking on the trees outside my window, I know it'll be a lovely day. When the early light softly illuminates my bedroom through the white cotton curtains, it puts me in a great mood. As a little kid, it made me feel like Cinderella or Snow White.

Today, however, was not one of those beautiful mornings.

The sound of Isabell puking in her adjoined bathroom pulled me out of sleep, reminding me I was not in my own bed, or my own house for that matter. Instead, my head was at the foot of Isabell's bed, which we had shared the night before.

I squinted my eyes back shut, cursing the open blinds in her room. It's like waking up from a coma with the doctor shining their flashlight straight into your pupils. Not that I know what that's like, exactly, but I can imagine.

The toilet flushed and soon after, Isabell trudged back into her room and slowly lowered herself to the bed. She sat up at the head of the bed, and I took special note of the rather frightening tangles in her hair.

"We are honest with each other, no matter what, right?" I asked her, my voice hoarse. She grunted and nodded in agreement. "Then I'm safe telling you, you look like crap, Izzie."

That earned me a squinted look, which I thought was a feeble attempt at a glare, but she followed it up with some strained laughter. "You don't look any better."

"You sounded awful, too. Are you okay?"

"Oh, yeah. Just wait until you move, Auggie. The second I did, I disrupted the force of my insides and I was punished for my deeds."

That was enough to convince me to stay put and shut up. She was right, too. We spent the better part of the morning in a state of complete disarray. I'll spare the details, and just say that we kept the bathroom fan perpetually on.

"Thank heavens you have your own bathroom and your parents' room and kitchen are both downstairs. No one has to know. I swear, Izzie, I'm never drinking that much ever again. I may never even *drink* again."

At that moment, there was a knock on the bedroom door. Isabell cleared her throat to rid of her croak and asked who it was.

"Brett. Can I come in for a second?" We allowed it, and he came in with a six pack of lemon-lime Gatorade and two plates of plain toast with butter. "Since you're both on death row, figured I'd share a couple tricks of the trade to remedy a hangover. Electrolytes. This is key. Alcohol dehydrates you, so next time make sure you're drinking a lot of water or at least have a few Gatorades on standby."

He handed us each a bottle, and we were eager to sip any elixir that would cure us.

"And, toast. Mild. Not likely to stir up a visceral reaction. Avoid foods or drinks with acidity, like orange juice or tomatoes. Bananas can be good. Just don't avoid eating. Find a way to snack. That sound good?"

Brett passed over the plates, and my stomach growled like an echo in an empty pit.

"Thanks, Brett," we chorused together. He laughed at our unison and assured we'd be better soon, before heading out the door.

We let the electrolytes and toast marinate for another hour before deeming ourselves officially recovered. Well, recovered enough to function outside of a zombie state of mind. It was after eleven in the morning when Isabell suggested we go to Comfort Zone, my mom's bakery. To avoid the appearance of mischief—and the smell—Isabell let me use her shower and borrow another set of clothes as we prepped to head to town.

It only took us about fifteen minutes to drive to Comfort Zone downtown. During that time, we re-hashed some of the main events of the party.

"So, what ended up happening with you and Landon last night?"

"Nothing." I shrugged in a half-assed attempt at indifference.

"Oh please! You guys were drawn like a moth to a flame, and he couldn't keep his eyes off you. Are you seriously telling me nothing happened?"

"I don't know what you want me to say, Izzie. We hung out a bit, sure, but that was it. Stacey was there, remember?"

"That's basically irrelevant, HBIC was trying to catch his attention, but he was already caught in a different trap, my friend."

There wasn't much I wanted to say to that. Any admission of truth would be an admission of guilt for maybe liking Landon in the tiniest possible way, which I was determined to avoid saying out loud.

We also talked about Tyler, and how grown up he seemed hosting the party without his parents there. I was certain her decade-long crush was very much in full swing, but made no move to suggest it. It'd just open me up for cross-examination. Plus, we had arrived at Comfort Zone.

Mom opened this place up a few years before I was born. For a while, she was a baker at various spots around town. When she noticed this corner store for lease, she decided just to go for it and try running her own business. She kind of jumped in head first, but somehow made it a success. Walking in the doors, a blind dog could understand why it's done so well.

The vibe of this place is extremely on brand. Growing up, I spent a lot of time here in lieu of summer daycare. The green sofa in the corner is where I would read my books while Mom worked, in between sneaking samples of all the different cookie doughs and ogling through the glass at the massive display case of baked goods. For me, it was home, and I felt safe here. Only in the last year have I realized it was Mom's intent all along: for people to have a place to relax, enjoy tasty food, and unwind with friends.

Isabell and I only made this discovery about nine months ago when I mentioned we go camping before junior year started.

"That's way out of my comfort zone," she had responded then with a snicker. Then she added, "hm."

I asked what she was thinking about, and she explained with a shy smile and a scrunched up nose. "Don't make fun of me, because this is really dumb. But your mom's bakery is called Comfort Zone. Is that a play on the phrase?"

"Huh." I usually thought of it as Mom's shop, not as Comfort Zone.

That night, I had asked Mom why she chose that name for the shop. "Oh," she had first responded, but then she used her hands as she spoke, like she was conducting an orchestra. "I had this vision of a lovely, quaint little bakery, or café, or what have you, that reminds people of a cozy place. Not too stimulating, not too fancy, with all the personable fixings of home."

Her vision was executed perfectly, and I felt relaxed by the atmosphere even in my hungover state. The pastel blue painted wall of picture frames to the left greeted us as we stepped sluggishly through the threshold in our sunglasses. As soon as the bell chimed, my mother was quick to charge over and give us each her signature big, tight, warm hug.

"Good morning you two! Or, I guess I should say afternoon. I haven't seen you since the school year ended yesterday, you're both seniors now! Ahh!"

Isabell beamed, and sighed dreamily. "Thanks, Jeanie, I still can't quite believe it."

"Your mother and I were just talking about our two babies growing up too fast for our liking," Mom said as she shook her head. She has been best friends with Isabell's mom, Tracey, since high school. When they found out they were pregnant with girls at the same time, they were over the moon—hence why Isabell and I are practically sisters.

"Well come on in and grab a seat at the bar, I'll make you girls whatever you'd like!" As if we were five years old, we darted to the seats with a wild eagerness, all traces of a hangover gone now. Mom ducked into the back to grab a few goodies while Isabell and I slunk into our seats.

"Did you do anything fun last night? Tell me about it!" Mom asked as she returned to the counter.

It was virtually pointless to hide that we had gone to a party. Something in the way she asked hinted that she already knew. Besides, Jeanie Moon was not known for her strict rules or harshness. I had little to fear.

"We went to Tyler's for a celebration of the seniors, it was cool."

"Auggie got in a heated debated with Landon a couple times, that was fun for me to watch."

"I did?" I asked, confused.

"Over the Ruggles treasure, remember?"

"I remember talking about it once . . ."

"Yes, that's true, but you also argued over it two other times. Whether the treasure was swept up into the Sac River, or stashed in the mountains, or if they even looted the treasure at all, and so it goes."

"The Ruggles brothers, huh?" Mom chimed in. I was grateful she didn't press more about Landon.

"You know about the treasure, too?"

"Know about it?" Mom laughed lightly. "Of course. Your father is big on the Ruggles Treasure."

"Guess that's no surprise, since he's a park ranger out at the lake. Don't you have to love history or something for that job?" Isabell clarified.

"He knows a lot, that's for sure. You should talk to him about it."

I made a mental note to ask him about the treasure as she served up two bagel breakfast sandwiches, each of us receiving a differently painted plate. After eating, we didn't stick around much longer.

As we got in the car, I grinned at my best friend. "Isabell. I have an idea for what we should do next."

With my directions, Isabell drove us to a trailhead in Old Shasta. A sign that said "Middle Creek Trail" greeted us as we hopped out of the car.

"Really? You want to go looking for the treasure right now?" Isabell mumbled.

"I don't know, aren't you interested at all?" When Isabell hesitated, I offered a compromise. "Do you want to just walk then, no treasure hunt? This trail leads down to the Sac River."

"I guess that's agreeable enough. We can bring another Gatorade."

As we started to walk, it was quickly clear that we hadn't thought this through. The first big heatwave of the summer was underway, and we were walking close to peak heat of the day on a paved path. Thankfully it was a bit shaded, but we were panting up a storm.

"At least we are sweating out the alcohol toxins," I offered.

"This is brutal. I'm not in that great of shape, unlike you and your cross country running, my golf game is mild."

"It's fine, Izzie. We can take a break and put our feet in the creek."

"True. Listen, it's our last summer together before our final year of high school. What are we going to do this summer, Auggie?"

"I feel like we need to do something big. A grand adventure."

"Ah, yes, zee grand adventure," Isabell deepened her voice to speak like a wise French man.

I laughed. "Seriously! I don't know, but this feels like the last year we can get away with things. Shouldn't we take that opportunity while we can?"

"You make a good point."

We walked for about an hour, maybe. Strolling along, we hardly passed a soul, save for a couple of cyclists. We were brainstorming all the different things we could do together. From kayaking down the river, to climbing Mount Lassen, to road-tripping to the Grand Canyon or to Vegas. The ideas grew more outrageous and more out of reach for two seventeen-year-olds, but we were having fun thinking about it.

After a good chuckle, we paused.

"You think we'll really just spend the summer floating in the lake?"

"Seems likely."

"I'm pretty okay with that."

As we turned the corner, we came face to face with two goons we didn't expect to see on this trail, during one of the hottest hours of the day.

"Landon?" I said at the same time Isabell asked, "Tyler?"

"Look what the cat dragged in. Meow," Landon teased.

"What are the odds we would run into you guys out here?" Tyler asked unknowingly. Landon and I knew, though. He crossed his arms, almost as if assuming some sort of Alpha stance. I put my hands on my hips.

"You wouldn't be looking for some kind of lost gold, would you?" he asked.

"Not that it's any of your business, but we are taking a nice little walk through the trees."

"An innocent walk? In this heat?"

"I happen to love the feeling of pavement so hot it could melt my shoes."

"Masochist."

I pushed Landon in the shoulder to shut him up.

"Well it's a good thing you guys aren't looking for the treasure. It'd be a waste of time, since we are going to find it soon," Landon said, shrugging like it was no big deal.

"What makes you so sure of that?" Isabell challenged. I resisted a smile. Landon had just provoked her. The two of us are pretty competitive as it is, but he may have just awoken the beast.

"Let's just say I have a bit of experience with local treasure hunts," Landon said. He was vague, but still maintained an aura of arrogance that was hard to distinguish from flirtation.

Isabell hummed and eyed me in her periphery.

Tyler looked between everyone like he had just started a movie halfway through. "Am I missing something here?" No one clued him in, though.

"What experience do you have that gives you an edge, Landon?"

"Hm, good question, August. It's so hard to pick just one thing . . ." He tapped his chin.

I scoffed. "Real convincing. I'll bet we could find that treasure before you easy peasy."

"Bring it on." Landon rose to the challenge, his brown eyes sparkling with a gold shimmer of excitement. "Are we doing this for real?"

"Heck yes, cowboy. Saddle up, it's going to be a ride." The longer we all talked, the easier it became for me to dish it right back to Landon. Isabell elbowed me and shook her head. "What?"

"Maybe we should make this a little more interesting." Apparently caught up on the banter, it was Tyler who was suggesting.

"Explain, Ty," Isabell prodded.

Landon took the reins back over. "A bet! Let's add a little wager, aye?"

"Huddle!" Isabell shouted, wrapped her around my shoulders and pulling me to the side. "What should we bet? That they have to go streaking through an area of our choice?"

"They are eighteen," I whispered. "That's actually against the law."

"Okay, good point, good point."

"Ooh! I've got it," I lowered my voice even quieter to keep it secret, and we went back to meet the boys.

"Name your poison."

"If we win," I started, and Isabell nodded me on. "You guys have to dye your hair a color of our choice for three months."

Landon and Tyler looked at each other, and touched their own luscious locks. Both of them had long hair. Tyler's sandy brown, frizzy hair was nearly to his shoulders, and Landon's black curls were a smidge shorter.

"And you can't cut it before the bet is completed!" Isabell added.

"If we win, you have to shave your eyebrows," Landon quipped.

I frowned in disgust, knowing full well I can't pull off that look thanks to the half-brow crisis of '15, the nightmare of eighth grade.

"That seems worse than the hair. Can we change our answer?" Isabell asked, looking back and forth between me and the guys.

"Sure." Tyler smiled.

"Doesn't bother me. We're going to win, so it won't matter," Landon teased, and Tyler laughed along with him.

Still, looking to a steely-eyed Isabell, a curious Tyler, and a daring Landon, I felt a surge of adrenaline.

"Deal."

"What are the terms of this agreement?" Isabell asked.

"First of all, we can't tell anyone about what we're doing," Landon lowered his voice, even though we were the only ones around.

"Why?"

He ruffled his hair. "Look, it's better like that. Then we don't have to deal with competing with more people."

"Seems reasonable, okay," Isabell agreed.

"Anything else?" We all sat on that for a second, and nothing came up.

"All is fair in love and war?" I extended my hand for him to accept my offer. Landon beamed a slightly crooked smile as he took my hand for a single, firm shake. In a flash, it was gone.

"May the force be with you." Tyler bowed his head graciously.

"And the odds ever in your favor." Isabell curtsied.

Meanwhile, Landon was still looking straight at me. "Let's play ball."

THREE

After parting ways with the boys, the first course of action Isabell and I took was to devise a plan. Something about those two—the current, or former, objects of our affection, or whatever—stirred the pot in our stomachs.

"It's like they think we're chumps. CHUMPS, I tell you," Isabell ranted in the car. "When, really, *they* are the chumps."

"Agreed! I mean, two months ago, everyone thought they were going to ask us to prom. Did that happen?"

"Nope."

"No it did not. We went with other people and were pretty much the last ones asked to go. Obviously, we aren't holding a grudge over that."

"Obviously not."

"But if we were, I would say that they should watch their backs. We are two scorned women on a mission."

When we returned to her car, she has shuffled a playlist. So far, the songs had entirely fit the mood. A loud bass dropped on the speaker, and Isabell smirked at me. With perfect timing, it hit right as we crested the hill into view of our beloved Whiskeytown Lake.

The lake is the quintessential experience for anyone and everyone in the area. Not only is it one of the most accessible swimming holes, but it has hiking and waterfalls galore. There's pretty much something for everyone, whether it's chilling out on the beach or kayaking or wakeboarding from the back of a boat.

Lucky for me, my dad is one of the supervising rangers. He's worked in this park since he was a teenage lifeguard, which was eons ago at this point. What that means, essentially, is I've had unrestricted access to the park my entire life. Secret beaches, rope swings, and hidden trails have been the hallmarks of my childhood.

Dad often takes me hiking with him, and he insists I know the park better than some of the rangers. He refers to me as his "little GPS," claiming he doesn't need a map when I'm around thanks to the photographic memory. I'm not sure exactly how or why I was born with a photographic memory, but it sure makes history class easy.

History. Today, Dad's job is especially handy because he can give me and Isabell a crash course lesson on some local history. Any information could help us beat the boys and keep our eyebrows.

"Hey, Dad!" I greeted as the two of us bounded into the ranger station.

"Hi Daniel."

"Girls, hi! I didn't expect to see you in here today. You're officially seniors now, that's exciting."

He asked about our last finals, and we filled him in. The two tests we took yesterday were our easiest ones, so we had just coasted through the day with summer on the brain.

"Do you have a minute to talk, Dad? We have some questions."

Dad held his hands up in a mock surrender. "What am I under investigation for?"

I rolled my eyes at his feeble joke attempt but still smiled. "Har har, good one."

He grinned and looked around. "Let me put a couple things away really quick and then I'll meet you both out on the wall?"

Isabell gave him a thumbs up on both our behalf, and we stepped outside. The information center is right off the highway, near the eastern corner of the lake. In the parking lot rests an old stone wall, from which there is a view of almost the entire lake, as well as the gorgeous mountains that create the basin for the reservoir. Your line of sight at the lake is filled with trees and water abundant, and on a bright day like this one, the water is a deep turquoise-blue.

"Lots of people are out boating today," Isabell observed.

"First day of summer, guess it makes sense."

"Plenty hot out for it," she commented as she twisted her hair into a bun.

The sound of a loud clap startled us both, and we turned around to see my dad rubbing his hands together. "Alright, girls, what can I do for you?"

"We want to know about the Ruggles brothers," we chimed in unison. Dad chuckled.

"You two sound more and more alike every day. The Ruggles. Good question, you know there's an interpretive sign about them down the Middle Creek Trail?" We hadn't walked that far on the trail today, so we didn't know that. "Well what do you want to know, fact or conspiracy?

"Fact," I said at the same time Isabell said, "Conspiracy." She raised her eyebrows at me and I changed my answer. "Actually, conspiracy sounds like a nice story. Let 'er rip, Dad."

"You both know that the two brothers robbed the stagecoach not too far from here, right?" We did, of course. "And then the older one, John, ran off with the bounty and left his brother for dead. They said it was about $5,000 worth of gold that they stole from the wagon. In today's market, the value of that treasure is probably closer to $100,000."

"Whoa," Isabell blinked.

"For reference, that's anywhere from two to four years of college, depending on where you go. So, there are two debated theories about the Ruggles. First being that John didn't actually toss it into Middle Creek. As a bit of a con man, many folks don't quite buy into the bit that he willingly confessed to where he stashed the treasure."

"Did he think they would get out of jail? Is that why people think he wasn't honest about the location?"

"Potentially. It's hard to speculate. With all the attention the brothers garnered from the town women, you'd think their freedom was a real possibility. Some folks suspect he fancied a lady in town. Some think he took the treasure with him down to Woodland to stow there, maybe with family or friends."

"What's the second theory?"

"Don't laugh at me," Dad paused to point between us, "but some people think that John Ruggles had some kind of supernatural power. That he hexed the treasure, and still guards it today."

Isabell hummed, and I squinted my eyes under my sunglasses. "Magic powers? Really, Dad?"

He shrugged in that all-knowing kind of way. "Just something I've heard."

"Daniel! Can we get your input on the schedule?"

"Sorry, girls. I have to go, we can talk more later. I do love talking treasure! See you at home, August."

"Well butter me up and call me a biscuit," I mimicked my dad and rubbed my hands together.

"We're really in for it, aren't we?"

Shortly after we left the lake, Isabell's mom called to remind her of her afternoon dentist appointment.

"Leave it to my mom to schedule me a dentist appointment on the very first day of summer. How much does that blow?" She was extremely reluctant to go, since we were itching to get after this whole Ruggles thing. There was little she could do about the appointment, and she made me *promise* not to do anything about the treasure hunt without her.

Unfortunately, it was difficult for me to keep that promise. It didn't help that when she dropped me off at the doorstep of my small green home, I was alone and left to my own vices. For the last few weeks, those vices had unfortunately revolved a bit around studying with a certain dark-haired boy. Today was no different, only this time, I had the determination to best him rather than boost him. Still, Isabell had asked me to wait, so I was going to try.

As the only child of two working parents, I've spent a fair share of time on my own. It's not that I have a problem keeping busy, but there is a lot of time to kill by my self. The closest thing I have to a sister is Isabell, but I'd guess she comes pretty darn close.

Well, Isabell and my yellow lab, Solo. He was named after Han Solo, but he was also the only puppy in his litter. After Isabell dropped me off, he was quick to greet and jump on me so his paws were on my shoulders.

I tied my long, dark brown hair into a loose top knot to throw the ball around for Solo. The goal wasn't to play for long, since it was excessively hot out and I didn't want him to overheat, but I needed to do anything to keep myself distracted from getting *too* ahead of Isabell on the treasure.

Solo, as expected, was eager to have a playmate for the moment. The backyard was somewhat shaded from all the fruit trees, so I sat on the steps of the back porch. Once Solo was panting a bit, I turned on the sprinkler that was attached to the hose and he went absolutely berserk over the cool water.

With sweat dripping down my own face, I itched to join him in the sprinkler. Instead, I caved to another craving and decided to dig through my house for any bit of history about the Ruggles. I stepped back inside and left Solo to frolic without me.

Of course, with Dad being the lead ranger at the lake, he often is compiling different resources to be incorporated into the park's programming. Not only that, but he reads . . . *a lot*. He loves to read historical texts just for fun in his spare time. Mom and I will be watching evening game shows together, and Dad will be sitting at his desk hunched over documents.

That's where I went first: the desk. Maybe Dad had something of interest tucked in here. I rifled through various stacks of folders and binders, which were very untidy, might I add. Scouring through the papers, I finally found a stack of manila folders labeled by year.

1849 . . . 1854 . . . 1862.

Jackpot: 1892. The year of the crime.

Just as I opened the folder, Solo barked at the front window. I jumped and clutched my chest from the sudden scare. Not that I was doing anything wrong, but Dad can be very particular about his desk. It needs to be kept 'a certain way,' though to me that certain way is somewhat of a disaster. To each their own, but regardless, someone was home. I scurried to my room, to stuff the folder underneath my mattress.

"Honey? You home?" It was Mom.

"Yeah, just a second," I called as I left my room to join her in the living room.

Our house was not that big, but the perfect size for the three of us. When you enter the house, you're met with the living room and dining room, and a view of the doorway to the kitchen and the hall with our bedrooms. I emerged from said hallway, to my mother smoothing out the velvet on our orange sofa.

"Auggie Jane, what on earth are we going to do about this couch?"

I shrugged. "It's gone back and forth from loved to hated so many times it's basically a work of art."

She pointed at me and squinted before carrying a few bags to the kitchen. "Very funny. Did you turn the sprinkler on or has that been on all day?"

"That was me, sorry. I just turned it on a few minutes ago. Solo looked a bit toasty."

Mom nodded and threw her hands up. "Ah, yes, okay. Okay that's good, thank you. I worry about that dog in this heat. You know I meant to hit the store on my way home to pick up a few things for dinner, but it slipped my mind." She moved through the kitchen somewhat frantically, which is nothing out of the ordinary. Despite her organization (a nice balance to Dad's mild messiness), Mom is often a bit frazzled and jumps quickly from one task or conversation to another.

"I'm sure we can scrounge up some food. Plus there's plenty of bread in the freezer still."

"From my baking spree a few weeks back?"

"Bingo."

She gave me a dramatic kiss on the side of the head before opening the freezer. "What will I ever do without you next year? You keep my head on straight sometimes, I swear. How does some barbecue chicken bread pudding sound for dinner?"

Just before six o'clock, my parents and I were seated around the table enjoying Mom's chicken meal and catching up on the day. My mind was fixated elsewhere, on the treasure hunt and the boy who started this game. Those golden-brown eyes that twinkled with mischief and confidence . . . oh, I'll show him.

"August?" Dad asked, and I blinked back to reality.

"Yeah? Sorry, what?"

"When are your final grades in?"

"Oh, I think by Monday. I'm not sure."

"Do you know how you did you on your tests?"

I took another bite. "I think well."

"What a relief for this year to be over," Mom said as she dabbed her mouth with a napkin. "You've worked so hard on your grades and at track and cross country. I'm so excited for you and your future, and to see how all this hard work pays off when you apply to colleges this fall!"

"Thanks Mom." I grinned, not that I exactly wanted to be talking about grades right now. I knew I ended the year with decent grades, but even though I wasn't worried about it, I was still ready to leave it behind. My phone buzzed in my pocket, but I ignored it. If there was one thing Mom and Dad loathed at the dinner table, it was texting.

"Should we plan some type of trip this summer?"

"Jeanie, you know that summer is busy at the lake. I can't take time off."

Mom didn't let that get her down. "Well maybe Auggie and I can take a little road trip and tour some universities."

Even though I was over talking about school, it didn't sound like the worst thing in the world to visit a few colleges. All the best ones in California were right along the coast, which made for an awesome road trip. Plus, Mom didn't go to college, and had been saying for years she couldn't wait to visit schools with me.

"Maybe in the car that's finally mine?" I asked hopefully. Despite the fact I got my license on my sixteenth birthday, I have hardly driven. My parents both need their cars to commute to work in opposite directions, and so there is never one available for me to drive. That's why Isabell always drives us when we go places. At the start of junior year, my parents promised me they would find me a used car by the start of senior year.

Dad and Mom exchanged a look, and Mom picked at her food.

"What was that?"

"What?"

"That look, you guys just exchanged a look."

"No we didn't, hon," Dad tried to assure.

"Yes, you did. I know what I saw. What's going on?" Again, they passed a glance of nervous eyes, before my mom crossed her hands and leaned her elbows on the table.

"Augustine," she started. When she didn't call me Auggie or Auggie Jane, I knew something was up. She is the only one to call me that, and she rarely uses my full name. No one does. No one ever does. "We are both terribly sorry. With my dad's passing last fall, and placing your grandmother in a care facility, we are a bit tighter for money than we anticipated."

My stomach dropped. I knew what was coming, but I still asked the question. "What does that mean then?"

Mom sighed, and Dad spoke up. "It means, we aren't able to afford another car, plus the insurance, this summer. We are both very sorry."

"Well can we change the insurance or anything? Aren't there different levels where we can save money?" I was desperate. There *had* to be other options we could explore. "It's not like I need anything fancy, just something with enough juice to drive to school and the lake and to the movies or something."

"I'm afraid not. We already downgraded our policy to one of the lowest tiers. Sorry, August. It's not in the cards for us."

Well, this wasn't the news I had been hoping for at the start of summer. I'd been waiting for this car for so long, and was beyond ready to have my own transportation. This seriously sucked. My instinct was to bite back a snide remark about fairness and freedom and confinement, but struggled with how to express it. After staring blankly at my plate for a moment, I looked to my parents to find the words to say.

Their eyes were fixated on me, and I succumbed to the cautious scrutiny. Mom especially, since her eyes were squinted slightly like she was bracing for impact. I swallowed the lump in my throat and brushed off the conversation best I could.

"Oh. Well. I guess I can survive. I've done it this long, haven't I? Driving around with Isabell has been fun anyway. I don't need a car." The only way I can get away with a lie is if there is a detection of truth in its words. This was yet another one of those times where I was not *technically* telling a lie. I did like hanging out with Isabell before and after school. "Besides, it still sounds fun to visit colleges this summer, Mom."

That seemed to ease a bit of the stiffness in the air, as the conversation derailed back to work schedules and ability to take a road trip. My phone vibrated again in my pocket, but I assumed it was just the reminder notification. It buzzed one more time.

Mom and Dad engaged in their own conversation that seemed to sense of some soft bickering about college visits and whatnot. Feeling a little low, I seized the opportunity to slide my phone out of my pocket and read my messages under the table.

Three texts from Isabell.

Hey! Do u have the shush-kabob on you? L and T started a group chat with us. Go look!

They want us to go to graduation.

I can pick u up in 30?

With Mom and Dad still talking in low voices, I took the risk to fire back a quick response. It seemed fun, and I was already itching to get out of the house. What a roller coaster of a dinner. I blew out a low breath, which caught the attention of my parents.

"You okay, Auggie Jane?" Mom asked.

"I'm good, I'm good. Um, I think Izzie and I might go to graduation tonight, so I'm just thinking about what I should wear." Not *technically* a lie.

"What about that little dark green thing you wore to your cousin's wedding last summer?"

"That's a good idea, thanks Mom. She's going to pick me up around seven, I'm guessing."

"So, soon. You better start getting ready, honey."

I shrugged, and scooped the last few bites of my dinner into my mouth to satisfy them both, even though my appetite had evaporated. "True. Then can I be excused?"

"Jean, I thought we were having a family night?"

"It's graduation, Daniel. Next year this will be her, so she might as well see what it's like and celebrate her friends." It wasn't unusual for my mom to be taking it easy on me, as Dad is definitely the stricter one. Tonight, with the car news, I could expect a little extra leniency.

"Thank you. Sorry, Dad. We can get a movie or something another night?"

Dad sighed. "Gone so soon." Once he sensed my hesitation, he laughed. "I'm kidding, go!"

I hurried to my room and locked door. There wasn't much to do to get ready for graduation. I'd just slip on the green dress Mom suggested and that would be the end.

Meanwhile, I searched for my shush-kabob. Though my parents were firmly against me having a smartphone before I turned eighteen, I bought an old one for fifty bucks off Russell a few months back. It doesn't call or anything, but when connected to the internet, I can message other smartphones in group chats. And I can still use my regular phone for basic calling and texting.

Since my parents were in the dark on my little purchase, Isabell and I named it the 'shush-kabob,' which we thought was pretty funny at the time. It dinged on my nightstand, and I rushed over to read the messages.

It was a group chat with Isabell, Tyler, and—of course—Landon. As Isabell had told me, the boys were inviting us to graduation. What I didn't expect was for her to play it off like we had way better things to do. Which, we did not. I chimed in for the first time.

Why does this seem like a subtle-but-obvious attempt to keep us from getting a leg up on the treasure?

Landon responded quickly to my message. *Your words cut me real deep, Auger. Maybe we just want you guys there because we like you.*

My heart beat loudly in my ears and my stomach twisted itself a little.

Isabell messaged back before I could collect my thoughts. *Do you ever turn off the schmoozing, Lanno? What are we, arm candy?*

. . . maybe.

I tried not to fixate too much on my chosen outfit and whether it classified me as arm candy. I shifted my focus to what had been nagging the back of my mind, and that was perusing the documents from Dad's desk before Isabell showed up.

Yanking the folder out from under my mattress, I tried my best to be quiet as I sifted through the papers. At first glance, I noticed several of the items were scanned copies of newspaper clippings: a lot of ads and excited headlines. It was also very text-dense, so I did a quick skim for dates in search of May, the month the Ruggles robbed the stagecoach. After leafing past several papers, I paused upon a black-and-white photograph of a house.

It was a familiar house—and a very large one. For one reason or another, it was stowed away in my memory. I squinted at the picture, trying to see any detail I could. There was a slender blond woman standing in front of the house. I flipped it over, and on the back it said:

Odette Dupont, 1892.

"Odette Dupont," I whispered the name aloud. "Is that French?"

Then, it clicked. French Gulch, where the French settlers landed during the gold rush. That's where I saw the house, last summer.

"August, Izzie's here!" Thankfully I knew what I was wearing. Otherwise, it would have been a stressful minute of prep. In response to Dad's alert, I tucked the picture of Odette into my small purse and stuffed the folder back under my mattress. After sliding into my green dress, I emerged from my room and dragged Isabell out the front door.

"Whoa there, Bessie. What's the rush? Wait, hold up. You look so cute! Love that dress."

We hopped in her car. "Thanks," I smiled at her endorsement. "So do you! Isabell and pink, birds of a feather. This dress is very you, and I love it." Her dress was bright, with spaghetti straps and a cinched waist that flowed just above her knees. There wasn't a single stand of her blond hair that was out of place. Curled to perfection— not unlike the woman, Odette, in the photograph.

"Oh stop," Isabell pretended to be coy with her dramatic hair flip.

"Sources say that someone else will also be taking notice. Tyyyyyler!"

"Interesting, I could say the same about you." Between the two of us, she certainly had the more traditionally feminine style and often looked very put together. Meanwhile, I wore a lot of dark colors and t-shirts.

"Wait. What are we doing? Landon and Tyler are the enemies of our mission. There shall be no fraternizing," I reminded her and myself.

"I didn't mention Landon specifically, is he on your mind?"

"Damn you." I fought back a smile while Isabell laughed at her own slyness.

"They did invite us. It does get you thinking."

"I still maintain they are trying to hold us back so we don't get out of the gate before them."

"If that theory is true, then it's working."

"Well, maybe not entirely. I did a little snooping through some of my dad's stuff," I pulled the photo of Odette and the man in front of the house out of my purse. "I know, you told me to wait for you before I did any digging for info, so I'm sorry for that. But I couldn't help it and I found this photo in a folder from my dad's desk."

"Please, I knew you wouldn't be able to keep that promise. There's little that could stop August Moon when she puts her mind to something. What do you make of the photo?"

At the next stop sign, I extended the photo for her to peek at. "Let the heavens bless you for your never-ending grace with me," I said as I bowed my head. Isabell snickered at that one as I started to explain the photo. "It's that old abandoned house way up out of French Gulch, that's all boarded up but they won't tear it down? We drove out there one night last summer, remember?"

"For the life of me, I cannot remember. But that's okay. Do you think the house has some kind of connection to the Ruggles?"

"It's probably nothing. Still, it was in my dad's binder. I do kind of want to look into Odette a bit, see if we can find something. Dad did say that there is a rumored woman that John Ruggles liked in town. It could be Odette, right?"

"How do you come to these kinds of conclusions?" Isabell shook her head in disbelief.

I tanked the idea and faced out the front window. "Definitely a bit ahead of myself here. It's probably not right, I don't know. Sometimes it's hard to tell if I'm seeing something that's actually there, or something I want to see."

"No," Isabell corrected. I turned back to her, and she was nodding her head in thought. "Knowing you, I'm sure we are on to something."

FOUR

"Is this your first Shasta graduation?"

"Yep, sure is. You've been to Brett's, but any others?"

"Just his, but that was years ago now. It's kind of interesting." Isabell shrugged. We were seated in one of the top rows, tucked into the corner of the football field stands. It had been a scorcher today, but the sun was beginning to set just as all the seniors marched down the bleachers. Finally, it was cooling off.

"Since we're just sitting here," I whispered, pulling out the photo out of my purse to show Isabell again. "There has to be more information on this woman. Why else would my dad stash this photo in between articles about the Ruggles brothers?"

Isabell snatched the picture for inspection, flipping it over to see the back. "Odette Dupont, huh?" She paused, staring at the photo. Something in her expression shifted as she stared at it. "Oh, hold up. Auggie, did you see that on the deck?"

"No, what?"

"Look at the deck, there's someone on it. Or am I just seeing things?"

I held the picture close to my face and blinked back at it. "Holy crap. How did I not see that?" Sure enough, standing on the wrap-around porch, lurking in the shadows, was a man. Due to the quality and the black-and-white nature of the photo, it was hard to make out the features. "I mean, it looks like a man. Right? I think that's a mustache. Is it too much of a long shot for it to be one of the Ruggles?"

"I don't know, maybe? Do you know what they look like?"

"No. Can we look them up on your phone?"

Isabell pulled open the search bar and a moment later we were hunched together over the screen. Old photos of the Ruggles were staring back at us. "That kind of looks like the same mustache," she shrugged, "but I can't say for sure."

Sighing, I held the picture back up to my eyes. *Who was that man in the background?* I tapped the face with my finger, and something weird happened.

The face moved. It scrunched up like I had just tickled its nose with a feather.

"Whoa," I whispered. The hair on the back of my neck stood up.

"What?"

"Isabell, this may sound crazy, but I think . . . the face moved."

"You're joking."

I wasn't joking. As I said it, the face disappeared from the photo all together.

"Isabell Trudeau, I swear I am not kidding around. It's gone now, look. The face is *gone*." I held the photo up for her to see, and she squinted at it.

"Maybe it wasn't actually there to begin with," she shrugged, handing the picture back to me.

"It was there, we both saw it!"

"Auggie, come on. It makes no sense that there would be something on the picture, and that it would magically disappear. We were probably just seeing what we wanted to see."

I sighed again, staring at the photo with enough intensity to bore holes in it. Still, the mysterious man did not return. Maybe we *had* just imagined it. Maybe I *was* seeing what I wanted to see.

"We'll do some research on Odette and see what comes up, okay? You said you hadn't looked into her yet, right?"

"Not yet. I found the photo right before you picked me up."

"Speaking of, any news on the car?" I slumped over at the mention, tucking the photo back into my purse. "Oh no."

I rubbed my hands together in my lap before slapping them on my knees. "No can do this summer, I guess. The cost of having my grandma in the home is too much of a money pinch. They can't swing another car. So it's not like I can even get mad about. At least not to their faces. I'm stifling all my annoyance."

"We have seen some cheapish ones online, I'm sure we can find something good that we can save for!"

"Thanks, Izzie. Maybe that's not a bad call. Dad is opposed to online car shopping because he thinks buying from the lot is less shady, though I kind of beg to differ. He'll probably be against it."

Isabell put her arm around my shoulder to give me a comforting pat. We watched on as the first of the three speeches finished and then clapped along with the crowd. The graduating class this year was about three-hundred or so, and they dotted the football field with their purple and white gowns.

Part of me felt a bit envious of them finishing with school. After the news about the car, I wanted nothing more than the freedom to get out of town. For a day? A week? The year? I don't know. If I had a car, I probably wouldn't *really* leave like that. But not having the option made me feel trapped. At least starting college next year was my way out, and that didn't depend on a car.

"Auggie!" Isabell gasped, catching my attention as she whispered. "I just realized something. The treasure."

"What of it?"

Isabell rolled her eyes as if the implication was obvious, but she wasn't annoyed. She was beaming. "The treasure can help you buy a car! If we beat Landon and Ty to it, we would have way more than enough money for you to buy a car."

I blinked at her, feeling like such an idiot. "How did I not think of that?"

Isabell did a small fist pump, which made me laugh a little. "I know, I'm a genius. Score for Izzie!"

"Wait. What if we don't even find the treasure?"

She didn't miss a beat, and beamed back at me. "We are going to find it, Auggie. Trust me, we will find it."

When we first arrived, I assumed that sitting through graduation would be about as exciting as a bowl of canned tomato soup. It didn't take long for me to realize I was wrong. Sure, I had had my moments of envying the seniors for getting out of dodge. Watching them walk across stage made it all too real, and soon, it would be our turn. It might look like some pompous walk across a stupid stage, but the moms crying around me and families standing to scream for their kid or brother or sister got me thinking.

"This is more emotional than I thought," I whispered to Isabell.

"Of all people, are you on the brink of tears here, Auggie?"

"Puh-lease! I just didn't realize graduation was such a big deal, if I'm honest."

Isabell chuckled. "We talk all the time about how we can't wait to get out of here, and *now* you're thinking it's a big deal? What did you think before?"

"I'm just talking about the walking part. The ceremonious nature of this is much more real and much less contrived than I pictured."

"You mean, watching Landon walk across stage it feels more real that he's leaving?"

"Yeah, exactly," I agreed absentmindedly. "Wait, no! That's not what I meant!" Isabell snickered deviously. "Landon's not even leaving next year," I added, hoping it would save me but instead Isabell raised her eyebrows. "I can't win here, can I?"

"Nope." She popped the 'p' and grinned.

After graduation, we waited a healthy and not at all desperate amount of time before plowing through the crowd to find the two boys down on the field. We spotted Landon before we made it onto the field. He was in the midst of taking a reluctant picture with his step-brother, Russell. They weren't on that friendly of terms, which was evident in the rigidity of their pose and the eye rolls of Russell's mom and Landon's dad.

As soon as he had the chance, Landon dipped from his brother, meeting Tyler with a hug. Isabell and I aimed for the two of them.

Landon was the first to see us, and he crossed his arms over his chest with a crooked grin. "Look who couldn't resist showing up," he teased. Much to my surprise, he uncrossed his arms to pull me in for a hug. "Thanks for coming."

"Congrats, Landon."

Tyler laughed. "Without you, he might not have made it. Best lab partner turned study buddy he could have asked for."

At that, Landon released me from the embrace. "Hey! I got by."

"Do you guys want to take a pic?" Tyler asked, looking wide-eyed at Isabell. He handed his phone over to someone nearby, and the four of us posed with the boys in the middle. "Can I get one with you, Izzie?"

"Let's not fraternize with the enemy here?" I reminded Isabell.

"Then I guess we better even the tally, Auger. You and me," he said, gesturing for me to come closer. When he smiled at me, I nearly groaned. That confidence of his would be the death of me, I swear. How do you un-attract yourself to a quality? Is that a thing?

No time to dwell. Landon handed his phone over to Tyler and slipped his arm around my waist. My heart raced in my ears so I took a deep breath through my smile. It was pretty short lived, because Landon dug his fingers into my side. As a reflex, I flinched away from the side tickle.

"Landon!" I squealed, hating the sound coming out of my mouth —especially when he kept his grip and poked me several more times. The small squeals didn't stop. "Okay, okay truce. Truce. Truce!"

Now he was laughing, but he released me. I hit him in the arm with my purse.

"I thought you said truce!" He defended after I swung at him.

"Yeah, until I realized I did nothing to instigate!"

He darted after me jokingly, but I hid behind Tyler and Isabell. I had forgotten about them for a second. To avoid Isabell's scrutiny, I stood up straighter, looping my arms through hers.

Besides, my game with Landon officially ended when I heard another high-pitched shriek. This one was intentional rather than instinctual, and I had a hunch who the culprit was.

"Lanny, we did it!"

"Lanny?" Isabell grimaced, and Tyler shook his head in disapproval. It was HBIC, jumping on to Landon for an overly zealous hug.

"We sure did." He laughed awkwardly, eyeing the three of us over Stacey's shoulder. Then the two of them started talking, and she had his attention.

"Bleh," I grumbled under my breath. Apparently it wasn't quiet enough, because both Ty and Isabell turned to look at me. Isabell was all-knowing, but Tyler was a bit slower. Before he could start to interpret what my sound effects were directed at, I cleared my throat to change the topic. "Maybe we should go?"

Isabell looked from me to Tyler. "Yeah, we probably should. Congrats again, Ty."

"Means a lot, Izzie. Thanks," he said. I slowly backed away from them and turned slightly, to give them an inch of space for anything to transpire. Obviously, I still kept my eye on them, in an attempt to decipher their conversation. Tyler and I met eyes, and that's when I turned away for good.

"You ready?" Isabell approached me a moment later.

I stole one last glance back at Landon, who was now posing for a picture with the evil-eyed mistress. "Am I ever."

After maneuvering through the crowd for a moment, I bumped shoulders with someone. "Oops, I'm sorry," I mumbled. Looking up, it was Russell, clad in a purple graduation gown. It was unzipped to display his dark blue tie, which made his light blue eyes pop that much more.

"Oh, no worries, August. I'm glad you came!"

I nodded awkwardly, not really sure what else to add. Isabell was standing right against my side, like my emotional support beam.

"Congrats, Russell."

"Yeah, congrats," Isabell added. "We have to go. See ya." She tugged me along and we were back to her car several minutes later. "You ever think that if you didn't go to prom with that guy, that things would be simpler for you and Landon?"

"Please, do not remind me of that night." I nearly shuddered. Going to prom with Landon's step-brother hadn't been the worst thing in the world. One of Russell's friends asked Isabell, so we all went together. But it did cause a bit of distance between me and Landon.

Of course, we had already been standing at an arm's length because he decided to go to prom with Stacey Higgins. After saying yes to Russell, that distance turned into the length of a football field. We'd just started to inch closer together the last few weeks, after he asked me to study with him and claimed I was his good luck charm.

There wasn't really anything wrong with Russell. He seemed relatively fine, but there was bad blood between him and Landon that I didn't want to get mixed up in. Evidently, I had, but whatever. Russell and I weren't close, and at prom we hardly hung out. But, considering Landon, it didn't feel right to be all buddy-buddy with Russell. When Isabell and I slid in the car, all thoughts of Russell had evaporated and I finally asked that lingered in my mind.

"So, what did you and Tyler talk about?"

"You."

"*Me*? I gave you both space so he could ask you out or at least exchange some kind of flirty banter, and this is how I'm repaid?"

She shrugged as she shifted into reverse. She stayed silent, baiting me. It worked.

"Well? What did you say?"

"He said you have nothing to worry about with HBIC."

If I had a drink, I would have spit it all over her dash to get my point across. "*What*? Did he think I was jealous? What did he say exactly?"

"He said, 'Tell August it's not what it looks like. Landon's not interested.'"

"Huh." I sat back in my seat, having just been on the edge of it.

"I know, right? Landon must like you."

"Did he say that?" I asked immediately. Regret caused me to smack myself in the forehead. "Why *would* he say that? I mean, at times I can hardly tell if he likes me or if I'm just his good luck charm or if we are mortal enemies."

Isabell laughed. "You are definitely not mortal enemies. Literally nothing points to you guys being enemies. It's all playful sass, also known as *flirting*. Besides, you *like* sass." I fought my own smile and shielded myself by turning up the radio.

My phone buzzed. When I pulled it out, I blinked back at the name on screen. "He texted me."

"And?"

I opened the message to see a picture of Landon laughing, poking me in the ribs, while I looked up at him with don't-you-dare eyes. It was actually a cute photo, to my surprise. In it, we appeared to have chemistry of people who know each other all too well.

This isn't over, the message read.

Then, another. *I am glad you came, btw. Sorry I didn't say goodbye.*

Isabell laughed. "With that mushy grin on your face, I'll assume it was a good one."

FIVE

If the week following graduation was any indicator of how summer would go, I'd say I was in for a slow boil. Seriously. A heatwave tore through that made all outdoor activity unbearable. Sprinklers, lakes, and pools were the only way to be outside. The second week of June marked our first days above 110 this year, with surely many more to come.

People don't expect for Northern California to be as hot as it is. Considering how large the state is, our town is pretty far north—only two hours from the Oregon border. Mom told me when I was young that since we are at the top of the valley, all the heat acquired from said valley doesn't have anywhere to go, so it just pools in Redding. The rationale makes sense. Here, we are at the start of the foothills, the gateway to the mountains. When you take in a 360 degree view in Redding, you've got mountains on about three-quarters of the view. I'd say that's pretty bowl-like.

For all the crap I give this place, and mope and groan about wanting to leave, it is nice to have hills and lakes nearby. But, it would be that much nicer if I had a vehicle to drive myself to said lakes and hills.

That's the other reason this week has been so-so. No car. With both Mom and Dad working all week, I've been stuck at home in boredom. They can't carpool, because their jobs are in opposite directions. To make matters worse, Isabell started her summer job. She's a camp counselor at a small operation downtown, from mid-morning to mid-afternoon every week day. After her shift, she's been pretty exhausted, so I've hardly spent any time with her.

Mom finally agreed to let me go into work with her. One of her employees called in sick for the Friday morning shift, and I offered to help out. She's usually against the idea of me coming in for a shift. Something along the lines of, "I don't want work stealing your childhood, Auggie Jane." If I want to work at the shop to make a little extra money, I must choose my moments wisely.

This moment in particular was strategic. I had something to do this afternoon, and I needed a car. If I was at Mom's shop, I could borrow hers on a break.

Since the shop opened at six, she knocked on my door to wake me up at 5 a.m. I don't completely mind early mornings, truth be told. During the school year, it's the bane of my existence. In the summer, however, it's kind of nice. Maybe it's the competitive side of me, but the idea of watching the sunrise and beating everyone to the day is pretty satisfying. It's calming, too.

Comfort Zone was popping from the second the doors opened, with bosses and assistants and the friendly do-gooders of the world picking up pastries and coffees for their respective workplaces. It was Friday, after all, so people were in jolly good moods. Just me, my mom, and twenty-something Ann ran the shop all morning, and we found our flow together so quickly that I wished my mother would let me work more often.

"Auggie, will you do me a favor and whip up some more cinnamon rolls? We are running pretty low. You remember how to make those, right?" Mom directed as she made a move to take over my station at the register.

"Yep, I got it." Mom started teaching me to bake when I was a little kid. The biscuits and cookies were second nature to me, but her cinnamon rolls were a bit trickier. It was her bestseller, and no matter how I tried, my batches never quite compared to hers.

Perhaps it was the shaping. Mine tend to turn out flat but hers are perfectly swirled and floofed up.

When this batch came out of the oven, it was no different. Mom, gracious as ever, smiled at them as they cooled on the grate. "Well done, Auggie!"

"They are pancakes, Mom."

Mom rolled her eyes and clicked her tongue at me. "They are not. You are too hard on yourself, these are fine! Same recipe, same color, same taste. Now go set them out on the display. I'll make the next batch."

Whether she really thought they weren't that bad or not, I didn't know. Besides, it was half-past ten, and the morning rush had fizzled. Instead of a line out the door, a few groups sat in huddled in plush chairs around the wooden tables. Since it was quieting down, I made my move.

"Mom, it's pretty slow out here. Can I bring Isabell a cinnamon roll to work?"

"Sure, honey." Mom granted my permission as she pulled a fresh rack out of the oven, an idyllic display of steaming rolls with concentric swirls and perfectly round domes. "Want to take a fresh one for her?"

"I'll just grab one in the front, thanks," I spun around to stuff a roll in a little bag. With Mom's keys in hand, I slid out the back door like a woman on a mission.

The plan wasn't to go see Isabell. The plan was to go to the library and try to dig up any dirt on Odette Dupont in the local history archives. Or, at the very least, more Ruggles brothers information.

The 1892 Ruggles folder at my house was not as fruitful as I hoped. There were letters to the aunt who lived near Sacramento, and John Ruggles appeared to make a stop somewhere around Corning an hour south of here. That's a lot of land for us to cover in a single summer. Considering there are plenty of places to dive into around town, the best way to save time is to explore the local options before trapezing around the entire north state.

As soon as I entered the library, I turned up the stairs to the top floor. My days spent home alone this week were working in my favor now. I had passed a lot of free time with endless research: on the Ruggles, county gold rush history, and local mining companies.

Despite having the reference numbers memorized, I pulled a note with the codes out of my back pocket. My phone rang as I unfolded the scrap of paper.

"Sweet heavens," I whispered before answering, eyes panning the room for any angry stares. "Hello?"

"Where is that cinnamon roll?" Isabell joked about my alibi. "Why are you whispering?"

"You're whispering back, Iz. I'm at the library."

"Oh, nice!" Now her voice was at normal volume. "Is that one outlaw book there you were hoping for?" Aside from Odette Dupont, one of my sources of interest was that Arizona Pete. It's never explicitly mentioned anywhere that he was an accomplice in the stagecoach robbery, but he was involved with the brothers during their bandit tour of the Sierra Nevada. There was a profile on him in a book featuring twelve notable crooks from the gold rush.

"I'm almost to the aisle, I think." Rounding the corner, I ran my index finger across the spines and plucked my book from the shelf.

"What was the other one you're grabbing?"

"A town history of French Gulch and the people. Someone local wrote it for a class out at the college. I shouldn't be on the phone in here," I whispered, noting a glare from an elderly lady at the end of the aisle. "Do you wanna hang out tonight and we can see what's up?"

There was a scream on the other end, but it sounded far away. "I'm on my ten right now and let me tell you, it's been a crap-munch of day. Can we chill and watch a movie or something? My brain is fried."

"What if I read this stuff and then tell you about it?" Down the aisle, a dark-haired man eyed me over his newspaper.

"Then we watch a movie?"

"Yeah, yeah. Just think, Isabell. The sooner we bust this case wide open, the sooner we can rub it in the face of the boys."

"Ooh. I do like that. I'll see you later, then."

I hung up my phone and narrowed my eyes at the dark-haired man before turning the other way. Heading two aisles over, I thumbed around for the second book, but couldn't find it. Strange. Walking in the library, I was almost one hundred percent sure it was shelved. Last night, when I checked the database, it was marked as such. I doubted this obscure book was taken within the last twelve hours.

Still, I waltzed over to the computer to double-check. Sure enough, it was listed as available, in the section I just browsed. Muttering under my breath I checked one more time, and it was there. A black-bound book with the title, *An Introduction to the Settlement of French Gulch*, etched in faded gold.

Weird. *How did I miss that?*

I tucked the books under my arm and headed to the checkout counter. On my way, I passed the desk the dark-haired man sat at, so I could dish an uncomfortable stare back at him. But he had vacated, and left his newspaper opened on the table. In the middle of the crossword puzzle, written in red ink, were the words A LA MORT.

I backed away from the table slowly, so if anyone was watching me, they wouldn't know I was alarmed. After a casual few steps back, I turned on my heel and beelined for the stairs. Outside, I double-checked my surroundings, and didn't see the man anywhere.

To busy myself on the walk to the car, I leafed through the pages of the top book, the one about French Gulch. A torn piece from a newspaper flittered to the ground. My stomach hollowed at the sight of red ink. I bent down, and touched it carefully, as if it were about to catch fire.

You better watch your back, kid.

In a flash, I was thanking my random good fortune for all the summers of overly intense card games with my crazy Uncle Joe. My poker face was mastered, and with the ominous feel of a person watching me from close by, my face remained unchanged. Instead, I shrugged and put it back in the book.

Once in the car, I locked the doors immediately and buckled up to drive. I drove around aimlessly for a few minutes to lose anyone that might be following me, but there wasn't much time left before Mom would be expecting me to return to the shop. I shoved the books under her seat along with the flat cinnamon roll and hurried inside.

Mom beamed at me, in a way it made me feel guilty, somehow. It didn't help that a menacing cloud was casting a shadow over my book findings. "Did she like your treat?"

My eyes note the pastry case, where my contributions remained untouched. "Yeah, she did."

"Great! I'm glad," she said with a wide smile.

I manned the register for the rest of the afternoon, keeping a keen eye on the door. Every time it jingled, my heart raced, anticipating the man from the library. But how would I know if it was him? I never did catch a look of his face. I wondered if those threatening messages were really meant for me. It had to be some kind of mistake, right?

To my knowledge, the man did not enter the shop door that day. Instead, each jingle was followed by an average customer in search of a scone or a cinnamon roll.

Maybe he didn't walk through those doors. But he was already living rent free in my mind, in the form of six, red words.

You better watch your back, kid.

SIX

Fridays are often the night my family gets together with Isabell's. The tradition ebbs and flows. Sometimes weeks pass between our hangouts. Sometimes our families will go together to Old Mill, which was the main staple while we were growing up. Other times, we pair off and do our own things. Tonight, Mom and Tracey had planned to enjoy a wine and cheese spread while their husbands grabbed a beer at the Old Mill.

Mom is rarely giddy, but Tracey tends to bring that bubbly excitement right out of her. The whole drive over to the Trudeaus, Mom chatted about the smoked pepper jack cheese she purchased, and how she knew Tracey was going to love it.

"I'm sure it will pair just lovely with some type of wine," Mom raved. In a normal circumstance, I might prod her a little more about the wine. Mom is not much of a drinker, let alone being a wine connoisseur. My mind was racing with other thoughts, so I didn't delve into the whole wine and cheese thing.

Instead, I was crafting an agenda for the night with Isabell. My black duffel bag, situated between my feet, contained not only my toothbrush, but the two library books and the red-penned note. I tapped my foot as we drove, thinking of how I would address these oddities to Isabell. She's all for friendly competition, but when there's real trouble involved, she isn't as game. Perhaps it would be better to keep it to myself? I couldn't decide.

"Jeanie, Auggie. Come on in!" Tracey greeted us before we even knocked on the door. Their little dachshund, Molly, barked and wagged her tail before licking my leg like a salt block. I picked her up and cooed at her. She wriggled in my arms like a worm as I scratched her belly.

Isabell descended the stairs when we entered, and my mom reached out to hug her. "Hi Izzie, you girls have any plans for the night?"

"Just watching a movie. I'm dead after this week," Isabell said as she slouched into my mom's hug. "We'll probably post up in the bonus room so we can just marathon our way to sleep."

Mom and Tracey grinned at each other. "It's just us girls here for a couple hours. Brett went with the dads to Old Mill for a beer. We thought it might be fun if you joined us for our wine and cheese sample."

"Seriously?" Isabell narrowed her eyes at the moms. I slowed the pace which I was rubbing Molly's belly.

"I can't tell if this is a joke."

"Just a small glass," Tracey clarified, though her and my mom pursed their lips to hid their still-growing smiles.

At seventeen, we didn't need that much convincing, despite our tough drinking recovery just over a week ago. Being granted *permission* to drink—drinking without fear of retribution—sat pretty high on the list of "things that shall not be refused." We tried to play it cool, but still beat the moms to the kitchen.

What was supposed to be a small glass turned out to be two decent sized glasses, thanks to our (momentarily) loosey-goosey moms and a sly-handed Isabell. I was unconvinced I liked the taste of it, it reminded me of tart, dry juice, but I did kind of like the warm feeling it gave my cheeks. An hour later, Isabell and I stumbled up to the second floor of the house while our moms opened themselves another bottle.

With sloppy laughter, we yanked armfuls of pillows and blankets from Isabell's bed and carried them to the bonus room. The bonus room is part of what makes spending the night at Isabell's house better than mine. I love my house a lot, but Isabell's is probably twice the size. At mine, there are two bedrooms, two bathrooms, and the dining-living room is pretty much one big room. In the Trudeau's house, there is a massive extra game room that has giant recliners and a big TV. It's also private from the rest of the house, since it's above the garage.

Once our blankets were in a heaping pile, we plopped down on to them. Isabell blew a stray hair out of her eye.

"I have something to confess, about our little arrangement with the boys," Isabell said in a low voice.

It reminded me that I also had something to tell her. "So do I."

"Wow, really?" She quirked her head to the side. "That's funny. You go first."

"I think we should check out Odette Dupont's house," I started. Perhaps it was the alcohol, but the worry of the Red Inked Menace was gradually dulling in my mind. It was either all in my head, or this person knew I was on to something and wanted me out of the way. Both options meant that I should just press on as usual. As least, that's what the wine haze told me. "Preferably at night, since it's kind of trespassing."

"Ooh, trespassing?" Isabell grinned devilishly. "Who are you?"

I waved her off. "I'm a girl who really wants to beat the boys and find money for a car, that's who. No one lives there anyway, who would we be hurting?"

"You know, this actually fits in well with my confession." She giggled, tapping her chin.

"How so?"

"So, it's 8:30, right? Around 10 o'clock, we will be having a few . . . *visitors*."

"Visitors? Oh no. Izzie, what did you do?"

She giggled more. "I may have mentioned the wine to Tyler and I may or may not have sent him a few bold messages under the table.

He and Landon are going to come by."

I slapped a hand against my forehead, which was much too spinny to be dealing with Isabell's poorly executed plan. "Izzie! Both of our moms are here, and our dads will be back soon. What were you thinking?"

"Hm. Should I have told them a later time?"

I groaned in response and picked up my phone to call Landon.

"Who are you calling?" she whispered.

"Oh hello there, Auger," a voice hummed on the other end.

"Hi. Listen. Don't come over here?"

"Wait a second—"

Isabell yanked the phone from my hand. "She's talking crazy. The plan is still on but just park down on the street like we planned. Yes . . . Yes . . ."

"Izzie!" I whisper-yelled at her, and she held up a finger to silence me.

"No . . . Fine, whatever. See ya." Then she hung up and handed the phone back to me. "Don't worry, I straightened it all out." Her chipper voice was so nonchalant, like she actually thought she fixed an issue.

"Don't worry? Are you crazy? My cheeks are flushed enough, I can't get in a car with him! Or, them."

"Think. We can go to Odette's house tonight, the boys can take us! We aren't exactly in condition to drive."

"Those two boys are our competition in this escapade, remember?"

"We don't have to tell them it's for the treasure. We can just say that we want to drive out to French Gulch. When we drive by, we remark on how creepy the house is so we can stop, but then you and I go back another time. This is our intel mission."

"What about getting caught? Our parents are downstairs. Do you know nothing about sneaking out?"

"Think again, mademoiselle. We'll just lock the door and leave the movie on. No one is going to come in and check on us. If for some reason someone does, we just make up the beds to look like we are laying here. It's not rocket science, come on. These are the oldest tricks in the book!"

The Red Inked Menace crept back into my mind. I knew Izzie was going to hate it, but I had to tell someone. "You know, there might be some bonuses to going with the boys tonight."

Isabell leaned forward on her elbow, like she was ready for the latest dish of gossip. "Oh-ho-ho, do tell."

I rolled my eyes. "It's not like that. I feel like you aren't going to like it. But, well, the thing is, um. I had a weird feeling someone was watching me at the library today," I started. I re-told her the whole thing. How a man with his newspaper had been eying me, the way the French Gulch book was off-shelf then was magically on-shelf, the red-penned note, everything.

In response, she shivered. "You're giving me goosebumps. Maybe it isn't such a good idea to go out there after all."

"What I'm wondering is if this actually has any connection to this whole treasure hunt. I mean, it's been unaccounted for since the 1890s. What are the odds that someone would be looking for it today, and on top of that, be following a teenager around?"

"Good point, Auggie. The note is pretty weird though. Definitely the most suspicious part."

"The note could have been a prank from a long time ago? I don't know. That guy in the library could have had nothing to do with it. I guess the newspaper just gave me the vibe of a detective movie, and the timing of it all was a little too coincidental."

Isabell blew out a deep sigh. "I think this calls for the mostly drank bottle of whiskey I found under Brett's bed." After the drinking we did last week, I couldn't say that whiskey appealed to me at all. Or any drinking, really. The wine from our moms had been enough. "I see that face. Come on, Auggie. A little liquid courage never hurt anyone, right?" I didn't argue, but I didn't agree. Instead, coughed out a lion's breath and nodded that it was time.

A little while later, my mom peeked in to say goodbye, meaning our dads had returned and my parents were leaving. By 9:45, the Trudeau house was still. I stopped drinking the whiskey after a small swig or two, but Isabell drank a little more. I feared that with her inhibited hand-eye coordination, she would stumble out of the house and foil our clean getaway.

She sighed and leaned her head on my shoulder as I contemplated our escape. "You know, we don't have to see them if you don't want to. I'd be okay with telling them to beat it, or whatever."

We were sitting on the floor, slumped against the couch. "It's not that big of a deal. I'll survive."

"Don't you want to see Landon just a little?"

"Maybe I've liked him before, and maybe he liked me. But nothing happened, and it was just lame to feel like I was crushing on him like a puppy dog all that time."

"Why are they so confusing?"

On cue, her phone rang: Ty. "Are you here? . . . Okay, we will be down soon." She hung up, then addressed me. "They're here," she informed me as she rubbed her nose. "We just have to find a way to sneak out through the window."

"Isabell, wait," I tugged her arm. "Can we not mention the whole library weirdness to the boys? I don't want to make mountains out of mole hills, or seem like we can't handle the competition."

She tapped her temple. "Noted. Smart."

We slid open the window, and Isabell carefully removed the screen, setting it outside. I climbed out first, and the two of us sat to inch down the roof until we got to the edge. I slid over on to my stomach until my legs were fully dangling from the gutter. I tucked a leg under the overhang until my left foot hit the wall. Once my right foot found where the gutter met against the side of the house, I wedged it in the crevice for support as I lowered down further. A fresh pile of dirt sat on the ground, and it looked to be a soft-ish landing. I took the chance and dropped on to it.

Stuck the landing.

"Auggie! There's no way I can do that," she whispered frantically down to me, clutching a bag to her chest that I didn't even realize she had. With how liberal she had been with the whiskey, I had to agree with her assessment.

My eyes scanned the area for anything of use, landing on an item partially obscured by the dark. "How convenient, there is a ladder leaned against the side here."

"God wants me to keep both my ankles unfractured, how blessed am I?" Isabell bowed her head to her chest.

I laughed at Isabell and propped the ladder, holding it steady while she descended. Once down, she laughed and we high-fived before trotting down her driveway. The boys were waiting at the bottom in Landon's truck, with an idled engine and shut off lights. The sight of them through the dashboard stirred up a whole new flurry of nerves. Since graduation, our contact with the boys had been scarce. Aside from a few playful jests in our four-way group chat, not much had transpired. I reminded myself I had nothing to be afraid of—until the shadowed image of Landon in the driver's seat nearly made me turn around. This had to be a bad idea.

Isabell, on the other hand, was like a drunken toddler as she slid into the backseat behind Tyler, effectively halting my plans to retreat. I followed after her.

"Hey August!"

"Isabell. Auger."

"Landon," Isabell and I chimed together, annunciating his voice in the same exact way.

He shuddered. "When you guys sync up like that, it reminds me of the twins in that one horror movie."

"*The Shining*?" we asked.

Landon glared over his shoulder, but his lips were pursed to suppress a smile. "Yes, that's the one."

"You don't like horror movies, Landon?" I leaned forward, resting my left elbow on the back of his driver's seat. The rush of climbing down the roof, running down the driveway, and riding in Landon's truck had pumped Isabell's liquid courage through my veins. I didn't have too much of it, but if I convinced myself I did, maybe the nerves would fade away.

"It's a love-hate thing," Tyler answered for him.

"I don't *really* mind them."

"It sounds like you might," Isabell joined in the teasing. Of the four of us, I'd suspect she hates horror films the most, but I didn't point that out.

"Do not," Landon said as he made a face. At only about six inches from his face, leaned against his seat, I had a front row showing to the devious glint in his eyes.

"Prove it, Mr. Tough Guy," I joked from my seat, feeding into his mischievous look. My nerves subsided the more we settled into our usual dynamic. The natural ribbing that Landon and I shoot back and forth put me very much at ease.

"What, you want to watch a scary movie right now?" He was grinning back at me now.

"No," Isabell and I were quick to quip. It wasn't just Isabell who hated horror films—neither of us were big fans. I can understand the adrenaline pump from a healthy dose of fear, but that doesn't mean I want to watch it play out on screen. Besides, doesn't the world have enough chaos? Why would I indulge a movie with all the blood and gore? No, thanks. I'll stick to heist movies that star George Clooney and cult classics from the 80s.

"Then how am I supposed to prove it?"

"I don't know, let's drive out to Whiskeytown. There's supposedly a few creepy, abandoned buildings out there," Isabell suggested.

"Have you guys been out to Boys Camp yet?" Tyler offered up.

"What is that again?" Isabell snapped her fingers as she tried to recall.

"It used to be a juvenile correction camp or something, but it was abandoned a couple years ago. Now people go there to vandalize and drink," I told her.

"No vandalizing for me," Isabell squirmed.

"Then where to?" Landon asked.

"Don't say 'the stars!'" Tyler pleaded, which made Isabell laugh.

"Yeah!" I shook my head at her and snorted by accident, which caused her to spiral into a fit of laughter that pulled me in with it. "What was that sound?" she asked through struggled breaths.

"I don't even know!"

Somehow we grew aware of the boys watching us, and our laughing faded away slowly. Maybe it was my placebo whiskey lenses, but they at least seemed amused.

Landon surveyed the vehicle and cranked on the engine. "To Boys Camp it is, then."

Summiting the hill just before Whiskeytown Lake is a refreshing crest in and of itself, but during the night, it's one of the most mystifying experiences one can have around here. At least, that's my *professional* opinion.

In moments like this one, where the moon hasn't quite set yet, its reflection makes the lake look like some kind of magical-realism photograph. A photo you want to dive right into. But, when the moon sets and the lake descends into further darkness, that's when the real magic happens. Maybe it's because of my last name that I feel such a connection to the night sky, but it always struck me with awe.

In complete darkness, the lake is hidden under a full canvas of stars. It's like a secret only you know about, a magnificent beast that you feel the indescribable urge to domesticate.

Thinking my stream of consciousness would make for delightful group conversation, I spoke up on that behalf. "Have you guys ever considered the domestication of a lake?"

"Of course," Isabell agreed, though her dramatic hand gestures said otherwise. Tyler peered over his shoulder to crinkle his nose at her.

"August, what does that even *mean*?"

"Whiskeytown is man-made. Does that make it domesticated? The land has always existed, but man made it a space to recreate specifically. Man 'tamed' it, so to say."

"Like a house cat?"

"Oh, Auggie," Isabell sighed, resting her head on my shoulder. "Whiskey brings out the philosopher in you."

"It brings out the philosopher in us all," Landon said.

Tyler scoffed. "Yeah, right! Last time you drank whiskey you were adamant that we could make a human slingshot."

"How did that play out?" I asked.

"We broke a window at Nuke's house. So in my defense, it worked."

"A job well done," I applauded.

The conversation shifted, but I continued to stare out the window, studying the landscape. It didn't matter how many times I've driven the length of this lake. I can't help but marvel at it. Night drives out here are a little more rare to come by, but don't sleep on the view. The sky was illuminated enough to make out the mountains that cradle the lake, Shasta Bally standing as the most resolute of the bunch.

When the moon is in the sky just right like this . . . man.

"August?"

I hummed a response, and the rest of them laughed. "Oh, sorry, was I zoned out?"

"Like an astronaut." Isabell laughed. "Get it? Because you were so spaced out?" Landon chortled at the lame joke.

"Nice one." Tyler smiled, reaching his hand back for an Isabell high five.

"Wait!" Isabell yelled, and Landon jerked the wheel at her outburst. "French Gulch! We should go up to French Gulch, right Auggie? That's a good plan, let's drive up there?"

"Holy . . ." Landon blew out a loud breath. "You just scared the shit out of me. I thought I was about to hit a person, or a deer."

"Oops, sorry. I got excited when I saw the French Gulch sign."

"Can't blame me for not picking up on that right away," Landon mumbled. "Would we rather go there than Boys Camp? There's not much to do up in French Gulch. Believe me, I would know."

"Oh yeah, you lived up here as a kid, right?" I asked.

"Yeah," he peered over his shoulder. "Good memory."

"We can always just drive around a little," Tyler suggested.

Landon shrugged. "Why not. I could go for a cruise."

The ascent up to French Gulch was dark, especially since the moon was now setting behind the mountains. Pulling in was no different. Town was quiet as we cruised around. Like all good horror films, it was almost too quiet. The type of quiet that makes anything out of the ordinary stick out like a sore thumb. In a still town, the smallest crunch of tires can cause suspecting folks to peek out their living room windows. All the lights were dimmed, though many of the lights were off entirely.

"This feels off." I fought off my pseudo-buzz, which had been gently subsiding, determined to pay more attention to the situation. As the first to vocalize concern, the others brushed off my worry.

"What's the worst that could happen?" Tyler asked.

"Someone could charge out with a pitchfork or a shotgun?" Landon joked.

"We aren't trespassing," Isabell reasoned, slurring her esses.

"Maybe we should find somewhere a little farther off the grid instead of the main street of town." Tyler suggested to Landon before turning to the backseat. "You okay, Izzie?"

"Me? Oh, I'm grrrrreat!"

"Great!" Tyler smiled, oblivious to just how much whiskey she drank before we slipped out to meet them.

"Yes, she's grrrrreat," I said, slinging my arm around her. She crashed into my side. "How much whiskey did you drink, you silly goose?"

"Shh," she said, though her voice was not quiet. She reached into her bag. "I brought the bottle with me."

I resisted a laugh. "Aren't you a sneaky one. Have you been drinking that this whole time?" She nodded like a proud toddler, and I just shook my head. No wonder she was so much more drunk than me. "How long was I looking out that window for?"

"Long enough for me to do this," she continued to whisper. She lifted the bottle to her lips and gulped.

"Izzie!" I laughed out loud. Both the boys peered back.

"So it wasn't my imagination. I *was* smelling whiskey."

Landon grinned. "Always trust your instinct when it comes to whiskey."

"Ooh! I know!" Isabell yelled, and I snorted at the way Landon flinched again. This time, he caught my eye in the mirror, and he gave me a playful eye roll. "Let's go to that one big, abandoned house just out of town!"

I flinched. With the obscurity of her suggestion, I wondered if our plot to scope out the scene was blatantly obvious to the boys.

"I know just the one you mean. The haunted one. I'm on it." Landon turned down the next street, and I was relieved that it didn't really take much convincing at all.

"Wait, that house is *haunted*?" Isabell's jaw dropped.

"Have you been before?" Landon asked, and Isabell shook her head with wide eyes. "Once you see it, you'll know it's haunted."

"You didn't tell me it was haunted," she whisper-yelled at me.

"I didn't know for sure, though it can be reasonably assumed that a house from the gold rush is haunted. It's probably at least 130 years old," I reminded her.

"Oh boy. Oh boy, oh boy, oh boy." She linked her arm with mine, tight enough for them to be a chain link. Before I could even start to convince her we would be fine, Tyler took the reigns. There's a certain gentleness about Tyler that makes you think he could diffuse any situation. He's quiet, but only because he's observing the situation. In this instance, he was very reassuring.

The house—Odette Dupont's, though the boys didn't know that —was in an abandoned part of the small town. A few other houses stood on her street, but they were scattered, and some were crumbling. The main thing they all seemed to have in common is that they were made of wood, and were tucked between the trees.

Whether it was the supernatural force of an isolated spirit or our own awe, when we pulled up and parked, the four of us stayed unmoved in our respective seats. It was like staring up at a giant, especially since it was too dark to make out any distinct features. Without any light, there was an additional aura of mystery. For me, that meant intrigue. For Isabell, that meant impending doom.

Two stories loomed over us, and from what I could tell there was a large, wrap-around front porch. The yard was big, and we had an open view of the front while the back was dark, giving the illusion that a dense forest stood behind the house. As if the house itself blew out a breath, wind whistled around the car, and a chill ran down my spine.

"Anyone else feel like the hair on their neck is standing up?" Tyler asked, scratching the back of his head.

Isabell shivered. "I do."

"Will you turn off the air for a minute, Landon?" He didn't fight me on it, and turned it off like he was trying not to disturb a force in the air. Observing my counterparts and the way they stared at the house, I threw my hands up. "Am I the only one who isn't buying into this ghost crap?"

Landon made a face at me. "I'm not buying it, but I am *curious*," he attempted to defend.

"What are the odds you go up and knock on the door?" I challenged, and Tyler chuckled under his breath.

"Walk up to the house, and knock?"

"That's what I said."

He blew out a breath, and looked at me devilishly. "I'd say the odds are one in two."

"Ooh!" Tyler grinned, and even Isabell perked up a bit. "So if you say the same number, Landon has to knock on the door, and if you say different, August has to?"

"Yep," Landon said, popping the 'p.'

I shook my head at him and pursed my lips. No way would I be the one to back down from this. "Fine. Ty, will you count us down?"

"Alright, ready? When I say three, say your number. One, two, three!"

"One!" I said at the same time Landon said, "two!"

"Crap," I mumbled. "This game always bites me in the butt."

"What's that I hear? A little fear?" Landon taunted, cupping a hand over his ear.

"I'm not scared, I'm just bitter that you lucked out. This time, at least." I crossed my arms and squinted at the house. I could have sworn I heard it groan, but quickly shrugged it off. It had to be my imagination, right?

"You're not seriously going to make her go up there, are you?" Isabell's arms mimicked mine as she stared Landon down.

"If there's one, absolute rule of 'what are the odds,' it's that you can't back out. No one in the history of the game ever has, and once someone does, the entire game falls apart."

"Maybe this is dumb. She could get in trouble," Tyler said.

"Oh come on! If I had lost, you guys would definitely make me do it," Landon pointed out, laughing.

The three of them looked to me, expecting me to take the side of Tyler and Isabell. The truth is, if I didn't want to do it, Landon wouldn't actually force me. He knows well enough by now that I feed into the taunting and provoking, but he's a lot of talk and not a lot of follow-through when it comes to his smack-talk.

"Yeah, well, that's because you'd need the push to do it. I don't." I bopped him on the nose and opened the car door.

Just as it was closing, I caught Landon's cheer. "Alright, that's my girl!" Or maybe he just said "atta girl?" It was hard to tell between his claps and the door shutting behind me.

It was mid-June, and the grass was already dry enough to crunch under my shoes. The yard was as overgrown and unkempt as one would picture a decades-long abandonment to be, and the weeds were scratching at my knees. Inching closer to the house, there was some semblance of a brick path that curved to the porch steps, but grass sprouted between the cracks.

Peering back at the car, I waved at my three friends who were sitting on the edge of their seats like puppy dogs waiting for their owner to return home. The wood creaked loudly beneath my feet as I stepped up, much louder than I would have expected. It was deep, and throaty, almost human-like. My moves were cautious. The closer I stepped, the more enveloped in darkness I became, and the more I felt like my breath was being pulled out of me.

I stared at the door and before I knocked, reached out to touch the splintered wood. Worn down and warm to the touch, I shifted to a fisted knock.

Nothing. My courage shrugged, so I tapped again with a little rhythm. Nothing, still.

"Guess no one is home," I spoke out loud.

"That's what I want you to think."

I blinked back at the door. Was that all in my head?

"Did you just say something?"

Nothing responded. I rolled my shoulders and cleared my throat, retreating one step to analyze the door from a little farther back. By now, my night vision had calibrated, so I could make out the loose door knob and the four padlocks barring the door shut. A wooden beam across the top of the door frame arch was carved with the name "Dupont."

Something caught the corner of my eye, and I swore it was a figure in the window. It vanished as quick as it appeared, and another small gust of air moved past me. I blinked back at the window in surprise.

"August!" Isabell called from the car, giving my heart a few fast beats. I turned to see her hanging out the window, beckoning to me wildly. "You're lingering and it's freaking me out!" With a last look between the door and the window, I spun around and jogged back to the car, rejoining Isabell in the backseat. She wrapped her arms dramatically around me. "I thought you were going to be swallowed up!"

I squealed when she fell back, arms still tight around my shoulders. "I'm fine, Iz!"

"Nice work, Auger," Landon tapped his hands together for a gentle golf clap.

"Yeah, job well done!"

I sat up and bowed my head in a mock curtsy. "Thank you, thank you." Landon kicked the car in gear, and gravel churned beneath the tires as we sped away. On my knees, I peered out the back window at the house. In an upstairs window, I had failed to see a twinkling ball of light behind the glass. *Was that what I saw in the front window?*

"Whoa," I whispered. My verbal recognition jinxed it, and the orb shrunk.

"What?" Isabell asked. Back in high alert, she frantically followed my line of vision back to the house. By now, the buzzing light was gone.

"The house," I started, but clamped my mouth shut to choose my next words carefully as we hit the main drag of town. "It's just, interesting, I guess." In a moment's notice, we were already outside of French Gulch and carving our way back to the highway.

"Interesting? Auggie. I'm convinced it's haunted. I don't think you could tell me otherwise. It's definitely creepy."

"I'll tell you what's creepy," Landon started. He then accelerated as he turned on to the highway. Isabell and I flopped around in the backseat like two fish. She hit her elbow on the window and muttered an 'ow!' under her breath.

"You guys should buckle up," Tyler said.

"Geez, what's creepy about skidding on to the highway?" I mumbled as I strapped on my seatbelt.

"Not that." Landon's voice was calm, and his eyes peeking at me in the rearview mirror were serious. "I think we're being followed."

SEVEN

"Followed? We're being *followed*?" Isabell started to pant. "Oh man. This isn't good."

"It might be my imagination. No reason to worry." I couldn't help but note that his voice lacked all its usual playfulness.

"We're okay!" Tyler agreed, much more upbeat than his counterpart. "Besides, Landon can lose 'em. He's gotten out of situations like this before."

"You have?" I raised an eyebrow at him in the mirror.

He shrugged like it was the most casual thing in the world. "A time or two."

"At least we're in good hands, I guess," Isabell grumbled. When she made a move to peek out the rear window, he stopped her.

"Try not to stare. We don't want whoever it is to know that we know. Act natural. We won't drive you right home. We'll lose the car first."

Déjà vu crashed like a wave over me as I recalled the unsettling encounters I had at the library. Now, a person trailed behind us in their car? At the very least, they followed us *from* French Gulch, which also happened to be the subject of the book which that the red-penned note fell. Was there a possible connection between these two things? My stomach sank, and the blood drained from my face.

"Wait a second, Landon," I piped up. "Who's followed you in the past?"

"Uh, people."

Tyler nodded back at me and spoke up himself. "Is there a chance it's those same people now?" The knots in my stomach loosened the slightest bit when Landon's eyes flashed to the rearview mirror again.

"What?" I couldn't help but question, even though he wasn't looking at me. Then he turned and gave me a nod so small I wasn't sure it happened.

"Has anyone else been followed lately?" He surveyed the car.

Isabell straightened up at the notion, and I shot her a sideways look with the smallest shake of my head. She sat back a little. "Not me!" Tyler shook his head no, too. He looked back at me in the mirror, then peered over his shoulder.

"August? Has someone been following you?"

I nearly froze. Even after discouraging Isabell from sharing what I had seen, it was hard to deny the feeling in my gut that something was wrong. My encounter at the library had been bizarre. But what did I have to gain from telling everyone? Reassurance that everything is okay? So there will be a lead to give the cops if I somehow go missing? Or will my friends be taken down with me? That felt like crazy talk. Odds are, these two incidences aren't connected. It's probably nothing.

Isabell tapped a finger on her knee as she waited for my answer, and I knew the boys would only grow more suspicious the longer I paused.

"Um, no. No, I can't say that I have been followed." It was *technically* the truth. I hadn't so much been followed, but threatened. Maybe. Despite my denial, Landon narrowed his eyes at me in the mirror, but he didn't press any further. The car was tailing us so close now that their lights were flashing bright in our car.

Landon surprised us all with a sharp turn off the highway.

"Good thing you buckled up," Tyler joked. As soon as we turned right, Landon whipped into the park headquarters. The suspect vehicle skid in behind us, and to our surprise, Landon parked the car.

We all started to shout at him. Isabell was frantic and panicked, I was firing off questions, and Tyler was calmly trying to ask him what was going on when the other car parked. A hooded man emerged and moved with a purpose over to our car.

"I know who it is, guys. It's fine," Landon quieted us.

I, however, was not satisfied that Landon knew this guy. Why would they harass us like that on purpose? Tailing us and flashing their lights? It was creepy. In fact, it caused a protective urge to spread through my veins. I rolled down my window and started to yell. "Hey, mister. Don't you know that it's —" I didn't get to finish my sentence because Landon had overruled my window powers. He locked it as soon as it started to lower and then he rolled it back up.

Isabell whispered my name while I grumbled Landon's, pushing the window button over and over and over, hoping to wear him down. "Come on, let me give him a piece of my mind. I can talk some shit, you know."

"Don't I know it," Landon tossed over his shoulder.

There was a fervent tapping on the window, startling us all. Landon lowered his window a crack.

"Seriously, Landon? That's some petty shit right there."

Isabell and I whipped our heads to each other. We recognized that voice, and it was not from a typically threatening person. Isabell relaxed ever so slightly, but my guard didn't slip.

"Russ just cut to the chase. What do you want?"

"Oh, Russell! Hey man, what's up?" Tyler leaned forward and waved, friendly as ever despite our scare.

Landon and his brother—*step*-brother, as he would clarify—do not like each other. That much has always been clear. Even in happy moments like graduation, they still couldn't muster a genuine grin. Today, in the heat of summer, their ice still can't be thawed.

I've never fully understood the reason why their hatred for each other has stayed so resolute all these years, and Landon hasn't elaborated. All I know is that Landon's dad and Russell's mom had an affair, and got hitched after their spouses divorced them for it. That all happened about ten or more years ago, and while Landon is very staunchly on his mother's side, he has still spent considerable time under the same roof as Russell at his dad's house.

"Ty! Didn't expect to see you, dude." Russell's grin could be made out through the window, since he left his headlights on. In spite of the strained relationship between Landon and Russell, they've both managed to maintain a friendship with Tyler. Not that Russell and Tyler are *good* friends, but rather have mutual interests that link them in the same crowd. Since Tyler and Russell played on the basketball team together all four years, they get along pretty well.

About a year ago, I asked Landon about that very thing.

"Does it bother you that they are friends?" We had been at the movies just the two of us, after finishing our homework together at my house, when Tyler and Russell entered with a few other teammates. Though we had been there for different movies, it still to run into the felt strange running into them.

Landon had responded by tossing a piece of popcorn in the air to catch in his mouth. Of course, he caught it, and tossed another.

"Nope." He popped the 'p' and flicked another piece into the air.

"So you and your brother—"

"Step."

"You and your step-brother hate each other, but you share a best friend? That's a little weird."

Landon shrugged, and when he threw another bite of popcorn in the air, I whacked it away with my hand. He laughed at me. "Hey! I was eight for eight!" I rolled my eyes at him, smiling. "Look, first of all, they are not 'besties,'" Landon joked, using air quotes around the word besties. "I've been friends with Ty since we played on the same city league baseball team in fifth grade. In high school, we became best friends. If Russ and Ty are friends, it's fine by me. I think the Russ is a snake, but whatever. Ty's not, and he's a good friend. Some things in a friendship are just best left unsaid, you know?"

"You know, that's pretty mature for a guy who ordered a suicide soda at the snack bar."

Landon had just grinned, flicking another piece of popcorn up to catch in his mouth.

Now, Russell leaned his arms against the door of Landon's car. He's a pretty tall guy, so he could talk directly through the crack in the window with ease. Landon huffed a loud puff before rolling down the window all the way. Once he did, Russell shifted his lean to the window sill. "What are you doing following me, Russ?"

"Oh, I didn't realize you had *girls* with you. Is that August?"

"Yes," Landon hissed through gritted teeth. "And Izzie."

"Hey, Russell," we chimed in unison. Isabell breathed a sigh of relief. She must have been holding it in for a while because it was a very heavy exhale.

"August, I didn't get to talk with you much at graduation." Russell nodded back to me. I forced a smile, but it felt like a frown. I may not have siblings, but Russell used the same tone of voice I'd heard from Isabell and Brett when they tried to rat each other out to their parents. Russell, I realized, was trying to get under Landon's skin.

"Can you not avoid my question for once, please?" Landon snapped.

"What was your question?" Russell played dumb, and Landon tightened his hands around the steering wheel.

"Why are you following me? How did you even know where I was?"

"I happened to be in French Gulch. Recognized your car, obviously."

"You just happened to be in French Gulch, at 11 p.m. on a Saturday?" As Landon interrogated, Russell nodded like a diligent student following along. "Alone?" Russell continued give non-verbal answers, and Landon scoffed. "Right."

"So what were you doing out there, anyway? Looking for something? Sharing secrets?"

Landon was quick to snap back. "Back off, Russ." I looked to my best friend, who seemed as confused as me. Something deeper was going on here.

"We were just trying to find a spot to hang out. It was no big deal," Tyler said as the ever cool cucumber. "You scared us, dude. We thought we were being stalked."

Tyler and Landon's differing takes on Russell were troubling. I trusted both of their inputs, so it was weird when they didn't align. I hardly knew Russell myself, despite agreeing to be his prom date a few months back. Even then, I did a lot more dancing and chatting with Isabell that night than with Russell. He was in the boys' year, not ours. Since I was close to Landon, I tended to stay away from him. Plus, he's a bit of a wild card. Rumor has it that he carried his dead pet squirrel in his backpack for a week earlier this year. Squirrel charmers aren't necessarily my cup of tea.

The way he stood in the window with his hood pulled over his head (in the heat, no less—after the sun sets, it can stay above 85 degrees until midnight), not immediately addressing Tyler's query, unsettled me. He simply stared at Tyler with vacant eyes, only to shift them to Landon a second later. It could have been my imagination, but I swore he raised an eyebrow. Like he was challenging Landon, or something.

"No harm, no foul. A simple mix up." I didn't even know what that meant, and felt my face subconsciously contort to one of disapproval. Russell looked back at me and Isabell. "Are we all okay here?"

Isabell elbowed me before I could say anything snarky, which was probably for the best. Russell smiled at us. An actual, genuine, *nice boy* smile. This whole interaction continued to baffle me. Next thing I knew, his face darkened as he curtly nodded at Landon. "See you round, Ty." I laughed in exasperation, earning me another elbow from my glowering best friend.

"What?" I mouthed.

Russell was off and away. Landon stayed parked until Russell flipped around and skirted out of the lot in his black sports car.

"Landon, what the hell was that?" I unbuckled and sat forward on the edge of my seat, so I was like the conscience on his shoulder.

"Just Russell being an ass like always."

"You should have let me at him. Like I said, I can talk some shit."

"Don't I know it," Landon repeated, with less of an edge. This time, the corners of his lips were turned up to a grin. I was glad to see him more like his usual self, so I threaded my fingers through his hair to ruffle it and give his head a little push forward.

He wasn't going to go any deeper than that, no matter how hard we tried. Isabell continued to ask how Russell knew we were there. Tyler agreed that it was pretty weird for him to be following us for no reason, and I did my best to pry into why Russell thought we were looking for something.

"Hold up, did you tell him about the treasure hunt?" With the way Isabell crossed her arms, I wasn't sure if a 'yes' answer would make her feel better or worse.

"What treasure hunt?" Landon turned back to us, his eyebrows scrunched together and darted between me and my backseat buddy.

"The one that the four of us are in battle for. Is there another treasure?" I asked.

"Right, yeah. I knew what you meant. Like I'd clue him into something like this." He kicked the car into gear and thus put a definitive end to the conversation about Russell.

To prep for departure, I slunk back into my seat and re-buckled my seatbelt. I cast one final glance out the window at the lake. It no longer held the same mystical glow of the moon, and instead looked like a black cauldron: brewing to cast a spell.

The next morning, I drove home in Mom's car. She had left it at the Trudeaus' to drive home with Dad, and now I could return at my leisure. I woke up on the earlier side, and since Isabell was groaning when I stirred, I dipped out while she slipped back to sleep. It wasn't unusual for us to not spend the day together after we slept at each other's houses. Besides, we already had plans to hang out tonight.

After returning from our evening of gallivanting with the boys, I had taken slight advantage of my best friend's half-drunk, half-tired stupor. The visit to Odette's old house clued me in that there was something suspicious going on in there, and I was sure that the only way to figure it out was to spend the night inside.

I had seized my opportunity last night as Isabell crawled under a blanket on the couch, prepping for some shut-eye.

"I have a brilliant idea."

"Can it wait until morning?"

"I'm too excited," I told her. When she sighed, I took that as a grant of permission and pounced on to the couch at her feet. "We should spend the night inside Odette Dupont's house. Tomorrow."

"You're joking."

"No, I'm serious. I had a feeling when I was up at the door, that there's *something there*."

"I'm sure there is, and I'm sure it's a ghost! You know I don't toy with supernatural beings."

"Please, Izzie! The boys probably have no clue that's why we went out to the house. We'd be pulling such a fast one on them, just think! It could be the leg up we need."

Mentioning our friendly competition with the boys was enough for Isabell to agree to the night in the spooky house. I slipped out the door early so she wouldn't have time to reconsider.

By the time I got home, my mom was already up and finishing the batch of croissants she had started from scratch yesterday afternoon. The buttery aromas floated to the door to greet me almost better than any hug could. I snatched one fresh off the baking sheet. More often than not, Mom is a great multi-tasker, especially while baking. Today she seemed a bit distracted, so after I nabbed a croissant, I was able to retreat quickly to my room.

The night shook me up a bit, but just enough. While the fleeting scare with the mysterious follower turned out to only be Russell, it did spark a reminder of the library incident. Now that I had some privacy, I was finally going to dive in to the books I rented and see what else I could dig up.

My day was spent reading through the French settlers book, since it was the best thing to do to pass my time. Every little thing felt important to understand, like it was all equipping me to march into battle. Against the boys, against some type of spirit, or anything, really.

She called me that afternoon and her words spread like nervous vomit through the phone.

"August. Okay, I've been thinking and dwelling all morning. I'm sorry. Ugh. I just can't go through with this."

"You can, trust me! It's going to be fine."

"What makes you think it's all going to be okay?"

"First things first, this house is basically in the middle of nowhere. There weren't even any signs of vandalism, as far as I could tell. People don't go there to cause trouble like they do at Boys Camp. And if trouble does come our way, I have my pepper spray and baseball bat packed and at the ready."

"Okay, okay. But what about ghosts? Can that protect us against ghosts? What will we do if we encounter some kind of spirit, and what if it's a mean spirit, and it kicks us out of the house? Or worse . . . traps us *in* the house."

"God forbid that happens, but if it does, we will just be terrible company. I've been told by my parents that I'm a sloppy dinner guest, I can bring some of that into play if we are held captive by evil spirits. We can drive them mad. Eventually, they will let us go because we are too much of a nuisance to keep around. Trust me."

EIGHT

It may have been *my* idea, but I was coming around to the thought that it may not necessarily be a *good* one. As Isabell and I stepped out of the car, Odette Dupont's old house loomed over us just like it had last night. We were arriving later tonight, judging by the fact the moon had long set. For that reason it was much darker, and more difficult to make out any distinct features of the house.

"Foreboding," I said aloud.

"Huh?"

"It's creepy. We can hardly even see the outline of the house, but we know it's there." Given Isabell's paranoia when it comes to paranormal superstition, I left out my own suspicions. If I told her about the orbs of light and shuffles of movement I saw last night, she'd flip. Granted, even without visual confirmation, it's realistic to infer that this place has at least one spirit walking the halls. It had strong vibes of abandonment issues left unsettled. Probably dead set on revenge in its afterlife.

"Are you trying to freak me out more? I'm hardly on board with this as it is."

Yeah, that settles it. I definitely won't relay my theory of ghostly revenge plots to Isabell.

"Of course I'm not. It's fine, Iz. I'm not worried." Her fears quieted, at least for the time being, so we grabbed our sleeping bags and backpacks before ascending the rickety stairs of the old wooden house. My baseball bat was resting on my shoulders, ready to go in a moment's notice.

"How is this thing still standing? Scratch that. *Why* is it still standing?"

"I guess Odette's great-niece owns it and has always been really clear about keeping it around. She's still alive, but in a home out on the coast." I had found that out this morning when I dug into the house's history online. There had been a petition to tear it down a few years back because people saw it as a fire hazard, but that's when Odette's next of kin came forward.

Isabell grumbled something to herself as we walked around the porch in search of an unlocked window or door. Several of them were boarded up, but we found a small pane on the side of the house that we were able to open and climb through. My feet creaked on the tattered floorboards as I landed inside. Isabell hesitated upon hearing the sound, so I extended my hand. Once she grabbed it, I pulled her into the belly of the beast.

If you've ever entered a house like this one at night, you probably know the feeling. You tiptoe around as if the slightest misstep will siphon you into the core of its very being, which was likely a pit of fire or a midnight swamp. You circle the perimeter of the rooms like you would a sleeping dragon, trying to read the etching of its face while you dare not wake it.

That's all strictly metaphorical, of course.

Out of instinct, Isabell fumbled for a light switch as soon as she set foot inside. Her breathing was as ragged as someone finishing their first marathon, made worse by the fact that the house had no electricity. I wasn't sure what she expected to happen, but kept my mouth shut.

"It's okay," I said instead. "That's why we brought our flashlights." With the guidance of our lights, we slowly glided our way through the main floor.

"I don't know, Auggie. This floor seems to be made out of brittle bones. It could give out on us literally any second." On our next step, the rugged hardwood groaned and Isabell yelped as she lurched for my arm. Before I knew it, my arm was enveloped by the fuzz of her pale-blue, oversized sweater.

Despite the fact that it was warm out, Isabell had insisted on wearing her sweater. Her rationale was that if the house *was* haunted, the spirits would keep the temperature down. I asked her what she would do if it wasn't cold in there, and she responded by saying she'd still be spooked, and her sweater would make her feel comfy and safe—her words.

"Geeeez, you planning to take me down with you if you go?" I tried to joke, and Isabell released my arm.

"Not intentionally, but if I'm going down, I sure as hell don't want to go alone. Seriously, this place *has* to be possessed." A small gust of wind blew through the house, and Isabell sharply inhaled. My heart skipped a beat, but I swallowed it.

What *was* that?

"It's okay, Iz. This house isn't really sealed, it's bound to be a little drafty."

"The way you rationalize crazy crap is beyond me. Don't you *know* fear? Hi, August, it's me. Nice to meet you." Isabell shook my hand and then wrapped both her arms around one of mine and ducked behind me. "You know I'm not usually this much of a scaredy-cat, but I don't mess with ghosts."

Ever since we were little kids, Isabell has pegged me as the brave one between us. When there was a spider in the corner, she'd call for me. When the other kids were rude on the playground, I'd stick up for her. When we wanted to race down the hill in shopping carts, I was the one to try it and consequently need stitches in my calf and a cast for my arm. If I felt a little fear in this house, I had to hold it in, if only for Isabell's sake. Losing my cool would no doubt send her spiraling out the door.

We kept inching further into the house. Past the wooden staircase and front entryway, we came to an arched opening that led to a sitting room. There wasn't much furniture in there, and the pieces that remained were covered with sheets.

Right, like that would protect it against half a century's worth of dust.

"How about here for our sleeping bags?" I suggested.

Isabell sighed. "Fine."

"I just want to put down my stuff."

"Are we *actually* going to sleep here, August?"

While interested in posting up for the night in this creepy, 150-year-old house, it didn't quite seem worth it to me if Isabell would be miserable. "We don't have to. I am curious about that hex thing my dad mentioned. But obviously I don't want to be hexed myself. At the least, it'd be nice if we could get some kind of clue for the Ruggles treasure."

"Can we make it quick? The hair on my neck is sticking straight up. Major heebie-jeebies. I want to leave."

"Oh, going so soon, are we?"

Isabell screamed, and I widened my eyes. There was no time for me to react as a spastic Isabell yanked me to the ground. As my heart rate settled down from its spike to 200, I at the culprits. There were two of them, both shining flashlights eerily on to their faces. Without the light, I still would have recognized that voice. I'd know it anywhere.

"Landon *Bennett* Jones. *What* the hell?" I snapped at him, crossing my arms and making a move to stand up. Landon pursed his lips to refrain from a snicker, which almost made me laugh for whatever reason. I turned to Isabell, who had instinctively crumbled to the floor and now rested in the fetal position. She had, of course, taken me down with her. I guess she wasn't kidding about that one.

Tyler was gracious enough to help her up, though he was frowning. "Sorry to scare you so bad. We meant it to be funny, but clearly it wasn't."

"It's okay, Ty. This is not unusual for me." She scoffed, in an odd attempt to seem carefree and casual. Bless her soul, I couldn't understand how she managed to stay cool despite a collapse to the ground. I offered my support for her to save face.

"When we went to Hawes last Halloween, the same thing happened in the middle of the corn maze," I clarified while Isabell straightened up, dusted off, and cleared her throat. "What are you guys doing here, anyhow?"

"We could be asking the same thing," Landon flashed his light back and forth between our eyes.

"We were here first, what's your story?" Isabell was back, playing the tough guy now.

He paced carefully, like a lawyer in a court room. "You see, last night, we were out and about in this very neighborhood like it was a normal Saturday night activity. And we started to think about your suggestion to come all the way out here, to an unknown house, for absolutely no reason."

"Your point being?" I tightened the fold of my arms, the perfect vision of a defensive witness called to the stand for interrogation.

"It was suspicious. Then Isabell was a little *too* eager about swinging by this particular house. We got to thinking maybe there was something of value to this place after all, and maybe we had been used by the two girls we trusted not to break our hearts." He put a hand over his heart and bowed his head.

"All's fair in love and war, remember?"

"Yes, I do believe that was the agreement," Landon continued with his mock-formal tone. "Doesn't stop the sting."

I had to laugh at him. "What is with you?"

"Nothing!" he tried, but he was fighting a smile. "You know, you should be grateful we're here. After the scare last night with Russell, we are two chivalrous gents who are valiantly protecting the maids-in-waiting."

"These maids don't need protecting," I corrected, thinking of the small arsenal I had toted to this house. It was a bit weird sneaking an aluminum baseball bat out of my house, but I had managed.

However, at the same time I spoke my peace, Isabell chirped her gratitude. "It's real nice of you guys to look out for us."

"Of course, Iz! Where are the sleeping bags set up?" Tyler was on board, since the consent had come from Isabell.

"In the other room," she said immediately, pointing to our sleeping bags.

"Isabell," I whispered as the boys moved to drop their stuff next to ours. "We don't want them to stay."

"Except . . . well, I kind of do?" She shrugged. I smacked a hand to my forehead like this was the biggest thwart to our mission. "I'm sorry! It's so creepy in here and it's slightly better knowing that Ty and Landon are here, too."

"Because we need the boys for safety?"

"No, no. Well, kind of, a little. No. Definitely not, I'm pretty sure your pepper spray and baseball bat are enough. It's a simple numbers game, Auggie." I glanced over to the other room, where the boys were making themselves well at home. "I mean, it's also *Landon*. Don't you wanna—"

"I was about to agree with you on them staying, but when you say it like that, I wanna crawl into a hole," I retorted.

"Fine, fine. Then, for me?"

"For you and Tyler?"

Isabell groaned. We had both been avoiding our respective truths long enough, but it was time to come clean. At least, it was time for *Isabell* to come clean. "If I say yes, will you agree to let them stay?"

I shrugged. "Sure."

She huffed at me and lowered her voice. "Yes, I like him. Okay? Now can they stay?"

"A-HA!" I yelled. "I knew it!" That earned me a prompt shushing from my best friend. There was no way I was going to blow her cover, no matter how obvious it may be to the untrained eye that they *both* liked each other. Her eyes were pleading, so I didn't make matters worse. Instead, I behaved.

"What do we do now that they are here? Do we even go ahead with the search?" she whispered.

"So, what's the plan? Are we trying to summon the ghost of Odette?" Landon called, and we waltzed over to where they were in the other room. I crossed my arms over my chest, wondering how *he* knew about Odette. I debated asking him just that, but Isabell spoke up first.

"What makes you ask that?" Isabell asked, wary.

"You haven't heard the rumors about this place?"

We shook our heads no. Landon nodded for Tyler to say it.

"The legend goes that after Odette Dupont died in this house, she never actually *left*."

"Uh-huh," I hummed, while Isabell shuddered beside me. Despite what I had experienced last night with the orb of light, I was still mostly unfazed. I wasn't going to let anything push us off course.

Landon picked up the story. "Neighbors said they have driven past this house, and seen the front porch rocking chairs swaying back and forth. Doesn't matter if it's windy or the calmest day of the year, they've seen the chair rocking."

"Maybe that house is slanted, Landon. Constant momentum," I pointed out, slowly waving my hand back and forth for effect.

"Then explain why they have also seen a female silhouette in the upstairs window? Not only that, but at the same time every single Wednesday? And the week of July 24th every year, they hear *undeniable* moaning from the house that echoes through this part of the canyon."

"Is that the day she died?" Isabell asked in a deep whisper.

"Beats me," Landon shrugged.

"Wait a second. July 24th? Actually?" I asked.

"Yeah, why?"

I shook my head in slight disbelief. "That's the day that Ruggles brothers were kidnapped from their jail cells and lynched."

Tyler blew out a low whistle, while Landon clicked his tongue. "Wow. Good memory, Auger. I couldn't even tell you the exact year. The 1880s to 90s would be my best bet."

"1892," I pinged like I was on a game show.

"You're a wizard."

"Does this mean that Odette could really have a connection to John Ruggles?" As Isabell's frightened question ended, the door to the living room slammed shut and a whirl of wind shot up through the floorboards. The door re-opened, and then teetered to and fro. "Oh boy."

We all stood frozen, and Landon was the first to speak. "Should we check this place out a bit more?"

"Can't hurt, right?"

"Can't hurt, Auggie?!" She gestured wildly about the room. "Am I the only one who witnessed what just happened?"

"Maybe we should split up into teams then," Landon suggested, which earned him a scoff from Isabell. "Ty and Isabell, you can join forces. August, we can be a team?"

"Isabell and I are a team. We are against you and Ty in this search, remember?" At this point I was standing closest to Landon, namely since Tyler was keeping an eye on a very worried Isabell.

Landon ducked his head down to whisper in my ear. "Tyler's got a big thing for Isabell. Maybe we can let them lean on each other, what do you say?"

I did a silent cheer for my best friend. Of course, based on previous observations this wasn't exactly new info, but it was still great to have it confirmed via Landon.. When my eyes fell on the two of them, I caved.

"Alright, fine. You good with that, Iz?" Isabell was surprised by my easy agreement, that much I could tell. But to refuse this idea would mean one of two things. One, that the boys made us nervous. Or two, that we didn't want anything to do with them. Since neither were true, try as we might to convince ourselves otherwise, it was time to get on with it.

"I'm a little freaked, but I guess it's a plan."

"Great!" Landon cheered with sarcastic, but somehow genuine, enthusiasm. He put his hands on my shoulders, and I jumped a little. "Better get after it then." He spun me around and gently ushered me out of the room. As soon as we were in the hall, I slid out of his touch, but he failed to noticed or react to my abruptness.

Instead, he got right to business. "Where do we start?"

"I guess at the stairs?"

The house was rather large, leading me to believe the Duponts had struck it rich during the gold rush. After all, big veins of quartz and gold had been discovered basically down the street from here back in the 1850s. This place was probably consider a mansion in its day: two stories, with the top as large as the bottom, just with higher ceilings. Hell, it was huge by today's standards even.

"Hey, Auger?" When he had my attention, he bolted. "Race you to the top!"

I dashed after him, my competitive bone itching to point out he had an unfair head start. "Wait!"

As I was scratching at his heels, his foot shot straight through the floorboard. There was no time for me to react, so I tripped and landed straight on top of him. Not even in a way that prompted any kind of heat or intimacy. It was a clumsy, tangled, messy fall.

"Are you guys okay?" Tyler called from the other room.

"We're fine!" I called back through gritted teeth.

"We *would* be, if you hadn't just kneed me where the sun don't shine." Landon strained for the words, and I thanked what was left of my lucky stars that it was dark in here. My face felt hot. At least my embarrassment could be kept a secret—nothing a little snark can't cover up.

"I wouldn't have kneed you if you hadn't stomped through the floor," I retorted as I stood. "Sorry, though," I admitted sheepishly, extending my hands in a peace offering to help him up. When he grabbed, I pulled, though he did most of the work. He grumbled under his breath as he stood upright. Once he was up, we nearly fell backwards down the stairs, but he slipped his hand around to my waist to steady us.

Not the touch I expected. Talk about intimate.

My stomach jittered as we were positioned in another stance of closeness. The paranoia also set in that my feelings for him were blatantly obvious, no matter how hard I tried to bury them. Goodness gracious, could he *hear* how hard my heart was beating right now?

I cleared my throat, as if that could kill my nerves. "Are you okay to go on?"

Landon coughed, and his sly grin formed even in the dark as he patted me on the back.

A pat on the back? What am I, a kid on a little league team?

I nearly frowned, but then he grabbed my hand to tug me up the stairs behind him. Just like that, I was right back to resisting any other pulls I subconsciously felt from Landon.

At the top of the stairs, we dropped our hands and looked back and forth down the hall. There was only one window, at the very far end. The hallway was long, with two smaller halls forming a mezzanine balcony above the staircase. With a quick scan, I noted there were eight doors total up here.

"This is bigger than I thought," Landon whispered. "Which end should we start on?"

"I guess the end opposite of the window?" I shrugged at the suggestion, not convinced it mattered where we started, and Landon agreed. We got to the first door at the end of the hall, and it turned out to be a nearly empty linen closet. After shining our lights inside, all we found were dust bunnies and an exceptionally old broom.

"Here?" Landon pointed to the adjacent door, and we went in. The bedroom inside was simple. A bed, vanity, wardrobe, and small nightstand. We rifled through some of the items, but the vanity was entirely empty, as was the wardrobe. Landon crouched down to check under the bed, leaning on it as he did. A thick puff of dust shot in the air as he put his hand on the sheet-less bed to stand back up.

"Holy mack," he choked out, waving his hand wildly.

"There's nothing in here, let's move on." I ignored his dust plume and gestured for us to roll out of the room. So far, we were down two doors, with six left to go. We made our way around the balcony overlooking the stairs. There were two normal doors, and a set of French doors. Once we were close enough to the rail, I peered over the edge. Tyler and Isabell were walking below with their arms linked together. He looked like he was escorting her at a Victorian ball.

"Looks like those two are getting along well," I whispered to Landon, ribbing him with my elbow.

"They owe it to us, you know. If we hadn't been lab partners in chemistry, I doubt you and I would have hung out much. And we dragged them along with us, so they got to meet."

"Isabell and I have known Tyler since elementary school."

"Right, but you and I brought them back together in high school, paving the way for this holy matrimony."

"Holy matrimony?" I raised my eyebrows at him.

He laughed quietly, wrinkling his nose. "Whatever." Something was different about Landon tonight, and it wouldn't take a genius to figure *what* it was. The guy was flirty as hell. The crucial question was *why*.

For the third time, he grabbed my hand as we moved into another room. This one was large and empty. It was U-shaped and looped around the French doors, and to the door across the stairs. The floor was old and a little rotted, or so I suspected with the crawling scent of mildew. Even still, it was a bit fancier than the rest of the house. Only after my eyes adjusted better to the room did it click.

A ballroom.

Two high, arched windows framed the main wall, and the two side walls were floor-to-ceiling mirrors. The reflection was all the more eerie with its caked on layer of aged grime.

"Whoa," Landon awed. "Check out this chandelier. Is it just me or does it seem like it's new?" He was standing directly under it.

He wasn't wrong. While the style was antique, it had a glimmer that made it look free of dust. "It's almost like a ghost swipes through to polish it every now and then," I said, chuckling at the idea.

"Damn. You aren't a *little* creeped out in here?"

I shrugged. "Not really."

Spookiness danced in the air, no doubt. But I didn't really mind it all that much. At this point, there wasn't any factual evidence to form a foundation of fear. Most of the things in here that were creepy simply due to the age of the house, aside from the sparkling chandelier.

Besides, I was carrying the group's perseverance on my back, for better or worse. My biggest fear was that, if I showed any alarm or hesitation, they would back out. And I wasn't about to let that happen—not just yet, anyway.

"You really keep squishing this good girl persona, you know," he joked. "And you aren't even trying."

I scoffed and rolled my eyes. "What good girl persona?"

"You get good grades and you're never in trouble. Isn't that what good girls do?"

"I'm never in trouble because I never get caught," I retorted. Not that I've stretched too far in the realm of trouble, but the idea applies nonetheless. As an only child, you either learn to be sneaky or you iron out your creases for good. "But hey, if this place is freaking you out, we can go," I taunted.

"Nah," he played it off, effectively launching us into a game of chicken. "I'm feeling good."

"Are you sure? You don't have to be brave for me, Lanno," I said in a rare moment of using his nickname.

He chuckled and ran a hand through his hair as he closed the gap between us. "I'm good right here. We can give the lovebirds some privacy."

"Hm, I see. Hiding behind Tyler so you can seem as tough as a bull or bison or some other macho animal."

"What?"

"The lovebird thing?"

"Now who said I was talking about those two?"

My face dropped in surprise, and I tried to gulp down the knot in my throat. "Weren't you?"

He just shrugged and surveyed the room, taking a small step back from me.

"Piano. Fancy sofas. A chandelier. If I didn't know any better, I'd say this is a ballroom." He eyes fell back on me. "But you already knew that, didn't you?" I returned his shrug, and he grinned. "Then maybe we should dance."

"Landon." This time I was less joke-y.

"Don't say my name like that!" He chided, but he still had that mischievous look. "Come on, why not?"

"It's not what we're here for." I had to keep my answers concise. If I said much more, my nerves would be too obvious. The choppy sentences were a double-edged sword though, because they made my voice seep with annoyance.

"Puh-lease," he scoffed. "You mean the clues? Do you *really* want to look for clues with me? How do you know I'm not sabotaging your efforts?"

I crossed my arms. "Are you?"

He put his hands up in surrender before moseying over to one of the sofas. Once there, he plopped down dramatically and dust shot up. His hacking sent me into a fit of laughter.

"Twice, that's twice you've let that happen!" I cackled, unable to stop myself. The dust wasn't even that funny. It certainly didn't warrant a doubled-over, knee-slapping laugh, but sometimes you just fall into the giggles and can't stop no matter how hard you try.

Landon had stood, and was now walking over to me in my hunched-over state. At this point I was struggling for air with my intense belly laughs, but I tried my best to stand up straight. One deep breath and I steadied myself to meet his eyes. When I did, I caught a glint of playfulness, and that sent me yet again.

"I'm sorry! I ... I can't," I sputtered out between laughs.

"Remember when I said this isn't over?"

That sobered me up. "Landon, wait, not now. I'm too weak from laughter and—" My point didn't matter. He made a dive around me, tickling and poking at my sides and try as I might, I could not control myself with laughter. This time, he was laughing with me. "Please, I beg! Truce! Truce, Landon, please."

He stopped pretty quick, but was still laughing. It subsided to make way for a crooked smile. Smug, even. "I'll stop on one condition. Dance with me."

My non-combative answer surprised us both. "Why not."

"Really?" He raised an eyebrow.

I rolled my eyes and made a slight move to exit his grasp. "But not if you waste any more time."

"Don't have to tell me twice." His right arm slid around my back, and his left hand grabbed mine. Not a moment later, he was leading us back and forth. I can admit, it was actually kind of nice.

If I am being brutally honest with myself, it was actually *very* nice.

"What made you say yes?" Landon asked after a second of our twirling around. He was quiet, like he was walking on eggshells.

"The move was cheesy. I took pity," I joked, and he laughed.

"I'll take what I can get."

I paused, debating a question that only felt natural to ask next. "Why did you ask me to dance?"

"You owe me a dance."

"*I* owe *you* one? Don't you think it should be the other way around?"

"You went to prom with my step-brother, knowing how much I don't like him. I think that puts you in the red."

I scoffed. "I only went with him because . . ." I trailed off. No way was I going to confess to Landon, not that easy. How could I admit out loud that I had expected him to ask me? I felt stupid enough that he went with Stacey. Reliving that humiliation two months later wasn't exactly on my to-do list.

"Because, why?"

I looked anywhere but at him. My head burned to answer his question, just to get it off my chest. If anything, so I could rid myself of this exasperation once and for all.

"Because, he asked me," I blurted. "I wasn't going to make him feel bad by saying no. Besides, I was one of the last people without a date, so I knew no one else was going to ask me."

When I finally looked up at Landon, he was staring off over my shoulder.

"I guess it is me who owes you the dance," he said simply. Confused, I angled my head up at him. My stare seemed to fluster him, and his next words sputtered out. "Well, uh. I did want to ask you. To prom. And I didn't. And then my . . . Russell, did, instead."

"Mm," I mumbled as I looked away. I didn't want to delve too much into this conversation. It was a perfectly pleasant moment we were having. Our chat dared to taint it, and we were already unraveling too much.

"She asked me before I could ask you. Otherwise, I would have." Of course, he was referencing Stacey. "But then you went with Russell, and I was at a loss. I was, you know, bummed?"

As he said the words, he gently squeezed me a smidge closer to him. A negligible amount to the untrained eye, but I knew, and my heart was pounding away. Factoring in his small confession, my insides had turned into a freaking zoo. Landon and I have never talked like this before. It was causing a seven car pile-up in my intestines.

"Oh."

"Oh?" He chuckled.

"Sorry. I guess I'm surprised."

He didn't add anything else—probably waiting on me to chime in, but that wasn't going to happen. My throat was constricted, and with his subtle pull there was certainly not enough room between us for Jesus.

Instead of answering with words, I gave in, and let my head rest on his chest. Standing at five-foot-six myself, Landon is a nice height for me. Coming up to his shoulders, it's easy to rest my head in the crook of his neck. There wasn't an expectation for him to respond to my move, but a moment later he rested his cheek on the top of my head.

Something felt fragile as we danced together, like either of us could move and shatter glass. A song began to play in my head, one I hadn't heard before. It was instrumental, purely piano, and it was a bit tense, almost like it was off-key. Haunting, but beautiful. Heartbroken, yet hopeful.

What a weird way to set the mood, I thought about my own subconscious. *Focus. You're dancing with Landon freaking Jones. Focus! Or, don't. Just relax, August. Relax.*

"August," Landon started, yanking me out of my mental pep talk. "Is it just me or is there music coming from the piano?"

NINE

My eyes, which I hadn't noticed were shut, blinked open in shock. Just like that, I was awakened from any spell I had been under. "That's real?"

We parted slightly, and I tilted my head to study his face. I couldn't help but think this sound just ruined any romance that had been brewing. With the spooky tune in the background, it'd be hard to get that feeling back.

Since it was difficult to tell what was happening, we broke apart to check the piano out up close, the air feeling cold with the space between us. While no figure sat at the bench, the keys appeared to be in play, as if invisible hands were tapping the white and black pads.

"What the . . ." Landon trailed. I was just as dumbfounded. I squinted, and took a small step closer. "Careful," he warned.

I nodded, reached out my hand, and swiped over where a person would sit. I touched nothing, but the playing stopped abruptly after three more notes played way out of tune.

"What did you do?" Landon whispered. I was thankful that his tone was more fearful than it was accusatory, because I had a gut feeling I had just messed something up terribly.

"I'm not sure."

The ground beneath our feet started to shake. With it, the dust was disturbed and began to fall in small then large pieces from the ceiling. The sound of a high-voltage current rippled through the air, seemingly from nowhere. I didn't even think this house had electricity, but it buzzed around us.

"Landon? What's happening?"

"I . . . I don't know."

"August!" It was Isabell, but her voice sounded distant. "Landon! August!"

"This isn't good," I said. The words came out more casual than how I felt. My heart was hammering in my chest. We were in deep shit, but it was surreal. Clouds of falling dust were swirling down, as if creating their own weather front.

"Come on. We have to go. Now." Landon tugged on my elbow, but I didn't budge. The shaking was all around us now, from the floors to the walls to the ceiling. But it was like my feet were cemented into the ground. "August, let's go!"

The doors to the room slammed shut. It grabbed Landon's attention, but not mine. My eyes were fixed on the piano. A figure appeared on the bench: a woman in a long white gown, a wedding dress. Her eyes glowed green, and as they glowered at me, I worried they would puncture my soul.

My sharp intake of breath caused Landon to turn back to me, just as the figment disappeared.

"Landon, I—"

"There's no time. This house could literally crumble any second, we need to get out of here. *Now.*"

I tore my eyes from the bench back to him. His hand was still gripping my elbow, his eyebrows scrunched together. For the first time, I was aware of how the house croaked and groaned as it rumbled beneath our feet.

I nodded breathlessly, but a faint crack caught our attention before our feet spun into motion. "What was that?"

"I don't know," he answered, and we frantically scanned the room for any signs of danger. "It almost sounded like it came from the ceiling," he added at the sound of another crack.

"The chandelier."

As if it had been waiting for its cue, the light flickered. The lights didn't even work in this house, yet there was the chandelier, flickering away. Without missing another beat, it snapped from the ceiling, yanking old, frayed wires and plugs down with it. We ducked and clutched each other for safety against the plummet of the chandelier. I could hear my own ragged breathing as I sat on the floor, arms around Landon. I was confused, but in tentative awe of the unearthly phenomenon.

The chandelier, in an event of supernatural surprise, did not break through the ballroom floor. As it hit the ground, it sounded like fragmenting crystal, and the impact simultaneously shattered the mirrored wall.

Landon, by some miracle, stayed rational while I drifted way off into space. He lifted me to my feet while I stared with a dropped jaw at the intact floor. A moment later, we were out the door and jogging down the stairs. Isabell called my name again, a mild distraction that caused me to look up and subsequently lose my footing.

I stumbled into the hole previously made by Landon, and a loud, vibrating grunt emerged from the cracks beneath my foot. With a twist of my ankle, I fell.

"Ow," I muttered, squinting at where my ankle was caught between the broken boards.

"Shit." Landon hurried to me, sliding his arms under my shoulders to help me back to a standing position. Once upright, I was able to wiggle my foot out from the jagged hole.

"We got the stuff, alright? Hurry up, you guys!" Isabell shouted at the bottom of the steps.

"Go ahead, I'll catch up," I called back to her and Tyler. Landon nodded them on, and the two of them dashed on to the side window we had entered through. Isabell was fighting against Tyler for a moment, insisting she wouldn't leave me in the house, but he spoke to her quietly and turned her shoulders toward the exit.

"Are you okay to walk, August? We gotta get out of here."

"Yeah, I'm good. I'm good. Let's go." On the way down, particles of wood were dropping from the ceiling in fits of antique dust. Something wet dripped on my leg, so as we made our way to the side window, I caught a glimpse of a handkerchief in the corner of my eye. I picked it up without thinking and stuffed it in my jean shorts pockets so I could clean myself up later.

Landon slid out the window first, then helped me before slamming the window shut. Isabell and Tyler were huddled together on the lawn, and when Landon and I emerged from the side of the house, she broke free and snatched me into one of her big, bone-crushing hugs.

The strangest thing, though. Almost immediately after our feet stepped off the porch, the house stopped shaking. The dust plume that had exploding from the windows and roof disappeared in a magic poof. Quicker than it started, it was over.

Like it didn't even happen in the first place.

TEN

From where Isabell and I stood, embraced in a sideways hug beside Landon and Tyler, the house sat the same as when we arrived a few hours ago. Tall, dark, and perhaps now more unidentifiable than ever. While it appeared unscathed by the disturbance of the force, something about it was also entirely different. Mystical . . . mythical, even.

"Holy crap," Isabell panted.

"What just happened?"

Landon and I looked at each other, taking a silent oath not to tell all that we saw in there. What was there to say, anyway? If I was going to speak up about seeing a ghost, now was my chance. The more I thought about it, the more the words were caught in the back of my throat, threatening to choke me. I had to cough to rid of the feeling, and swallow to stuff it back down.

Besides, what if it wasn't really a ghost? What if that figment was just my imagination? I'm not a big believer in ghosts, but I couldn't make sense of what I saw. So how could I put it in to words? Between me and Isabell, I was the grounded one. What happens when the supporting rock crumbles?

Landon paced back and forth a few small steps at a time, running his hand down his face and through his hair. Tyler, normally very even keel, was wringing his hands together and holding his breath.

Or so it seemed, at least. In contrast to Isabell, whose breathing was shallow, Tyler's exhales were long and almost forceful.

"What the hell is going on?" Tyler's restrained stress was out of character, and caused Isabell to jump and dart her eyes side to side, judging everyone's reaction. Landon stopped pacing and put his hands on his waist.

Isabell loosened her grip on me, and her step back forced me to stand on my own. I felt a twinge in my ankle and wobbled slightly. "Ow," I whispered, shifting my weight to my left foot. No one seemed to hear me, though, because Isabell started to rant.

"You guys, this is *not* good. That was a freaking train wreck in there!"

"We made it out okay," Landon tried. Isabell threw her arms in the air.

"The house almost collapsed!" She emphasized this by gesturing wildly to the house. "With us in it. We must have angered a spirit or something. I know that wasn't all in my head. There was dust crumbling from the ceiling and everything shaking. Candlesticks falling and vases shattering. Dishes were flying out of the cabinet and smashing into the walls! Expensive China, too! None of that was normal. It really has me questioning this whole treasure hunt thing." She stopped flailing her arms and crossed them tightly over her chest. "And we don't even know what happened! What if it follows us and haunts us for the rest of our lives? What if—"

I grabbed her shoulder and made her face me. "Isabell. Breathe."

"You breathe!"

"Breathe with me." My voice was calm. I exaggerated a long breath in my nose, then out my mouth. She didn't follow, so I started again and beckoned for her to join. For the second round, she did, and we synced our breath for a few cycles. "Better?"

"Yeah, thanks."

"Good, good." I stepped back, and my ankle almost gave out. "Ow."

"Are you okay, August?"

I looked down at my foot, but was unable to make anything out in the dark. "I think so, I just felt a sting. I'm okay."

"Shit, that's from that fall you took isn't it?"

"I guess. I'm sure it's fine, guys." The fall had slipped my mind in all the chaos. Now that everyone was looking at me, I remember the wetness around my ankle. "I just cut it on some splintered wood."

"It looked like you twisted it. Maybe you need to sit down." As Landon suggested I sit on the car, Isabell picked up a rock.

"This is what you get for hurting my best friend!" She cried as she chucked it at the house. Typically not the athletic one, this particular throw of hers had remarkable aim, and she ended up hitting a second-story window.

"Izzie!" Tyler gasped.

"Ooookay," she backpedaled, "I immediately regret that decision."

I looked to Landon. His lips were pursed in thought as he stared up at the house. A sound from the door caused me to whip my head back to the house. The front door burst open, so aggressively that it hit the wall of the house. A dense flurry of dust funneled out the door, whooshing through the air straight toward us. Everyone scattered from its path, but I was spellbound, just like I had been in that ballroom. So I remained, taking a small step back only for my ankle to give out on me.

I fell backwards to the ground, and the force spurred closer to me. Hiding my eyes in the crook of my elbow, I braced for impact. I uncovered my eyes when I heard footsteps. It was Landon, running back to me.

Before it could come in contact with me, Landon shot the contents of a water bottle straight at the moving cloud. In contact with water, it fizzled with a sad little hissing sound, and what was left of it retreated to the house. It slammed the door shut behind it, and from our distant spot we could heard the sound of locks snapping into place.

We all exhaled together when chaos was surrendered and peace was restored. They were all checking in with each other, but I was still fixated on the house. There was a strange glow in the upstairs room that only I seemed to notice. In a second, it was gone.

"Whoa," Tyler blinked in astonishment.

"What was that?" Isabell's voice was getting higher and higher in pitch. My eyes darted to them, wondering if they saw the same orb radiating upstairs. But they were all looking at each other, and I realized I was in fact the only one to see the light.

"Are you really okay?" Landon asked again, sticking out his hands to help me back to my feet. My ankle almost gave out again, and he steadied me. "Shit, is that your ankle? We need to check that out. Maybe you really twisted when you fell."

"That's exactly what happened. I'm sure it's okay, I just need to walk it off. I'm more concerned about that cloud of dust that just came after me." My ankle was throbbing now that the adrenaline was dying down a little. But I was sure the pain would subside eventually. How often do we make mountains out of mole hills with injuries? And not even have so much as a bruise to show for it?

"Here, use my arm as a crutch," Landon offered. I raised my eyebrows at him when he stuck out his arm like a gentleman at a ball. He shrugged, as if the action meant nothing, even though my stomach flipped. He responded to my hesitation with a simple, "I don't mind."

I linked my arm through his. Perhaps it was embarrassing and not the most ideal of circumstances for physical proximity, but I kind of enjoyed it in spite of myself. "I'm holding you to those words, you know."

"Auggie, I feel like we need to get you and, well, all of us to safety and away from this death trap of a house. I just . . . I gotta get out of here," Isabell shuddered.

A flashing light caught all our attention, but it wasn't coming from the house. It was from the main road, and blinking red and blue. I could feel the blood drain from my face.

"Shit." Landon spat under his breath.

"Oh no, is that a cop?" Isabell whispered, covering her mouth with her hands and then biting her nails. "My parents are going to kill me if they find out we got in trouble with a cop."

"Let's play it low, alright? I'll take the lead," Landon stood up a little straighter. I started to slide my arm out of his grip. He let me go, but I was sensitive to his eyes following me. Hobbling over to his truck, I leaned back on the front corner just in time for the squad car to pull up next to us.

Two men hopped out of the car, with shoulders much straighter and broader than Landon or Tyler. Our two boys were tall, but they didn't have the bulk that the two officers did. Isabell pattered over to me before the cops sauntered up. The comfort of my best friend, even if she was breathing heavily, was nice to have by my side in our first run-in with the authorities.

"We got a call about some potential trespassing in the neighborhood. You kids wouldn't know anything about that, would you?"

"No, sir. We just heard this was a great spot for stars after the moon sets. I'm Landon." With one hand in his jean pockets, he extended the other for a firm handshake.

"I'm Officer Johns," the driver of the car said, returning the shake with a single, curt tug. "This here is my partner, Officer Adkins. You're telling me you're only here for the stars?"

"Yes, sir."

"A-ha," Officer Johns said. He flipped open a small spiral notepad. "We got a call that some teenagers were messing around in the old house at the end of the street. You're aware this is private property, right?"

"Sorry, sir. We didn't see a sign or anything marking it as private or posted. I used to live in French Gulch, a few years back, and would ride my bike by. I never saw anyone here, so I figured it was abandoned. I didn't think anyone would notice or be too bothered."

"Evidently, someone was." It was Officer Adkins, for the first time. The way he said it made the hair on the back of my neck stand up, thinking of someone following us again. Isabell must have had the same thought, because she grabbed my wrist.

"I'm really sorry about that, officers. We're leaving right now, right guys?"

Together, the three of us chorused in agreement to confirm that we'd get out of there. Really, anything to stay out of trouble with the cops.

"We're just going to take a look around, make sure nothing seems out of whack on the house."

Well, shoot. The house was just nearly destroyed. Not that we did it, but if it was trashed inside, we'd look guilty. As they marched up toward the house, Isabell whispered to me. "I mean, it was basically falling down before we even got here. What do they think they'll find?"

"Hopefully they won't think too much of the shattered chandelier."

"Maybe they won't go inside," Landon whispered back.

We watched on as the cops surveyed the perimeter of the porch. They poked their batons at the windows, exchanged words between themselves, and shined their flashlights inside the house. Thank goodness Isabell and Tyler grabbed the sleeping bags. Inside, they would have been incriminating.

"The side window was open." Tyler covered his mouth, thinking us doomed.

"We have Landon to thank for that. He closed it," I assured, and Tyler clapped Landon on the back.

The two cops secured the rest of the perimeter, making their way all the way around the porch and to the front door. They appeared to be checking the security of the house. They shined a light on the door and the locks, and pushed to see if it would open. It didn't budge.

Without looking at us, the cops trekked back down the overgrown path to where us four stood. Their voices were low, the only sound to be heard beside the wind at this hour.

"Well," Officer Johns began. "We didn't see any signs of forced entry or vandalism on the house, or anything out of the ordinary for that matter."

"Does that mean we can go?" Isabell chimed in. Officer Adkins eyed her eagerness, but they must have interpreted it as innocence because they granted us the right to leave.

"Consider it a warning. Don't let us catch you out here again, you hear?"

"Yes sir," Landon spoke for us. We all agreed with a thank you as the cops spun back to their squad car. Only then did we let out a sigh of relief.

"Let's get out of here, I'm more ready than *ever*."

"Do you guys want to meet at the visitor center lot?" Landon suggested under his breath. "There's a lot to unpack here and we should make sure everyone is okay once we are a safe distance from this damned house."

"Sure, sure," Isabell nodded absentmindedly.

"You shouldn't get behind the wheel, you're shaking," Tyler commented. His attentiveness to her did not escape me, despite the anxiety that lingered in the air. She did look distraught, even in the dark. Her fidgeting was constant.

"Alright Ty, you drive Izzie's car and August can come with me," Landon directed. I looked to Isabell who shrugged very discreetly and tucked her hair behind her ears. When they moved toward Isabell's car, Landon opened the passenger side door of his truck for me. I gave Isabell a small wave through the window of Landon's car, which she returned.

As Landon flipped a three-point turn, I resisted a look back at the house. It didn't last long. I succumbed and turned for another glimpse before we disappeared through the trees. The radio was playing 80s rock music. I had to admit, its techno beats and heavy bass contributed to the feeling that we were driving out of battle.

I thudded my head against the backrest, noting Landon's vanilla air freshener that was hanging from the mirror. I could tell it was new. The smell was strong, and I didn't remember seeing it yesterday when we cruised out to Odette's. I wasn't sure I liked it. It covered up his usual woodsy scent, and the faint aroma of black licorice from all the candies he ate.

Landon was watching me. I knew because of the way I felt slightly self-conscious, and how I refrained from looking back at him. I finally snapped with a, "what?"

"I don't know, I just . . . What the hell happened in there?" He ruffled up his hair and returned his hand to the wheel with a thump.

"I swear, I'm hearing that question on repeat. Why does everyone think I know what it was?"

"We were in that room together. Ty and Izzie don't know what happened in that room. With the piano, the chandelier. It really felt like the ghost was in that room, but I didn't see one. Is there something we should do about it? Do we need to cleanse our auras now or some shit?"

"Cleanse our auras?"

"You know, with sage or whatever. Or garlic? Or is that for vampires?"

I snorted, and covered my mouth to hide the horrible sound. His nervousness was unexpected, and since it was Landon, it was extra endearing to see him unsure of himself. I had to shake my head to empty it of such thoughts. Now was not the time.

"I'm by no means an expert on how to rid ourselves of the spirits that may follow and haunt us for all eternity. But I will say that I don't think Odette will be leaving that house."

"Maybe. I guess. But did you see a ghost? Or anything like that?"

I just sighed, and adjusted myself in my seat. "That house really shook you up, didn't it?"

He rolled his shoulders and sat up a little straighter. "No. Well, I thought it was going to cave in on us. And that scared the crap out of me. Then your foot was caught, and I was really worried. I'm not gonna lie about that."

It occurred to me we weren't addressing our concern with the cops. With some paranormal trouble under our belt, I didn't necessarily want to add legal issues to the list. If problems extended outside of Odette's house, I'd surely be grounded for the rest of the decade.

But Landon's worry for our well-being softened like a melting ice cream cone, and I sighed. I'd rather forget about it for the night and restore peace to our universe. "I'm okay, Landon. You are too. Maybe that's all that matters right now."

"You haven't even looked at your foot yet."

"I know it's okay," I tried to brush it off, but he was right. I hadn't checked it out, and it was aching.

"Just check on it, August." He clicked on the overhead light and I resigned, pulling the handkerchief out of my pocket that I had managed to nab in the house. When I reached down to take off my shoe and sock, Landon was quick to interject.

"What's that?"

"Just something I grabbed in the house."

"No, I mean the little swirly thing on the cloth. Is there a star on it?"

I flipped over the hanky, which must have been white at some point but was dingy and yellow now. The edges were made of lace, and in the corner there was a black stitching just as Landon had described: three swirls, and a star. I held it up. "What about it?"

He flicked his eyes back and forth between the road and the hanky, before mumbling a dismissal under his breath. Not wanting to question him further, I set it down on the middle console so I could have both hands to pry off my shoe. I tried without untying it and whimpered a small 'ow.'

"It looks swollen," Landon noted as I loosened my shoe. He was right. My ankle bone was non-existent with the swelling.

"Shoot. That was fast."

"Why don't you prop it up on the dash. Elevate it until we get to the visitor center." Not in the mood to fight him on that, I stuck my socked foot up by the windshield and turned the light back off. He kept talking. "I've got to be honest."

My stomach shifted. If you have to preface something as honesty, it's usually to lessen some kind of blow. I had to wonder if it was really the right time for such openness, but found myself giving in again. "Alright?"

"I'm not sure Tyler will be game to keep going after the treasure." The notion surprised me. I was under the impression the stakes were higher than ever. Landon picked up on my shock, and explained. "As you know, he's pretty mellow. The guy's going to school to be a teacher, for crying out loud. I don't think this is his jam."

"Huh."

"Do you think Izzie will stick with it?"

I hadn't really thought about that either, and it had me feeling blindsided all of a sudden. "I don't know. I'd hope so, but I guess I can't blame her if she backs out because of tonight."

Not to mention she has her family vacations coming up in the next week or so. I'd be on my own for a bit at that point, anyway. It's the permanent self-removal that never crossed my mind.

"Yeah. I can say the same about Ty."

I tapped my thumbs on the door and clicked my tongue. "So. Theoretically. If that were to happen, hypothetically, what would we do?" He asked what I meant, and I resisted a grunt of annoyance. "Would *we* keep looking? Would the bet be off?"

"Oh. I don't know."

I didn't want to push it. Mainly because if I did, and he continued to be on the fence, I'd feel pretty lame. So I kept my mouth shut, and wondered whether this treasure would ever be found. Or, moreover, whether I'd *ever* get my own car.

Déjà vu flooded over me as we whipped into the visitor center parking lot for the second night in a row. Isabell and Tyler were already there, standing outside her car. My stomach sank at the sight of Isabell's crossed arms and crinkled eyebrows. Maybe she really didn't want to be involved anymore.

I slipped on my shoe as Landon turned off the engine. When I stepped out of the car, my ankle was stiffer than I recalled it being and I stumbled a little, limping the rest of the way over to Tyler and Isabell.

She rushed over. "Is it bad?"

"A bit swollen, hard to move. But it'll be fine," I assured for the umpteenth time. Everyone else seemed more worried about it than I did. I just wanted to move on. Isabell paused and nodded absentmindedly. I patted her arm. "Iz, it's okay. Really."

"I just don't like it. It's all the ghost's fault. What's our next move with this ghost?"

"What *can* we do? Besides not going back there, of course," Tyler added. It was clear they had talked about their mutual concern in the car, because their eyes were flipping back and forth between me and Landon for answers.

"I'm not really sure if there is anything," I told them. "Hopefully it's done and we've left it behind. Now, we can move forward with the hunt."

Isabell was quick to quip back. "But did we really leave it behind? Odette could have a connection to the Ruggles. It feels a lot like we just put a target on our backs for a ghost to hit."

"The two might not be connected," Tyler mediated. He seemed torn: between continuing and staying out of it. In the literal sense, he was swaying side to side.

"It sure felt paranormal in there. But did anyone see a ghost?" Landon asked.

The group shrugged and stayed quiet.

"Maybe we need to sleep it off. We can meet up tomorrow once we have a clear head. Breakfast? We can get some pancakes, or something." Landon's idea to grab a casual flapjack and talk about the ghost and treasure sounded kind of nice to me, but I wasn't sure Isabell would be on board for such a nonchalant rendezvous.

"Is there more to talk about? It's pretty clear to me. Something doesn't want us here. I won't go as far to say it actually was trying to kill us, but it felt like it *could* kill us, if it wanted to. Besides . . . Auggie, didn't your dad say something about a hex?"

"Technically, *yes*, but I am pretty sure he was just messing with us."

Tyler shivered. "Yikes. That sounds bad. We're hexed now?"

"He more or less said the treasure was hexed. I'm sure Odette would know more, if we could find a way to go back sometime and —"

"Go *back*?" Isabell shook her head, and Tyler shuffled his feet.

I slouched a little at the scrutiny, and debated keeping my next thought in my head. "Not that I'm trying to defend the ghost that just tried to hurt us, but do you think her reaction was warranted? We did break into her house."

I regretted that pretty much immediately. The three of them stopped and stared at me like I had just lost my mind. Shrinking down further, I held up my hands in mock surrender.

Landon broke the awkward silence with a smack of his lips. "Let's put a pin in that thought. August, I think you should get off that ankle, and we should all head home for the night and get some sleep. Breakfast tomorrow, at 10 a.m.?"

"I'm in," I agreed first. Isabell threw up her hands, which was a reluctant yes. Tyler shrugged, seemingly in for it.

"Then it's settled," Landon breathed out, running his hands through his hair. "You guys okay to get back?" He was looking at me, but gestured with his head over to Isabell, who was biting her nails and staring off into space.

"We'll be fine. I can drive her car. Or we can just sit in the car and gather our wits together. But either way, we'll be fine," I repeated. It dawned on me just how many time I'd said that tonight, and I wondered when it would lose all meaning. "You guys should go."

Tyler stuffed his hands in his pockets and they said their goodbyes. I spun Isabell around and ushered her over to the passenger door of her car.

"I'm okay to drive."

"Really, Iz, I don't mind."

"No, no. It'll be good for me to clear my head a little." I let her be, and we slid into the car.

There was obviously a lot on her mind as we hit the highway. The glow of the dashboard illuminated her face, which looked like it was bracing for impact. I started to open my mouth and closed it a few times. As much as I wanted to know what she was thinking about, I was too nervous to ask. I wasn't ready to hear it if she *actually* wanted to back out of the hunt.

"Do you want to go home or stay at mine?"

It wasn't the first thing I expected her to ask, but I was grateful for normal conversation. "Maybe mine. Are you cool being by yourself though?"

Isabell shrugged, and sighed. "I'll just turn on my Scooby-Doo night light. It's best used in times like these. Look, Auggie . . ."

Please don't be quitting, please don't be quitting.

"I'm feeling very weird about this whole treasure thing now. I want you to get your car really bad, but I didn't think it would be this stressful. I swear this night aged me five years. If we went to the store and tried to buy alcohol, they probably wouldn't even card me because I'm starting to grey after tonight."

I tried not to laugh, but a snicker came out. Isabell whipped her head to me and I pursed my lips to stop any further chuckles. "I'm serious!"

This time, I didn't hold back my laughter. "I know you are!"

"Whatever," she rolled her eyes, but she was smiling and we started to relax a little.

"So you aren't quitting?"

She sighed. "I think if it was just you and me, I might be. But there's some strength in numbers, and since Ty and Landon are in the know, I feel a little better. If either of them were to quit, that's when I'll seriously doubt myself."

"Either of them? Or just Ty?"

"For starters, we both know that Ty and I are the most likely to back out. You won't quit just because of what happened with the house. Landon won't either because he's in a game of chicken with you."

"Shut up!"

"It's true. He doesn't want to you to think he's a wimp."

"Whatever." I blew it off as she turned right off the highway. "Did anything happen with you and Ty tonight? Before the house started to cave in?"

"Well, not exactly. He did hold my hand as we walked around. I know you'll hate me for saying this, but it was nice that he was there when trouble hit. He really got in the zone to get us out of there. It was pretty hot."

"Ooh! Okay, okay. That's definitely forward progress!"

"I'll tell you more later." She grinned as she pulled on to my street. We were running out of time. "What about you and Landon?"

I thought back over the night. What a crazy whirlwind. I didn't even consider the possibility of the boys showing up, and then they did. Isabell held hands with Tyler. Landon and I danced in an ancient ballroom. I almost cringed thinking about it. Had I just been a complete idiot for doing that? Then, I remembered our conversation, and the embarrassment subsided a smidge.

"He told me he did want to ask me to prom. HBIC asked him first."

"What? No WAY!" Isabell shouted, all previous fear out the window at the news of the latest gossip.

"Right? I was shocked, too." We were in my driveway, so any other catching up would simply have to wait. It was probably for the best—then I wouldn't fall in the dangerous trap of speculating Landon's feelings without having all the information. Isabell only fed those types of conspiracies, and she'd just tumble with me even deeper into the rabbit hole of dwelling.

"I'll be extra curious to see how breakfast goes tomorrow. You better believe I'll be watching Landon like a hawk. We'll see what I can figure out." I rolled my eyes and laughed as she parked in front of my little green house. "Want me to wait until you get in?"

"It's fine," I noted, my brain dinging again at the little F-word. "The side door is always unlocked." I tapped my thumb on the door handle before turning back to her. "Iz, you sure you aren't quitting this thing?"

She sighed. "I'm not quitting right now, August. But I know that there isn't much that would make you bow down, and that's just not my limit. I can't promise that if things get worse, I'll still think it's a good idea to stay."

That night, as I laid in bed trying to sleep, I couldn't switch off my brain. I was thinking a lot about what Isabell said, and wondered what it would even take for me to want to quit. I didn't have an answer, and until I did, I'd play the game as long as I could.

ELEVEN

The next morning, I was itching to get going. Instead of hitching a ride with Isabell to breakfast, I joined my mom again in opening Comfort Zone. Sundays could always use extra hands, so she didn't even object when I was up and ready to go a few minutes after five. Well, she did give me a sigh, but also motioned for me to scoot on out the door.

While Fridays are for the benevolent office folk, Sundays are for the families. The rate that the shop sells out of breakfast cookies and chocolate croissants is higher than any other day. Tables were full of kids leaving trails of crumbs and parents picking up cups of coffee before their kids could knock them over. It was a bit of a zoo, and when I caught my mom's eye she was beaming. Days like these were her bread and butter, chatting warmly with kids and laughing with the regulars.

The sound of a plate shattering on the floored echoed throughout the cafe, causing a momentary lapse of silence as everyone turned to the culprit. A little boy, no older than three years old, was standing on his chair. His tiny, cinnamon-roll-sticky hands were holding him up on the table. He simply smiled, while his mother mouthed 'sorry.' The whole place erupted into a cheer, as they usually do when a dish breaks, and the boy's mother gave a small bow.

Meanwhile, I grabbed the broom and dust pan so Mom, the baker, and the barista could help the line that was spewing out the door. For me, cleaning was better than helping customers. I am perfectly capable of being *nice* to customers, but it's so exhausting. Best leave that to Mom, the ray of sunshine.

"So sorry about that," the mom apologized as she rubbed the back of her bouncing toddler.

"Not a problem. It happens every weekend, so you're not alone."

The toddler started to climb down from the table, toward the shattered glass, when his mom pulled him back and onto her lap. He twisted and whined in her arms, resisting the hold. I worked twice as fast to sweep up all the glass, feeling like I had a front-row seat to the looming temper tantrum.

"I'll get out of your hair. Can I get you guys anything else?"

She smiled at me. "We're okay. Right, buddy?"

I nodded and backpedaled to the counter where my mom and the others assisted the line. "Auggie, are you limping?" Mom asked, scrutinizing me up and down. I had been walking all over the shop this morning, and she had finally looked at me long enough to notice. Here I was thinking that I could get away with the limping and no one would know.

"Am I?" I played dumb.

"Yes, you are. Did something happen to your leg?" She peered over the side of the counter, and I braced myself for her gasp. "Auggie Jane! What happened to your ankle?"

Crap. I had worn socks that cover my ankles specifically to cover up any swelling or bruising, but there was a blackish-blue line shooting up my Achilles. So much for hiding it. "Oh, that's weird."

"Augustine," she warned. "I can see how swollen it is through your sock. Tell me the truth."

I groaned. "I stumbled into a hole last night and twisted it, alright?"

"You need to get that checked out." I started to protest, and she cut me off. "It's your last season of cross country this fall. What if you can't run? Or hurt it worse so you can't run ever run again? Is that what you want?"

Moms always know best, and mine was a master of delivering hard truths gently. I knew she was right, but I didn't want her know that. "Well, yeah, if I can, *obviously*," I grumbled my response.

"Then take care of that ankle! After you're back from breakfast with your friends, we'll head to urgent care to get it checked out. We need to make sure it's not broken." She picked something up off the counter and bopped me on the head with it. "Someone left this for you, by the way." A small envelope was between two of her fingers, and she held it out to me.

That's weird. "Who was it?"

"I couldn't say, sorry honey. I was doing too many things at once to pay any attention. I assumed you were expecting something."

Gingerly, I plucked the envelope from her grasp. My name was written on the front, in bold, red ink. The blood in my neck ran cold as I surveyed the room. It was hard to be nonchalant about it, but I tried. My skin crawled just thinking about someone watching me. Nothing stood out as suspicious, so I took a couple deep breaths and fled out the back door with Mom's keys.

Only once I was locked in the safety of her car did I open the envelope. Inside was a note written on thick cardstock.

Maybe I wasn't clear before.

When I said 'watch your back,' what I really meant was: you better stay the hell away from our gold. If you don't? Well. You better be prepared to watch your back, kid.

And your friends, too.

Without moving, I glanced in the rearview and then flicked my eyes to the side mirrors. I saw nothing. No one lurking in the back alley, no cars. Just me.

I pushed the note to my chest, as if I was shielding it from the world and tucking it away like a dangerous secret. Like it wasn't already burned into my mind for eternity, I read it four more times, just to make sure I got the message right. My fingers were tensing up around the card.

It might—just might—be time to tell Landon about this one.

By the time I showed up, Tyler and Isabell were already there. My mind was still racing, but seeing the two of them standing awkwardly together gave me a minor distraction. As I parked, Isabell was shifting her weight back and forth between her feet, and Tyler was leaning rigid against the railing of the steps. They were both craning their necks to scope around the parking lot. My phone buzzed in the cup holder. It was a message from Isabell.

It's just me and Ty here. Where are u?! Hurry up please!!!!!!!

I tucked the note in my back pocket with my phone and grabbed my wallet mid-scurry out of the car. Isabell's face visibly relaxed once she spotted me, and Tyler offered an ever-friendly smile and hello. Isabell was quick to comment on my approach.

"You're limping."

I looked down at my ankle. "Yeah. Mom's making me go to the doctor with her after this. It's whatever. Should we go in and get a table? It looks busy."

We shuffled inside, but didn't have to wait too long for a seat. Sliding into a booth, Isabell and I claimed one side and left the other for the boys. Holding up a menu to hide my face, I scoured the dining area. Was there anyone spying on our table? Glaring over their cup of coffee?

"What's with you?" Isabell asked under her breath, startling me.

"Nothing."

"You seem a little jumpy."

"Do you think your ankle is broken, August?" Tyler interjected, not having head our whispers.

"Um, I'm not sure. I think it's just a sprain."

"That darn rickety, old, falling apart house! I should have known something like that would happen, and now you're hurt and you're a runner so of course an ankle injury is extra bad, and we have a ghost that will probably haunt us for the rest of our life and—"

"Iz, chill. Deep breaths, remember? You can't forget to breathe."

As she started her cycle of inhales and exhales, Tyler looked over our shoulders. "Hey, look who decided to show up!"

I didn't need to turn around to know it was Landon. He slid in the booth, sitting directly across from me. He mumbled a low hello to everyone at the table, along with a curt nod. His dark hair was wet, and curling up a bit.

Despite myself, I thought that he looked pretty . . . hot with wet hair. With my terrible knack for inappropriate thoughts at inconvenient times, my face flushed. I tried to force my attraction to him out of my mind completely.

He leaned his elbows on the table, sitting on the edge of the seat, like he was ready to bolt at any minute. I did my best not to analyze each movement he made.

The four of us sat without saying a word. It was awkward—plain and simple. I was still ducked behind my menu. Then there was Landon, now staring at me between soaked strands of hair, tapping his finger on the table.

Tyler cleared his throat. "So."

Isabell let out a strained sigh, looking back and forth between me and Landon.

"Are we ready for food over here?" the waitress said. Her question popped our weird bubble, and we all ordered pancakes and waffles. She was gone in a flash, putting us right back in to our fit of silence.

"What's the 4-1-1, Landon?" Isabell smacked her menu down on the counter, and Landon raised an eyebrow. "You are the one who wanted to chat. So what's your plan? Your course of action?"

He slumped against the back of the booth. "I don't know. How's everyone doing? We've all had some time to think about the haunt. Are you guys feeling better? Worse?"

Given Isabell's rant moments before Landon walked in the door, I figured this question would grind her gears a little.

"The *haunt*? The way you say that makes me think that we are going to keep being haunted by this ghost forever. Is that what you're saying?" Isabell was already stressed, so I crouched lower behind my menu, saving my input until I was directly called upon. Or, until I disagreed strongly enough to post my rebuttal.

"Oof, I hope not," Tyler chimed.

"That ghost seemed like she was defending her home, not trying to torture teenagers for all eternity. Pretty much the second we stepped out the door all was normal again. Unless the treasure is in the house, then we can easily avoid a situation like last night."

The front door of the restaurant chimed open, and Landon's eyes flickered over to the door as he sat up a little straighter.

"Okay," Isabell started, following Landon's eyes to the door. "Then why are you so edgy?"

"I'm not edgy."

"Sorry, dude. You *are* a little edgy."

Landon ruffled his hair, and I could make out a *"shit, shit, shit,"* under his breath.

My attention was caught when he strung a string of more curse words together. I lowered my menu so it was no longer shielding my face. "Landon, what's wrong?"

His eyes met mine for the first time today, and it sunk a ship in my stomach. When he pulled his eyes away, he turned to everyone else. "You guys aren't going to like it."

"Is it about the ghost?" Isabell was the first to ask.

"I wish," he snorted as he pulled something out of his pocket. After doing a survey of the perimeter, he gently set something on the middle of the table. At the sight of the envelope, a lump caught in my throat. "I found this on my windshield this morning," he told us as he tapped the envelope with his index finger.

Isabell's eyes burned the side of my head, but I was fixated on Landon. When he looked at me again, he gestured for me to look at the envelope. The pounding of my heart was rising up my throat and to my ears, and I controlled my hand just enough to grab the paper without trembling.

Isabell lowered her voice. "I can't watch this," she said as she folded her arms on the table and hung her head.

The front read "Mr. Jones" in red ink. I blew out a puff of air, which sent a few loose strands of out of my eyes.

"Tell that little bitch to get her nose out of it. She don't belong. Deal with it, Lanno. Or else."

"Any idea what that's about?" he asked after I read it over several times. I felt like a little kid all over again: caught for something, given a chance to fess up.

I huffed and tossed the car back on the table before massaging my temples. "You know, they used some pretty nice paper for such threatening messages. Wouldn't normal printer paper do the trick just fine?"

"Not the response I was hoping for," Landon said. He sighed as Tyler picked up the card.

"Whoa." Tyler blinked at the letter.

"Let me see." Isabell snatched it from his hands, only to drop it like it was poisonous seconds later. Which, come to think, maybe it was. "Bleck! No *thank* you. What is this about?"

Landon shot me an expectant, but subtle look, like he knew I had something to confess. His eyebrow quipped up, egging me on. Isabell and Tyler were soon staring me down as well. Isabell, of course, knew about my first note, but the second was a mystery to all. If Landon shared his, I figured I should share mine, but I still had to groan about it.

"Fine, fine. It's about me. I guess I'm the little bitch, which is rude."

"But what does it mean? What's it talking about?"

With impeccable timing, our waitress arrived and set down our food. We all smiled politely at her, but she seemed uncomfortable with the way we were all looking at each other. The tension at the table could have been cut with a knife.

I sighed and re-told the story of the library incident. In particular, the note, and how I felt like someone was watching me. How it was written in the same red ink as my second note, which was delivered at my mom's shop this morning.

"A second note?" Isabell breathed, fanning herself with the menu in front of her.

I scratched the side of my neck before grabbing the envelope out of my pocket and setting it on top of Landon's. Without hesitation, Landon was the first to reach for it. He rubbed his face and Ty leaned to read it over Landon's shoulder.

"You shouldn't read it, Iz," Tyler tried to warn her. Of course, she practically lurched over the table to pry it from Landon's hands. Once she read it, she hit me on the head with it.

"Ah! What's that for?"

She gestured back and forth between me and the card before tossing it in the air. "How can I possibly eat my pancakes now?"

When a silence fell over us, all that was left to do was mull it over and eat. I sighed before being the first to dig into my plate of blueberry pancakes. The rest of the group was slower, and watching my every move, but they soon joined in for a stoic meal. Weird silences usually don't bother me much, but I had to speak up.

"The way I see it, these notes just mean that we're getting closer. We're on the right track. And this person, whoever they are, is few steps behind us."

"And that means?"

"We can't give up," I finished. "We must have been on to something with Odette, otherwise we wouldn't be getting these notes. I don't exactly know where we're supposed to go from here, but it has to mean that we're close. It has to."

"I don't know," Isabell was picking apart her pancakes with her fork like she was searching for a hidden prize in them. She lowered her voice to a whisper and angled herself toward me for privacy. "I did not expect this when I signed up to join a treasure hunt. I thought it would be a friendly, maybe slightly flirty, competition with the boys, not a police-involving, ghost-terrorizing type of thing."

The words tumbled out of me in a bit of a panic. "Are you saying you're out?"

Isabell gave it pause, and I widened my eyes at her. The hesitation was killing me. Doing this whole thing without my best friend hardly seemed worth it. Finally, she rolled her eyes and continued her whispering. "No, not exactly. But I am thinking about it. I'm not sure how long I can hang on for."

"So what are we going to do about this?" I addressed the group again, picking up the red-inked paper from the table and flapping it around like a mad woman.

"If no one's out," Landon lowered his gaze around the table, "then I just say we stick together. No one goes off on their own, or wanders down dark alleyways or the aisles of the library alone. We should have each other's backs."

Isabell narrowed her eyes and nodded.

"Ride or die," Tyler hummed and lightened the mood by pounding himself on the chest twice. Isabell cracked her first grin all meal, while Landon shoved him and I laughed.

When all subsided, I asked a question through a mouthful of syrup-saturated pancakes. "Um, is this a bad time to ask if the bet's off?" Landon threw a grape at me and Tyler tossed his napkin.

Beside me Isabell shrugged, having my back as per usual. "That's a good question."

"I guess it makes sense to call it," Ty agreed.

"Such a shame." I shook my head, and gestured between myself and Isabell. "Because we were totally winning."

"Whatever." Landon tried to seem annoyed, but he leaned toward me, smiling. "What do we do now, modern mystery gang?"

"Not it," my best friend said as she shoved a massive bite into her mouth.

"This whole treasure thing is your forte, Lanno," Tyler noted. I almost rolled my eyes, thinking that Landon and I had to at least be comparable in our success. "I'm just following your lead."

The so-called lead then turned to me, resting his chin in his hand. "This one's the real mastermind. What do you think, August?"

I tapped the table, hoping I looked casual under Landon's piercing eyes. The forefront of my mind was ushering me to go back to Odette's. The picture of her and the wonky nature of the house just made me feel like there was something we could learn there. Our time had been cut short by the chaos, and we really didn't search for clues at all. But, this crowd was sensitive to Odette's house, and timing is everything.

"Um. Let's see. Should we scope out Middle Creek a bit more? Sift through some bushes and rocks? It's not too far from Old Shasta. So maybe we can visit the park, too. See if any of the workers can fill in our gaps of knowledge?"

"Sounds like a good idea. Should we go now?"

"I can't. I'm helping my mom out at the shop today. But all day tomorrow I'm free."

"Me too," Tyler piped up. "Well, I'm free until the afternoon."

"I work tomorrow, but by all means, you guys should go without me." Isabell hardly looked up as she spoke. She was busy pouring an ungodly amount of syrup onto her food.

"Are you sure, Izzie?" Tyler asked, frowning a little.

"Yeah, yeah. I need to refuel the engine," she said, referring to her need to take a slight break from the hunt.

"Us three, tomorrow morning then?" Landon pointed at us all.

"It's a plan," I agreed, chomping on another bite of pancakes. We all loosened up a bit after that, but the two notes still sat in the middle of the table. Though we didn't mention them anymore, I noticed all our eyes landed on them at one point or another.

While no one cared to admit it, or dwell on it, it was looming over us.

TWELVE

"You're *sure* you're okay with me, Landon, and Ty doing something without you?" The boys were on their way to pick me up as we spoke, but I had to call Isabell one more time. If she said no, I still had enough time to cancel last minute on them.

But she did not refuse. "Totally. I've told you this like a dozen times already. It's fine, I promise. Just make some progress on that treasure."

I sighed through the phone. I was sitting in my room with the contents of Dad's 1892 folder splayed out all over my floor. This type of stuff—history, puzzles, recall—was my jam. I loved the excitement, and only wished Isabell was on my side of the fence rather than clinging to the fence itself.

The whole treasure hunt was a lot more fun with Isabell, but her interest was fading rapidly. Soon enough, I knew it would just be me and the boys. Even if she didn't quit, she was going on vacation in like a week, and she'd at least be out of commission during that time. But I felt like I'd lose her sooner.

Without her, I was some kind of imposter, tagging along with the boys on their little adventure. Sure, I helped get the ball rolling here, but at the same time, I imagined it'd be weird to stick around without Isabell. I didn't want to overstay my welcome, with Landon of all people. That's another reason I need Isabell. She's my buffer.

No Isabell means no best friend to have my back, to shift my focus onto when my eyes lingered on Landon for too long.

"Are *you* fine with going? Didn't the doctor tell you to stay off your ankle for two weeks or something?"

"Yes, but I think she meant just to take it easy and not do anything too strenuous or walk too much. Besides, I have my boot."

"Should have known you won't be taking the rest seriously."

"Ha, ha," I sneered.

"Anyway, Auggie," she shifted the tone of her voice, sounding like she was up to no good. "Now you can spend more quality time with Landon."

"How do you figure?"

"Things are heating up. Your dance in Odette's—which was basically straight out of a rom-com—definitely stirred the pot. I mean, come on, he said he wished he could have taken you to prom. And before you say anything, I know, you hate the idea of prom. But that aside, he wanted *you* to be his *date*."

"That was two months ago. His feelings about me could have changed," I pointed out. He's now done with high school, and I'm stuck trying to grow up. He's effortlessly cool and comfortable, while I'm relentlessly upset over nothing. It just didn't make any sense.

To Isabell, that didn't seem to matter. Even through the phone, I imagined her shrugging, unfazed by me. "You guys just have each other's backs. With the ankle and everything, and the note, and the looks back and forth. Don't think I've missed that, Auggie. From both of you."

"Whatever."

"Just admit it."

"Admit what?" I played dumb, hoping she'd give up.

"Shut up, you know what I'm talking about! You like Landon. You *still* like Landon. Just admit it!"

I huffed on my end, and she hummed on hers. "*Why* won't you admit it?" She wasn't accusing me of anything. She didn't sound annoyed and impatient. On the contrary, she sounded curious, and genuine.

The question actually stumped me. Why *can't* I admit it, even to my best friend? Aside from the fact it felt stupid to even *think* about saying it out loud, I couldn't pinpoint my resistance. I grumbled gibberish under my breath, which bought me enough time for Landon's car to pull into my driveway.

"Speak of the devil, he just got here. I'll fill you in on everything after you're off of work, okay?" In an uncharacteristic move, I shoved the contents of the folder under my bed instead of packing the folder neatly and stowing it away.

She sighed. "You're lucky, he got you off the hook here." I just laughed as I grabbed my packed little backpack, but she got in one more sentence before I hung up. "This conversation isn't over!"

Still limping, but less so in my boot, I half-skipped out of the front door after giving my dog a quick scratch on the head. I hobbled down the stairs, my strange movements catching Landon's attention, and he jumped out of his truck.

"August, slow down. You don't want to overdo it." He hurried to my side, and offered his arm as a crutch. I eyed it warily and waved him off.

"I'm fine, I'm fine. Let's get this show on the road."

"Are you even okay to walk? The trail is what, a mile or two long? That's kind of far on a sprained ankle."

"I'll be okay. Not my usual speedy self, but that just means it'll be easier for you to keep up with me," I teased as he opened the passenger door for me. He rolled his eyes. I looked in the backseat, expecting to see Tyler. "Hey, where's Ty?"

"Driving separate. Where are your parents?"

"Work."

"Do you spend a lot of time here alone?"

"In the summer, mostly." I didn't elaborate as he slid into his own seat. Since we were alone, it was easy to dwell on the final notes of my conversation with Isabell. Here I was, spending 'quality time' with Landon, and there wasn't a single word in my whole brain. I cleared my throat, and he looked over at me confused. I smiled awkwardly.

"So. This road sure needs to be paved again, am I right?"

"What?"

"Nothing," I answered curtly, as if saying that word would erase my random question. Besides, they just had done a bunch of construction on it last summer. It was almost good as new. Stupid, stupid, *stupid*.

He chuckled, and didn't comment on the construction. I wasn't sure if I should be thankful or more embarrassed.

"You know, there is something I wanted to talk to you about." My stomach, already a little twisted, tightened more at his cryptic lead-in. "Remember what we talked about in the house?"

My mind instantly went to the chat we had while we were dancing, where he said he wanted me to be his date to prom. I tried to take a deep breath in, but it was shallow. "We talked a lot in the house. What little chat you referring to?"

"You know? Our talk upstairs?"

"While we were dancing?" I asked, sneaking a peak at him. He blinked out ahead, opening his mouth and closing it. I shifted my gaze back to the road.

"Oh, I actually meant about Tyler and Izzie."

My heart stopped beating in my chest. I felt too exposed sitting beside him, and wished for a rock to hide under. All I could must up was a single syllable.

"Oh."

"We can talk about that other talk though," he offered up quickly.

"No. No, no," I stopped him, not wanting to wind down that track. Here I was, thinking we weren't done with that conversation, replaying it in my head over and over, but it had already poofed out of his brain. "What were you going to say about Isabell and Ty?"

He sighed and scratched the back of his neck. "Well. We should get them together. Ty seriously likes Izzie. We were joking about them being love birds, but does she really like him, too?"

"If she does, do you think we could set them up?"

He grinned, all the tension from a moment ago fading away. "Most definitely. I've been trying to kick his butt into action, but this is the key I was missing. With you on my side, I think it's a slam dunk. He'll *have* to ask her out after that."

"I've always thought it's so obvious they like each other. Why can't they just come out and open with it?" I threw my hands up as I talked, like an impassioned Italian chef.

Landon grew still, and the silence was short but stiff. "Yeah," he agreed, pausing before he continued. "Why do you think that is?"

I shrugged. "Fear of rejection, maybe."

"Is that so?"

"Or maybe they don't think it will work out."

"Hm."

Turning to him, his eyebrows were all scrunched up as he stared ahead. It confused me. "What? What's wrong?" I asked.

He hummed like he didn't know what I meant.

"Aren't we just chatting about why it hasn't worked yet? No harm in that. Overall, I thought we were feeling good about them. Now you seem kind of lost in thought over it, and not in a fun way."

"Oh. Yeah, yeah. Sorry. Maybe this isn't a good idea after all."

What could I have said that bothered him? I wracked my brain pondering what just went wrong. We were in agreement on getting them together, that was good. After that, all I did was speculate on why they never got together. Somewhere along the way, he started his stoic staring out the window. Maybe he wanted more faith in Tyler and Isabell? I couldn't be sure. I mean, I could muster up some hope for their relationship and assure him of it.

I knew how much Isabell liked Tyler, and how long she's liked him. They really could work out, I did believe that. She's my best friend, of course I want her to be happy and in love. Did he think I was being a shitty friend to Isabell with my theories? This confusion was starting to make my head hurt.

We didn't talk for the rest of the drive, which was probably a good thing. Maybe he needed space and some quiet. Thankfully,

Tyler was already there when we arrived, leaning against the side of his car. He greeted us with a wave and his signature warm smile.

"Hey guys!" He walked over with his hands in his pockets. "It's not even ten yet, and it's 90 degrees! I'm glad we're out here early," he said. His eyes widened when I stepped out of the car. "Whoa, August. You got a boot. Are you sure you're fine to walk?"

"Yeah, I'm fine," I assured. It felt like my hundredth time saying it.

"Really? It's hot to me and I'm not carrying around a black tank on my foot. Does it hurt?"

"No, I'm good. Thanks Ty!" I started to walk toward the path, but sensed they weren't following me. I turned around, feeling like a child waiting for Mom and Dad to hurry up so I could go to the playground. "Let's go, boys! If the girl with the sprained ankle is beating you, you're moving too slow."

"Yes ma'am." Tyler's feet spun to motion. Landon ruffled his hair and looked around the small dirt lot before he followed, too.

I didn't plan to slow down for them, but walking with the boot was more difficult than I expected. Since getting the dumb thing yesterday, I had hardly walked outside of my house. I underestimated how a few steps around the house would transfer over to a small hike.

"You okay?" Landon asked as he and Tyler quickly caught up to me.

"I'm fine," I grumbled mid-hobble. The more we walked, the more they pulled away and the tighter my boot felt. Plus, my foot was sweating like a pig in there. With a heavy breath, I slowed down my pace. It was no use trying to keep up, let alone exhaust myself over it. After a few minutes, I rounded a bend in the paved path to see Landon and Tyler posted up in the shade.

"Remember this spot?"

I scanned the area, and a memory hit me from a day just as hot as this one. "Is this where we made the bet originally?"

"Izzie was so into it, it cracks me up when she gets so competitive," Tyler said with a chuckle. I looked to Landon, who gave the slightest shake of the head as if to ward me off. After shooting him my most innocent smile, I turned to Tyler.

"Tyler, I have to ask something."

"What's up?" He looked up. In the corner of my eye, I saw Landon cover his mouth with his hand.

But I charged full steam ahead. I wasn't going to miss a beat. "Do you like Isabell?"

"Of course, August!" Tyler smiled. "She's great!"

"Not like that. Do you *like* her? As in, want to *date* her?"

"Oh," he faltered. "Um, why are you asking this?"

"Because, I'm her best friend."

"No offense, August, but that's exactly why I'm nervous that you're asking." He stuffed his hands into his pockets. "Am I bothering her? Oh crap, I'm bothering her, huh? I've been coming on way too strong and now she feels weird."

"Geez. Of course not. You've both been tiptoeing across thin ice together and you just need someone to come in and smash it for you. That's me."

"Smash the ice?"

"Break the ice, stir the pot, light a fire under your ass, whatever floats your boat. Are you picking up what I'm putting down here?" The wheels were turning in Tyler's head while his best friend kicked pebbles off the path. So much for double-teaming this one, I was on my own.

Finally, I watched his eyes click. "Oh. *Oh*. You mean, Izzie likes me?" I nodded slowly. "You really think she'd say yes if I asked her out?"

I rolled my eyes and shoved him playfully in the shoulder. "Yes, really! It's about time!"

He smiled a bit wider before frowning. If Landon was paying any attention at all, he certainly didn't show it. His sudden amusement with gravel, plus his impatient scanning of the trail, made it seem like he'd do just about anything to get out of there. I stared him down, but he was too deep in his own head to notice.

"I don't know if I can do it." Tyler's switch of gears caught even Landon's ear. He pivoted his head toward us, furrowing his brow.

"What do you mean, Ty?" he asked.

"Izzie and I are great friends. We have so much in common, and I've known her since elementary school. What if I ask her out and we are just horrible together? Would we stop being friends after that?"

"Maybe." Landon sighed and rubbed his face with his hands. I resisted throwing my arms in the air in surrender. If he wasn't going to *help*, he could at least not make things *worse*.

"That's what I'm afraid of! Even a tiny chance of ruining our friendship feels a bit too risky for me. I don't want to lose Izzie if we go on a date and I totally mess it up."

Now the three of us were a muddled mess of sighs and head scratches. What felt so hopeful an hour ago was now a small but irreparable tear in the fabric of our group. Sure, this wasn't anything big yet, but it felt like opening a can of worms. The lid was cracked, and things we were already spilling out. It would only get worse, unless I could fix it for the better.

"Ty, Ty, listen to me. You can't possibly know if it'll work out with Izzie. That's the unfortunate part about dating. You've just got to be real with yourself about your feelings for her. If it's just a small dollop of a crush, then do us both a favor and spare her the future heartbreak. But, if you think this has the potential to be something real, that's a different story. Would you rather live with awkward friendship, knowing you shot your shot, or never even take that shot in the first place?"

He blew out a breath and looked up at the sky. "You make some good points."

"And, Ty, who knows? Maybe you take the shot, and things never get weird. Things could work out, you know."

Tyler pushed his sunglasses further up the bridge of his nose and crossed his arms. "You really think so?"

After spewing out my little speech, I had to sit on my own words for a moment. Hyping him up was so instinctive, I wasn't sure what had come over me. I almost cringed imagining how cheesy it sounded to these two boys. Gross.

Then I averted my gaze to Landon, who had stopped his kicking of pebbles and taken off his sunglasses, the sun fully illuminating his eyes. They were burning gold right at me, with an undecipherable seriousness that made the butterflies in stomach beg to burst through my throat.

With my gaze fixated on Landon, I responded to Tyler. "I really do," I affirmed.

Post-heart-to-heart, the three of us continued our journey down to the river. Perhaps there was a bit more pep in our step, but we mostly acted like nothing had happened. I was still hobbling along, but thankfully the boys slowed down enough for me to stick with them.

As we inched closer to the merging point of the trails, the boys started rummaging through the bushes for any type of clue or a sign that something had been buried. I tried to help out, but it was a bit difficult to bushwhack with a clunky boot weighing me down.

Now it was my turn to kick pebbles. It felt like I was sitting on the sidelines of a game I should be playing. If only there was a magic spell to mend my wounds, then I could get right into those bushes and show the boys up from down.

After my first efforts in the shrubs failed, Landon had escorted me to a rock. He gave me a small pat on the shoulder like some sort of consolation prize.

"Don't patronize me!"

He laughed at that one. "I'm not, promise! I meant it to be comforting, is that not how it felt?" I crossed my arms, and he placed his hand back on my shoulder. "We got this, Auger. You can be our eyes."

Thirty minutes of rock-picking later, Landon trotted back over to me.

"Any luck?" I asked, hopeful for a positive report.

"Unfortunately, no. But I did find this," he pulled a penny out of his pocket and held it out. "For you. It's a lucky penny."

"Heads up?"

He grinned. "You bet. I was thinking if you tucked it into that boot of yours, it might heal a little quicker or something."

"Oh, really?" I stared at the penny with wide eyes.

Landon dropped his hand and shrugged. "Nevermind, that was stupid."

"No, no. It's not stupid at all," I refuted. Grabbing his hand, I pulled it open to take the penny. "I love it, actually." I flipped it over a few times in my hand. "1999, that's the year you were born."

"Dare I say, a lucky coincidence?"

I laughed, even though the joke wasn't that great. It just made me want to laugh. "This is super nice of you, Landon. Thank you." I pinched the penny and waved it around as I spoke.

"You've got a nice laugh, Auger. It's the kind of laugh that makes me wish I was a little funnier." I unintentionally snorted and shook my head. "Maybe not *that* laugh."

I shoved his shoulder and he tipped over slightly, laughing himself.

"Landon!" Tyler called. "I need you show me poison oak again. I think I'm in the thick of it here."

He turned to look at me. "See what you're leaving me with? Heal that foot. It's not the same without you busting my chops in the shrubs."

I made a face. "When have we ever been in the shrubs?"

"Exactly," he said as he bopped me on the nose with finger. He then ran off down the path, toward the sound of Tyler's voice. As he approached the spot, he looked over his shoulder at me. I didn't look away, or make a face.

Instead, I sat up a little straighter and smiled. And he smiled right back.

THIRTEEN

After two hours of searching the trail, the three of us were still empty-handed. All that tromping around in the bushes didn't lead to any big discoveries or pots of gold, as much as we had been hoping. Personally, my only contribution was sitting in the shade on a rock. By the end, my restlessness had kicked in full swing and I was chomping at the bit to leave.

Once we made it back to the cars, we hitched it just down the road to the former gold rush settlement of Old Shasta. Now, it's a state park, and you can have picnics and check out the museum and all that jazz. Might as well scope out the scene, ask a park employee some questions, and snoop around.

At least, that's what I thought we should do. I was ready to get down to business as soon as Landon and I parked in front of the ancient jail. When Tyler pulled in next to us, I had already hopped out of the car.

"What's our first move?" Tyler asked as he locked his car.

"Lunch," Landon decreed as he dug around in his back seat.

"Hallelujah!" Tyler rubbed his hands together. "I'm starving."

"Lunch? But I didn't bring anything." I frowned, just as my stomach growled. No one told me to bring food. And since I was standing empty-handed and empty-bellied, my annoyance grew at an alarming rate.

Landon grinned cheekily. "That's okay, Auger. I brought enough for you, too."

"Are you just saying that because you feel bad that I'll go hungry if you don't share?" I crossed my arms. I hated the feeling of not being included in the plans. Dumb as it sounds, I felt left out not having a lunch with me. It was the elementary school cafeteria all over again.

Landon chuckled as he plucked out a re-usable grocery bag from the trunk. "Of course not. I made you a PB&J."

"What kind of J?"

"Strawberry, obviously," he sassed, but he was smiling.

"The best combo! Thanks, Lando." I beamed.

Both Tyler and Landon stopped in their tracks, and turned to stare at me like I had grown a third head. "Did she just call you ..."

"I think she did."

"Lanno? What's the big deal, it's your name, isn't it?"

"Yeah, but you don't call me that."

"He's right, you don't call him that."

I sighed in exasperation before brushing past them toward the grass and benches. They shuffled to follow, and I shook my head.

"This is why we need Isabell here," I told them. "She balances us out."

It was an unfortunate moment to lose my balance. I slid on some loose gravel and mumbled a few curses under breath. So much for my commanding exit.

"Here, use my arm. Your boot doesn't have the best grip."

"Chivalry isn't dead after all," I joked, grabbing his arm. Not that I needed his help *entirely*, but it was a nice gesture. And I didn't necessarily want to refuse, or argue about it. "Thanks. I'll try not to take you down if I tumble."

Tyler picked out a table for us under a big, shady oak. Landon handed me a metal tin that had been packed with a sandwich and then set a peach in front of me.

"It's a crispy one," he said with a grin..

"Really? That was thoughtful. Thanks!" Picking up the peach, it was in fact firm. I was a little surprised he remembered, but then again we had spent most of our school lunches together the last year and a half.

"Are you being sarcastic?" Tyler grimaced across the table with his tuna sandwich hovering just in front of his mouth.

I took a big chomp out of the hard peach, making a similar sound to biting an onion. "Nope."

"You like hard peaches? Are you an animal?" Tyler nearly gagged. "Landon, you knew about this? And you kept her around?"

Landon unwrapped his sandwich with a quirky smile before looking at me. "I think it's funny."

"August." Tyler raised an eyebrow. He set down his sandwich, leaned forward on the table, and stared directly into my eyes. "Human beings do not agree on anything, okay? Like, anything. For goodness' sake, there are people out there legitimately arguing that Earth is flat. The one thing humans can all agree on, is that peaches are best when they're juicy."

I shrugged and ripped out another crunchy bite of the peach.

He shivered like he was trying to exorcise a demon from his body. "I feel like I just lost a tiny piece of my sanity." He shook his head, laughing a little.

"Are you questioning our friendship?"

He squinted, trying to figure me out, or something. But he was fighting a smile, and waved me off. "Yeah, whatever. You're cool. Well, 95% cool." He smiled, but quickly faltered. "Heads up," he muttered under his breath.

Before Landon and I could turn around, a person descended upon us.

"Hey, brother, how's it hanging?"

Landon hung his head. "Russ," he mumbled. "Can I help you?"

"Didn't realize August and Tyler would be here too. What's up guys?"

Tyler and I nodded our small hellos. But as it often is between the two brothers, awkward tension quickly prevailed. Casual conversation was unnecessary.

"Are you keeping tabs on me now?" Landon spat.

"Of course not." Russell gestured to the highway behind him. "Thought I saw your car. You know, that Tahoe bumper sticker is a big tell. I was on my way out to the lake to meet a few friends. Dropped in for a quick 'howdy-do.' I imagine you aren't just casually hanging out here. Unless you're on a third grade field trip again?"

"Sounds like you *are* keeping tabs," Landon quipped back. Tyler and I exchanged lowered glances, commiserating on our mutual discomfort. If he wasn't here with me, I'd feel much, *much* more awkward.

"You haven't been around your dad's lately. I miss you." Russell drew a line down his cheek while jutting out his lower lip. I knew he was joking, but sometimes his jokes have an underlying tone of authenticity. It can be really difficult to decipher Russell's intent for that reason. I still wasn't even sure if he asked me to prom jokingly, seriously, or to get under Landon's skin.

Landon scoffed. "Have *you* been around there? Last I heard you were skipping off with Ed this summer."

"Who's Ed?" I blurted.

"Russ's dad," Landon answered. To dull any additional awkwardness I had caused, I slouched and took another bite of peach. Of course, I made an obvious crunching sound.

"Was that sound your peach?" Russell asked, his lips turned up. "Are you eating an unripe peach?"

"Aren't you supposedly meeting friends at the lake?" Landon interjected. "I don't want you to keep them waiting."

Russell didn't have an answer for that. At least, not with words. He looked between the three of us, pausing on each of our faces. Finally, after scanning the table several times over, he clicked his tongue. With an abrupt bow, he backed away. Only once he was out of sight did we breathe a sigh of relief. The deep exhale felt like a thaw after sitting through that mini ice age.

"What was that about?" Tyler asked as he popped open a bag of chips.

Landon sighed. "Sorry. He just pisses me off so damn much."

"I might regret asking, but what's the deal with you two? He *obviously* knows what buttons to push," I gave him a poke in the chest for emphasis, and was grateful when he smiled. "But did you just hate living together as middle schoolers or something? Swore yourselves in as mortal enemies for life?"

Tyler shook his head the tiniest bit, warning me of a danger zone. Landon chuckled, but it didn't meet his eyes. "I wish it were that simple. We've got some family crap that runs pretty deep, I guess you could say. I won't dive in to it, but there's been some backstabbing and stealing and . . . yeah. I just can't stand that guy. His family sucks, too."

"Okay," I nodded, fine with putting it to rest. I reached my hand back up to rub a few circles on his back.

"Shit," he mumbled. "I'm sorry, Ty. I hate putting you in the middle."

Tyler was shoving chips onto his tuna sandwich, and he shrugged. "It's alright. Now we're out of high school, I probably won't be seeing much more of him. We were really only friends because of basketball."

I pursed my lips, trying to picture the situation from Landon's perspective. I couldn't be best friends with someone Isabell hated, and I know she's the same way. Maybe guys are different. They fight different, it seems. For girls, loyalty and cattiness are the rallying war cries. We can tell from the tone of voice if a girl hates us. Hanging out with the enemy is taking a definitive side, and thus one of the most overt ways of causing drama. That's when evil looks become ammo in the arsenal.

But guys? Whole new world for me. Landon and Tyler aren't fighting, but Landon and Russell are, and Tyler is friends with both of them? My head hurt trying to follow such casual madness.

"You guys baffle me," I settled on saying, rubbing my forehead. "Are we going to find a ranger or what?"

Tyler checked his watch. "I have to get home. But let me know what you find, okay?"

"See ya, Ty." Landon flipped him a two fingered wave as he stood from the table. Since we weren't in any rush, Landon and I took our time eating lunch before getting back to business.

Once we were finished, we crossed the highway to check out the ghost town ruins. We stopped at all the park signs, which retold the history of the settlement and the merchants. It wasn't really necessary for the treasure hunt, but Landon's eyes were gleaming like a kid in a candy shop reading them, so I just went with it.

"Ooh, look. It's the 'cold storage room.' I remember this! They used to shuttle snow off Shasta Bally, carting it all the way over here to the butcher shop. Meat's gotta have ice, right?"

"This used to be a butcher shop?" I raised my eyebrows at the small, hillside dig-out. There was hardly enough room in there for a table and chairs let alone an entire meat display.

"It burned down in 1878," Landon pointed at the date on the sign. "Up until then, I think it was a butcher shop. But after the fire, this was all that survived."

"Huh. That's pretty cool, actually." I peeked through the iron-clad gate guarding the cold storage room. It was just an empty chamber, not much to see.

"Oh, look, they're opening the museum." He nodded back across the street, where the museum was opening. We crossed the highway again and tromped up the wooden ramp to the entrance. As we waited to be let in, Landon's eyes were wide.

"When was the last time you were here?" I asked him. He was acting like this was his favorite place in the world. You'd think we were waiting in line for a ride at an amusement park.

"Probably as a little kid. I've been wanting to come back, though."

"Third Monday of the month is free," the park person greeted, gesturing for us to move into the museum. We skittered on in, and right away started our mosey about the room.

As to be expected, a lot of old artifacts decorated the walls and filled the displays. Photos in black, white, and sepia color schemes, framed documents, and accessories behind glass. I stared through a case at a pocket watch, which was frozen on the time 12:36.

The watch tripped me up a bit. How strange that watch can be stuck in time, but time is still moving on. My mind wandered to Odette, and her house—it was also kind of stuck in time. Here, at the museum, we viewed history from present day. But at Odette's, it was different. There, dwelled a person, or a ghost, or something, *engulfed* by its history. They say that living in the past is what depresses you, but could the same thing apply to ghosts? Is that what purgatory is like, being unable to escape what troubled you in the past?

I tapped on the glass case that held the gold pocket watch. Could Odette be lonely out there? Before I fell down that rabbit hole, Landon's beckoning drew me away.

"August, check this out," he said, waving. I stepped over to him, where he was pointing at a framed newspaper clipping on the wall. Next to the clipping was a photograph. "It's about the Ruggles, and their hanging."

"Whoa," I squinted. "Is that really a picture of them being hung? Wait, I've read this article."

"Where on Earth have you seen this?"

"It was printed in a newspaper the day after the matter. But I didn't see the picture."

"The wild, wild, west," Landon joked with a terrible western accent. "Don't matter if yer set for trial, townfolk can come in and steal ya right from yer jail bed!"

"It was a lawless time, that's for sure," a voice spoke behind us. Landon ran a hand through his hair and cleared his throat. I almost jumped, but then seeing that it was a park employee, I let out a breath. It was a guy, probably close to thirty years old.

"No kidding. This story is crazy. You know much about the Ruggles?"

I stiffened at his question, fearing some kind of exposure of our mission. But Landon was smooth as ever, crossing his arms and tilting his chin toward the framed newspaper.

"I'm afraid not, aside from the article. I've heard a few conspiracies, but, you know, that's not the type of history we want to be spreading 'round here." The guy laughed and mirrored Landon, folding his arms across his chest. Just above his arms, his name tag read 'Dan Evans.'

"Conspiracies are just interesting stories. And I love a good story. Let's hear it." Landon grinned, egging Dan on.

Dan played coy for a moment, but ultimately his eagerness matched Landon's. "Okay, okay. So get this. Rumor is that the treasure they stole hasn't been found."

"You don't say. That's something," Landon said, feigning surprise. He looked down at me with a growing smile that made me forget my place. My cheeks flushed despite myself, and only Dan's voice pulled me back.

"Right? After 120 years or so, it's still sitting out there somewhere. A lot of folks have their own theories for how thing went down with Johnny boy. Some say he stashed it near the scene of the crime, but I say that's a load. Why would he hide it right where he found it? Plain sight ain't as good a spot as people think."

I tried to control the narrowing of my eyes at Dan, but couldn't help it. A glare begged to be shot at him. Something in his voice I simply didn't trust. Dan reached up to stroke his reddish-brown, straggly beard. He shuffled his red high-topped feet from side to side, like he was preparing to pitch the idea of his life.

"Unless he didn't think he had time to haul it and hide it," Landon pointed out.

"It's one theory, yep. Another is that he hid out in the hills 'round here for a week or so, up Whiskey Creek in the abandoned mine there, before fleeing south. Some say he found a lady who stowed him away for a bit, others say he took the goods with him to Woodland, where he was caught."

"You don't say," Landon scratched behind his ear and nodded along. It was information we already knew, but Landon played along like it was brand new.

Dan put his hands up to suggest his innocence. "Hard to tell truth from rumor," he flicked his eyes to me, quipping up a single brow, "but the speculation can be just as fun as finding treasure, right?"

I couldn't be bothered to hide my grimace. The glint in his eyes rubbed me way wrong. Something was off.

Landon chuckled. "Right."

Studying Landon's face, I couldn't tell if he trusted Dan or was hiding his skepticism. Not wanting to give my own thoughts away, I forced my gaze back on Dan. He stared Landon straight in the eyes, then me again. It sent a shudder down my spine.

"If there's anything else I can do for you, ask." He dipped his head in a curt nod.

"We will. Thanks, man."

Once Dan backed away and we turned our backs to him, I tugged on Landon's arm. "Do you trust that guy?" I huffed under my breath.

He looked over his shoulder, where Dan disappeared behind a curtain. "Sure, why not?"

I pursed my lips, keeping my eyes forward at the article. "It feels off. He was wearing red high tops."

"So?"

"Park people don't wear red high tops, it's too flashy. Not an earthy tone."

"I don't know. He seems fine to me. Whiskey Creek is the only new lead we have that's in the county. Shouldn't we check it out?"

I resisted a frown when I peeked in the direction Dan vanished.

"August," he lowered his voice. "What if he's right? Are you in, or not?"

There was an itchy feeling on the back of my neck, but I wasn't about to stand down. "Yeah, I'm in."

Shortly after, Landon drove me home. It was hardly early afternoon, which had me resenting the fact I'd be home alone again. Dad usually worked at the park until dinner in the summer, sometimes later, and Mom still had a few hours before she closed up shop.

"What are you up to for the rest of the day?" I asked as we pulled on to my street.

"I have to pick up my little sister from her volleyball camp out at the college in about an hour, but that's it. What about you?"

"Not a thing. What do you and your sister usually do when it's just the two of you? You have two sisters, right?"

"Yeah, the two. I don't know, we do normal stuff like play cards or monopoly or fight about what to watch on TV."

"I wish I had someone to do normal stuff with. I get so bored during the summer when it's just me by myself all the time." The words alone were making me slouch as we crept closer and closer to my driveway, but I kept talking. "The no-car thing adds a serious hurdle for any type of social activity. Thanks for picking me up and dropping me off."

"Don't mention it." He turned up my driveway, and paused before saying, "I'm sorry."

My gut fluttered at his sincerity, spreading warmth to my cheeks. "What are you apologizing for? You didn't do anything wrong."

"I don't know, I guess I'm sorry you get lonely here. That sucks."

"Landon," I started, clamping my mouth shut and re-opening it. "Thank you."

"For what?"

I shrugged and played with the hem of my shirt. "For making me feel understood, I guess? That's hard to come by these days." I chuckled, but it wasn't funny at all. It sounded ridiculous to say out loud.

"Yeah," he whispered. "Of course."

Before I could work up the courage to look at him, and drag out this moment a bit longer, my house came in to view. My dad's car was parked out front—a rarity on a summer weekday afternoon. It briefly distracted me from Landon.

"Guess my dad's home." I smiled, voice a little higher. Turning to him, I was taken aback by his eyes on me, flickering with an unknown intensity. "What?" I asked on impulse, my voice suddenly breathless.

He blinked a few times, and his gaze switched back to normal. But I felt just as hypnotized under this look. His eyes were golden, and playful, and completely Landon. *That* was what got me every time. Being looked at by *him*. Feeling *seen*.

"Should we shoot for Whiskey Creek on Thursday?" I tried asking.

"Thursday it is. Whiskey Creek. Named for liquid gold. Now, maybe there's *actual gold* in it. Who would have thought?"

"I guess it is fitting." I unbuckled. "Maybe Dan led us to water after all, pun unintended. I'll see you Thursday?"

"Wait."

My hand was already on the door handle, but I stopped. He opened his mouth, then closed it. Then opened, and closed it, just like I had a few minutes ago. His eyes were scanning my face like he was searching for an answer to some unknown question.

With a loud heartbeat in my chest and a building silence, there was enough tension to burst my eardrums. Still, I couldn't really look away from him. With every look in this freaking car ride, I felt like I was more and more under a spell. I'm pretty sure I didn't blink once.

What was he going to say?

"Um." He cleared his throat, and my stomach lurched. "Want me to wait for you to get in?"

One of my eyebrows quipped up, and back down as I suppressed a grin. I gestured toward the house. "My dad's here. Even if the front door is locked, the side door is always open. Thanks, Lanno," I gave him a little shove on the shoulder and popped out of the car. I couldn't linger any longer in that charged atmosphere.

He rolled his eyes. "Bye."

As I hobbled to the front porch steps, I stopped. Landon was still parked, both hands on the wheel, looking right at me. He offered a sheepish grin and a cute little wave. It was impossible not to smile back, so I did, and waved before darting to the side door of the house.

The cheeky grin remained on my face as I entered the house and leaned back against the front door. My dad's voice on the phone in the kitchen grabbed my attention, and I pinched my cheek to sober my nerves up and head to my room. Passing by the dining room table, something caught my eye and caused a double take.

It was the folder, labeled 1892.

All the contents inside were, for once, neatly organized.

"Crap," I muttered.

A phone beeped. Booted footsteps entered the dining room with a slow, foreboding rhythm. "Might I ask what you were doing with these?"

FOURTEEN

"Look, Dad—" I started. But he held up a finger, stopping me in my tracks.

"You know how I feel about my desk. It's the one space in this house that I like to keep a certain way. Between the patchy couch and the drawers full of tangled yarn and the end of the table that usually has a tower of textbooks. I love that you and your mother have your space, but the desk is mine."

I sighed. Dad's desk was like his little man-cave. Our house was small, without much room for privacy. Well, unless you're here all day by yourself. "I know, I know. I'm sorry, Dad."

"On top of that," he continued, opening the folder and leafing through the contents. "You picked out the folder from 1892, with contents about the Ruggles, just a week or two after you asked me about it. Coincidence?" He shrugged.

"It's been so boring. I'm here alone while you and Mom both work. I can't help my curiosity, especially when there's nothing around to distract it," I tried to reason.

Dad picked up the folder and tapped it on the table a few times. "I'm not mad, you know."

"Just disappointed?"

He chuckled, and a little tension rolled off my shoulders. "I should have been more clear about the Ruggles treasure when you asked. I was ineffective. The thing about the gold rush, August, is that it inspired a frenzy. It was far away from the rest of the country, and people were rushing in from all over the world for a slice of the cake. You know what that means?"

"That people were losing their minds?"

"Yes, in part. But moreover, that people were greedy," he corrected. "They'd do anything to get ahead, to make easy money. Quite contrary to a lot of American ideals at the time, of honorable work ethic. It's the original get-rich-quick scheme."

"What does this have to do with the Ruggles?" I didn't mind the history lesson, but it felt like a roundabout way to get to his point. I'd rather just skip to the end and have him ground me or whatever was going to happen.

Now it was Dad's turn to sigh at me. "Part of that gold rush greed still exists today. When folks catch a whiff that others are hunting for lost gold of that time—believe me, it happens more often than you think—it's like it awakens the dead. People get swept up in the romantics of it."

"Point being?"

He put a hand on my shoulder. "Stirring up myths of lost gold pulls people out of the wood work. You'd be surprised by how many folks around here have familial ties to the gold rush, and think there's hidden treasure they're entitled to."

"Dad, no offense, but I seriously don't know what you're getting at."

He sighed. "Searching for conspiracy gold around here is dangerous. People get up in arms about it, with old debts to settle and deep, generational, inter-family feuds. Stay away from the Ruggles treasure, August. I mean it. It's for your own good."

With that, he picked up the folder, patted my shoulder, and returned to the kitchen, a way of telling me it was not up for negotiation.

"That's oddly cryptic and vague," I called after him with a frown.

"Just trust me on this one, okay? I have to get back to the park. Call me if you need anything, I'll be back around six tonight," he shouted back at me.

"Okay," I grumbled. "Bye."

As he shut the back door, I blew out what my mom would call a 'dramatic huff' and plopped belly first on to the patchy sofa. I heard the sound of Dad's truck revving to life outside, followed by churning gravel before it faded the distance. I trudged over to the door and let Solo in. It was against the rules, but if no one was around to see it, then I really didn't care.

Once my dad left, I debated calling Isabell about a hundred times. I had the compulsive need to tell her about my dad's warning, for just the sake of getting it off my chest. However, knowing she was on the fence about this whole thing put *me* on the fence as to whether I should tell her. It was eerie messaging, even for me. They say ignorance is bliss, but what kind of friend would I be if I kept her in the dark about Dad's caution? And his second warning, no less.

She tells me I'm the fearless one, and sure, I do push the boundaries. But as the only child of my parents, I have this crippling need to make sure I don't disappoint them. If I screw up, there isn't anyone else to draw the focus away. My mom looks at me with those big, sad, how-could-you eyes, and my dad delivers the sentence.

Besides, Dad wouldn't tell me something was dangerous if it wasn't true. He's got the same adventure-thirst that I do, but more extreme. If it's too outrageous for him, then it must be too far-fetched for me.

Telling Isabell felt like the nail in the coffin of the treasure hunt. I doubted she'd want to continue. I tossed my phone on to the adjacent chair and rubbed my eyes. Solo was so happy to be inside he was sitting on the ground with his two front paws on the couch, tongue hanging and tail wagging. His innocence was the perfect distraction from all the insanity in my head.

No. Looking at Solo, I decided that no, I would not tell Isabell about my talk with Dad. I'd suffer in silence on this one.

My phone rang on the other chair, and I perked up at the sound. It was Isabell, leading me to think that my phone was somehow reading my thoughts.

"Sup, are you off work for the day?" I answered, slouching back in to the couch.

"Hey, yep. Heading home now. One of the kids was driving me up a wall because he kept trying to eat glitter. I need something to cheer me up, so I called to see how the day went with Lanno and Ty."

"Oh, right," I trailed, her question reminding me of my chat with Tyler. My mouth hung open as I debated giving her the full scoop. Unless I knew for certain Tyler would ask her out, I didn't want to get her hopes up. Plus, it's nice to be surprised with a date.

"It was fine," I settled on saying. "Landon thinks we nabbed a lead from a park guide, but I think the guy was full of it."

"What did this person say?"

I snorted. "Nothing of substance. Blah blah blah, the treasure stowed somewhere near Whiskey Creek, blah blah blah. He seemed like he was pulling it out of his ass."

"Uh-huh."

"I know, I know. I'm being harsh, but it's true, Iz. You'd think it too if you had been there," I defended. "In any case, Landon doesn't see the harm in checking it out, so we were thinking of going Thursday if you and Ty are in."

"I guess Landon's right. Why not? Sounds good to me," she agreed, and I imagined her shrugging on the other end like it wasn't a big deal. A pang of guilt buzzed in my gut. "So did any sparks fly between you and Landon?"

Her topic change only intensified my twisting confliction, and I chuckled. "Oh, Landon. You know what? I will say, he was very thoughtful of how I was getting around in this darned boot. He lent me a hand a few times, and he even packed me a PB&J to eat at lunch."

Isabell awed and cooed though the phone. "That is too cute! Did he make it with your favorite jam? I know you have some big opinions about jam."

"As a matter of fact, he did." I laughed, and she gave me a little cheer. "Ty seemed to be missing you out there."

"Oh, Tyler," she said, sighing wistfully. "That beautiful, confusing boy." Before I could decipher what exactly she meant by that, she continued. "Shoot, Auggie, I have to run. A cop is tailing me and my hands are sweating, I better focus. Do you wanna go on a burger run later? Say ten o'clock?"

"I'm in. Drive safe," I said as I hung up.

Good, this was good. I'll be seeing her later tonight, which gave me plenty of time to decide whether I should fill her in on Dad's concern. Or, about Tyler's hidden torch for her. *Plenty* of time.

When I told my parents that Isabell and I were doing a late-night fast food run, they hardly gave it a second thought. They rarely question my plans with Isabell, and we've been doing these burger runs since we got our licenses a year and a half ago. Better yet, Mom offered to let me take her car, so I actually got to drive us for once.

The trek across town from our houses takes over twenty minutes, so after I picked Isabell up, we had a lot of time to catch up on the boys and the treasure. It dawned on us that we still hadn't debriefed the night in Odette's haunted house. For the most part, our experiences were pretty separate, and I had no clue what happened with her and Ty in there.

"So he didn't actually reach for my hand," Isabell clarified as we pulled in to the parking lot of the burger joint. "There was a creak upstairs, probably from you and Landon, and I grabbed his hand out of instinct. But he didn't pull away, so that's a good sign."

I smiled with my eyes still on the road. She was going to be over the moon once Tyler asked her out. "Sounds like a budding roman*c*e," I remarked, pronouncing the word with an accent.

She groaned. "If only. It's already three weeks into summer. He's moving to Berkeley this fall. Would he really want to be dating a high school girl? Doubtful. I feel like it may be time for me to move on."

I nearly swerved us into the curb before guffawing at her. "What? Seriously? But you've liked him for so long, and we're spending all this time with him. Now you want to move on?"

"Exactly. I've liked him forever, and now that we're hanging out more, he still hasn't made any kind of move. Doesn't that make me look pathetic?"

If Isabell really thought that, I couldn't help but wonder if I looked equally pathetic for my crush on Landon. It's almost the exact same situation. Should I be giving up too? I debated asking her, but stopped myself. We were working through *her* issue. We should tackle one boy crisis at a time.

Besides, her guy confirmed his interest. She can't give up now.

"I think it means you're closer than ever to dating him for real," I reasoned with her. "Just give it until the end of the summer or something. No reason to give up on him when we meet up with him multiple times per week."

"That's an oddly hopeless-romantic thing for you to say."

I scoffed, parking the car. "I believe in romance, and love."

"You're a skeptic, Auggie," she laughed.

"Not true, I love you," I point out.

"Aw!" Isabell cooed, unbuckling her seatbelt to lurch over and wrap her arms around me.

"Whatever," I joked, hugging her back. "Let's go get some milkshakes and fries."

As one of the favorite high school hangout spots, it was pretty busy, even for almost eleven at night. A lot of school apparel decorated the group: Shasta letterman jackets, Hornets sweatshirts, things like that. Russell was among the crowd. He gave us a curt nod from across the room, but didn't approach us. Girls were dressed cute, and Isabell and I huddled together in our sport shorts and baggy tees. After ordering our usual—two milkshakes, chocolate and Neapolitan, and two orders of fries, regular and savage style—we hustled to a back table where we could watch everyone else in our own bubble.

"I do love it here," Isabell started. "But high school just wasn't where I was meant to shine."

I studied my best friend. She was undeniably beautiful, but she also was happy-go-lucky, and smart, and fun. She could really shine anywhere, so in some ways, I wasn't sure what she meant. Then again, we were just middle of the road at our high school. We were in the blending-in-slightly-on-the-outside crowd, the two of us. Neither popular nor disliked. It's not the worst place to be, but it's hard to feel like you belong with a position like that.

"Guess next year we'll be getting out of here." I shrugged. "It'll be nice to start over. No parental rules looming overhead."

"Right," she snickered. "Because we break our parents' rules *so* often."

"We snuck out your bedroom window last week, did we not?"

"Well, see, that's . . . different?" she tried, but I snickered at her effort.

Our order was called, and Isabell rushed up to get it. She returned and tossed the tray down in the middle of the table. We popped off both our milkshake lids, mine the chocolate one, and started to dip the regular French fries.

"Wherever we go, I can't imagine leaving California. It's not the same swirling your fries in other fast food shakes."

I bowed my head like what she had just said was gospel. When I lifted it back up, I frowned. "HBIC. Incoming."

Stacey Higgins was walking through the door, dressed like she was here to pre-game a party. Two friends walked in behind her, and when Stacey saw us, she grinned before strolling to our table.

"How cute. Mommy and Daddy give you permission to be out past curfew?" Stacey mocked. Isabell and I looked at each other with raised eyebrows. "Or are you having a little sleepover party, and getting a milkshake in your PJs was a must-do before TP-ing the neighbor's house?"

I stifled a laugh, and Isabell snorted on a cheesy fry. We tried to ignore her, but she crossed her arms and pressed on. "While you do your best to not blow milkshake out your nose, I'll be over there, waiting for Landon."

My face fell, and it must have been obvious because Stacey's grin only grew as she gave me a prissy little wave. "Toodles," she said, beaming as she spun on her heel and off on her broom.

"I don't know what that girl's damage is. I always thought the HBICs in movies and TV shows were total crap. Fake. Non-existent. Lo-and-behold, they exist in real life, too."

I made a sound to get the bad taste out of my mouth. "What's her deal? What does Landon even see in her?"

"I'm sure she's saying that to rile you up. There's no way he would—"

"Speak of the devil," I muttered when I caught sight of Landon approaching the doors. Isabell jerked her head so fast I thought she'd get whiplash. She quickly cowered back over the table with wide eyes.

"Want me to let him have a piece of my mind?" she offered, which made me laugh again.

"You're a better hype-woman than a smack-talker. Thanks for having my back though." I shook my head, smiling though my appetite had been lost. "He's coming over here," I lowered my voice. Isabell's eyes bulged again as she stuffed a handful of animal fries in her mouth right when Landon stopped at our table.

"Hey," he greeted us casually, as if he had nowhere else to be. "I heard a lot of people were meeting up here before heading out to a bonfire at The Ranch, but didn't expect to see you guys. Are you going, too?"

The Ranch was an infamous party spot. It wasn't even an actual ranch, but a spot way out in the boonies down some old dirt road that high schoolers would go to throw massive ragers and bonfires. We, of course, had never gone.

The moment he spoke the words, Isabell dribbled secret sauce on to her old t-shirt. She wiped it with a napkin, but a grease stain remained. I answered Landon for us, trying not to burst into laughter at the sight of my disheveled best friend.

"Nah, we're here for the fries."

Isabell hummed in support next to me. "Besides, Lanno, Stacey seems to think you're here for *her*."

He frowned and looked side to side without moving his head. He resembled a deer in the headlights—a cute look on him. "Is she here? Did she say that?"

The mere mention of her name was like a spell to materialize her out of thin air. She strolled up right behind him. "Lanny, the rest of us are outside," she said as Isabell signed H-B-I-C from across the table. I made a face like I had just smelled something nasty.

Stacey tugged on his arm a little as he rolled his eyes to the ceiling. "I'll be right back," he said to us as she physically pulled him away.

Isabell dropped more sauce on to her shirt. "Crap," she mumbled.

"Whatever. Maybe he really does like her," I copied her grumble. Peering out the window, Stacey still had her hand on his arm. I could have sworn he was grimacing, but maybe I was just seeing what I wanted to see. He turned to look inside, right at me, so I swiveled back to Isabell.

Ten minutes and a few stolen glances at Landon later, Isabell and I had picked over the rest of our fries and tossed our trash before taking off. When we stepped outside the front door, Landon jogged over to greet us.

"Your posse let you go for a moment?" Isabell joked. I nearly cringed.

"Ha, ha. I thought I'd see if you guys wanted to come out to the bonfire. You're already here, aren't you?

Isabell looked down at herself, in her greasy tee and bright pink rubber shoes. "As much as I'm dressed to impress, I may pass tonight."

I chuckled. "Yeah, not tonight. I don't think my mom would like it too much if I spun her car around town till the wee hours of the morning."

He gave us a small smile. "I gotcha. It'd be more fun if you guys were there, but I get it. Let me walk you guys to your car."

We didn't argue with him, and my mood perked up the tiniest bit. Isabell kept addressing him. "So August told me that the next move is to check out Whiskey Creek? Do we have any other specifics?"

"Not really. Heard through the grapevine that there's an abandoned mine shaft up there. I'm betting that's the place to start. We were shooting for Thursday, right August?" he asked, and I nodded.

"Sweet. The closer we get, the closer we are to putting the stress of this whole thing behind us." Isabell gestured manically before letting her arms dangle by her side.

Once we arrived at my mom's car, I smiled at Landon. "Thanks for walking us out, Landon. Maybe next time we'll join you out at The Ranch."

"Yeah, that'd be nice." He smiled a little more. I opened my mouth to say something else, but Isabell cleared her throat and grabbed our attention.

"Um, uh-uh," she stuttered, her voice quiet. "You guys?"

I turned around, and she was facing the windshield of my mom's car, about six feet back from it. Peering past her shoulder, my blood ran cold. There was a familiar envelope, the third of its kind, tucked under the blade. Rushing past her, I plucked the envelope out as the two of them crowded around me. When I unfolded it, the same red ink greeted me as the other times. I took a deep breath before I read it out loud, trying to stop my hands from shaking.

"*I can do a lot worse than this*," I read, my heart thumping in my chest. "I can do a lot worse than what?"

"Uh-oh," Landon whispered. He was pointing to the back window, which was shattered.

"The tires. They're flat," Isabell observed. I ran to kneel next to the back tire, careful not to kneel on any glass. Sure enough, the tire had been slashed. My stomach plummeted to my feet, and I felt the blood drain from my face.

"Crap on a stick!" I spat.

"The front one too. Oh, oh oh *oh*. There's a knife in the front tire," Isabell gasped. She jumped back from the car a few steps and covered her mouth.

"What?"

"Knife. Front tire! Oh no, oh no," she shuddered. Rubbing her hands together, she paced back and forth while I moved in for a closer look at the blade. Landon crouched beside me, his arm up against mine.

"Shit. I'm sorry, August."

I covered my face with my hands, hoping it would wake me up from this nightmare. "I am so dead. As *if* my parents will ever let me have a car now. What am I going to do? How will I even pay for this? Aren't new tires, like, really expensive? And a window repair? That must be even more," I said as I twirled the ends of my hair. I couldn't take my eyes off the knife.

"Maybe your insurance will cover it," Landon tried, offering a consolatory smile.

My frown deepened, and I rested my chin on my hand. "I'm pretty sure my parents have the worst insurance possible."

Isabell sighed, and Landon went as far as wrapping an arm around me. I mustered a smile for him, since the gesture did a lot to make me feel better. I reached up and grabbed his hand, its warmth instantly spreading to mine.

"Hey, Landon, we're leaving. Let's go!" someone called from the outdoor patio.

"I'm bowing out. Another time!" he shouted back with my hands still in his. The person threw their arms up and shrugged before rejoining the congregating group. Soon, they all called for him, and he huffed in annoyance. To my dismay, he stood up, leaving a cold patch where he once was.

He waved them onward with big arm motions, just as his phone started to ring in his pocket. He pulled it out and rolled his eyes before answering.

"Hey Stacey . . . No, I'm not coming . . . Yeah, I'm serious . . . Just go ahead without me, alright? . . . Um, maybe another time." He shrugged at me as he hung up the phone.

"Thanks, Landon," I told him, though it felt like a massive understatement.

"No problem. My cousin's a mechanic, I'll call him and see if he can tow it to his shop. They can fix it up with new tires, replace the window, and have it ready to roll in no time. Stay right here." He held up a finger as he whipped out his phone to make a call. He didn't go too far, just a few steps away to pace and fill in his cousin, but it was enough space that Isabell fell apart with fear.

"This is a tangible, physical threat," she whisper-yelled. "Don't even try to say that this is okay! This. Is. Not. O. Kay. We're minors, which I'm pretty sure makes this threat even more of a crime, probably, I'm sure. And it's the third one," she started to laugh, but not because it was funny. "Oh my gosh. We are being threatened, for *real*. We hardly escaped a ghost and now, well, who knows if we'll escape this because we don't even know what or who *it is*. Oh, hell. Could it be the ghost?"

I slumped into a seated position and Isabell's chuckling died down. My back was against the front tire, my ear next to the stiff blade. It technically wasn't flat yet, since the knife was keeping the hole semi-plugged. I tilted my head to get a better look at the blade before I answered her back.

"Whoever it is means business, obviously. They're trying to send a message, along with their actual messages," I thought out loud, flapping the envelope in my hand.

"It's stalking, too. How do they keeping finding us? Or you, I should say."

My attention turned back to her. "You haven't gotten any letters, have you?"

"Oh trust me, Auggie. If I got any personally, I'd have fled for Timbuktu by now."

I chuckled a little, and her posture eased up. Angling my head toward the fixed knife, I squinted at it before flipping open my phone for a little light. Landon rejoined us as I started to scrutinize.

"Okay, my cousin is bringing a tow truck over right now. He should be here pretty soon. Once we load up your mom's car, I can drive you both home. What are you doing?" He was raising an eyebrow at me, and I flipped my phone shut.

"You guys don't think that whoever stabbed the tire would have been so stupid as to leave their personal knife with a personal engraving, do you?" I asked.

"That would be pretty dumb," Isabell snorted half-heartedly.

"It says 'Love, Roseanne.' Unless there's a manufacturer named Love, Roseanne, I'm assuming this knife is one of a kind."

"What? Let me see." Landon knelt, and shone his phone light on to the knife. He froze and then sighed. "It would be very dumb. But some people are just, really, really, dumb," he said before continuing to mumble a few choice words under his breath.

My eyes moved to Isabell, who shrugged like she wasn't sure what was going on. We sat in silence for a moment and Landon stared at the ground, running his hand through his hair a few times.

"I'm sorry, really sorry. I should have known." He rubbed a hand down his face and shook his head.

"You should have known what, Landon?" I asked, resting a hand on his shoulder for comfort.

He looked to me, face full of disappointment. "I'm saying," he coughed, "what I'm saying is . . . I know who's been sending the notes."

FIFTEEN

Once Landon admitted to knowing the culprit, Isabell and I stared at him for an uncomfortable amount of time. What an anticlimactic way to uncover the offender's identity. A simple 'Love, Roseanne' engraving? It felt too easy. Something was off.

"Landon, how? How do you know? How *sure* are you?" I broke the silence after what felt like hours. Isabell, meanwhile, stayed frozen in place.

"Let's just say, it's someone who hates my family. My family's sworn enemy."

"Okay, sworn enemy or not, why do they care that we're searching for the Ruggles gold?"

He rubbed his hands together before pinching the bridge of his nose. "It's complicated, alright? And probably a misunderstanding. I'll fix it, don't worry."

"This person seems crazy, Landon. It'd be dangerous to try talking any sense in to them. What is there to misunderstand here, anyway?"

"I'll fix it," he repeated, resolute. Then, he finally turned to me. "I promise."

Struggling to understand his cryptic answers, I held his eyes like they'd clue me in on the secret. All the ambiguity lately was driving me mad. First my dad, now Landon. It's like I'm being left in the dark, fully unarmed. But before I could interrogate him, bright lights flashed at us. I had to cover my face to avoid going blind.

"That's him. Buff's here." Landon breathed a sigh of relief as he stood to wave the truck over.

"Buff?" Isabell whispered to me.

Buff parked the tow truck in the middle of the lot. When he hopped out, it was clear that his name suited him well. He was tall, with broad shoulders and a strong chest—the kind of guy that slings chains around like a lasso. Without a hello, he jumped right in, asking questions about what happened and assessing the tires. While Buff loaded up my mom's car, I worked on filling out a form with my info. On his way out, Buff tipped his hat and said he'd be in touch first thing tomorrow. All was said and done in about twenty minutes.

My mom's car hitched a ride out of the lot, and I helplessly watched on. I locked in any feelings of panic by crossing my arms. My mind raced over all the possible scenarios that could unfold tomorrow morning with Mom and Dad. They could say it's no big deal, that their insurance will cover it. Or they could ground me for a month. Or they could take away my license. Or they could send me to a tower far, far away until I've learned my lesson, or until a prince climbs up my hair, or until I turn to dust.

Was there best-case scenario that didn't suck?

The state of purgatory before punishment, I hoped, was more torturous than what was to come. Isabell rested her hand on my shoulder, but didn't say a word.

"Come on," Landon said as he motion to his car. "Let me drive you guys home."

The car ride was silent, save for the low hum of the radio. I didn't have the energy for chit-chat. For goodness' sake, I didn't even have it in me to pester Landon. If I opened my mouth, I knew I'd end up whining about my situation. I would feel more pathetic word vomiting my misery everywhere, so it was best just to zip my lips.

Landon was stiff as a board at the wheel, like any sudden movement would cause an eruption. In the backseat, Isabell whistled the tune to the radio. I didn't *want* to talk, but the walking on eggshells was just as aggravating.

Isabell's house was the first stop. Before hopping out of the car, she hugged me from behind the seat and said she'd call tomorrow after work. Once she was out the door with her whistling, the air tightened between me and Landon.

It seemed like we would go the entire drive to my place without speaking, until Landon startled me by blowing out a breath like a horse. "Look, I'm sure my cousin can cut you a deal on the tires. It'll all work out."

I rested my elbow on the door and propped my head on my hand. "Summer can really suck, you know?"

"I'm not sure I do."

"After tonight, I doubt either of my parents will let me drive their cars ever again. They'll probably take my phone, ground me, or both. So I'll be even more bored at home by myself all day."

"Well when you put it like that, that really—"

"Sucks?" I finished for him.

He chuckled a little, and I couldn't resist joining him. "Yeah. That really sucks," he agreed. I lifted my head and fiddled with a loose hem of my ratty shirt. "You know what? If you're about to be grounded for the rest of the summer, maybe we should break a few more rules tonight."

"What?" I laughed, waving him off.

"Seriously! You want to throw glass bottles off the Clear Creek Bridge? Or break 100 miles per hour driving by the lake? I'm all for it. We could stay out long enough to catch the sunrise from the parking garage. Come on, your parents would never know. What's the worst they could do, ground you more?"

"With that logic, might as well treat it like the last night of freedom I'll ever have in my life. Go all out."

Our snickers subsided to lingering smiles and a contented peace.

"I wish I could," I told him as we turned on to my street.

"Me, too."

I asked him to stop at the bottom of the driveway, not wanting to wake my (hopefully) sleeping parents with the sound of his truck.

"Want me to wait for you to get in?" he asked, nodding at my house up the hill.

"The side door is always unlocked. I'm fine," I said, nodding. "It was pretty cool of you to help us out tonight, so. You know. Thank you. I know you left your friends and, well, Stacey, high and dry." Even saying her name made my stomach twist.

He scoffed. "I didn't even know Stacey was going to be there, for the record."

I reached for the handle, but stopped. "Before I go. I need some peace of mind, or it will drive me crazy."

"August, trust me. I don't have a thing for Stacey. I actually—"

"No not about that. About the letters. How do you know who it is? How are you going to fix it?"

He thudded his head back against the seat and rubbed his eyes. "I just know. I have to talk to a few people before I do anything. Like I've said, it's complicated. I would tell you if I could, but—"

"If you did you'd have to kill me?"

He tilted his eyes toward the ceiling and shook his head slightly. "Believe me, you're the last person I'd ever want to hurt."

When I averted my eyes down to the center console, his hand reached up to tuck a strand of my hair behind my ears. For a second, I thought it was my imagination.

But was I imagining the way his fingers wove in to my hair? The gentle pressure on the back of my head, as he pulled me in? It was happening so fast, but so slow all at once. His face was only inches from mine now, his eyes lowered to my lips.

My whole body was buzzing as he dipped down past my lips to my cheek, where he planted one soft kiss, followed by another. I swear I levitated in my seat, and dared to look at him out of the corner of my eye as he pulled back. Still not convinced it was real, I touched my cheek at the same time that he rested his forehead on mine.

I worried I was panting like a dog, and I could not tear my eyes from his. His intoxicating breath fanned my face, and my bones grew weak. I craved more from him, and my eyes fluttered closed. Just when I felt him moving in, a sound sent us both reeling.

It was a ringing phone, firing off in my back pocket. Landon jerked back just as I did, and I fumbled to silence the call. Once I did, I pursed my lips. Would he be upset? I had to admit, I was a little upset myself. Or did that interruption just make things permanently awkward?

Forcing a glance his way, Landon was staring out the front window. He must have felt my eyes, because he turned my way. My anxiety continued to build. How would he react?

He narrowed his eyes at me and seemed to be fighting off a grin. That was all it took for us to both burst out laughing. It may have been riddled with nervous energy, but it was laughter nonetheless.

As it died down, I found myself sighing at the sight of my driveway.

"Well," I whispered, facing him again, "I guess I better get going."

His eyes blazed back at me, and he smacked his lips. "Are you going to remember me if you're grounded for eternity?" He grinned.

I was dreaming. Most definitely. I had to be. I rolled my eyes, and I stepped out of the car.

Peering back in, I flashed him an all-knowing smile. "Goodnight, Landon."

***

As to be expected, sleep that night was difficult to come by. Between the damage to the car, my impending doom, and my moment with Landon, my mind didn't know which direction to go. Well, it did. It picked Landon, replaying our time in the car over and over and over again.

I immediately texted Isabell about Landon—partially because she was the call that interrupted, but I also had to get it off my chest before I burst. My brain was turning to mush. Should I be excited? Hopeful? Cautious? Horrified? Needless to say, Isabell flipped out.

But I had a million other things to dwell on. For instance, Mom and Dad were sure to notice that the car was missing in the driveway. They'd likely assume I stayed out all night, and proceed to flood my phone with angry voicemails. That scenario couldn't end well. If I had any chance of lessening my sentence, then it was imperative to come clean and beat them to the punch.

If I could add a little sugar to the chaos, that couldn't hurt, either.

Thankfully, Mom wakes up way before Dad, so I could deal with her first. She tends to take it a little easier. To do something nice for her, I tiptoed to the kitchen around 4:30. In the midst of prepping her coffee, I also packed her a bag of her favorite snacks. When she stepped out around five, I scared the living spirit out of her.

"Augustine Moon, you about sent me to the grave. What are you doing up at this hour?"

"I made you coffee," I whispered back.

She put a hand on her hip and smiled in the dim-lit kitchen. "Oh, honey, that was so thoughtful. What brought this on? You didn't need to trouble yourself. You must be tired. I'm sure it was late when you got back. I didn't even hear you. "

I cleared my throat. There wasn't much time to tell her before she would be walking out the door. Though I tried to plot a tactful way to tell her, I ended up blurting it out in a flub that sounded like one big word.

"Your car isn't here."

She yawned. "Don't be silly."

I was too afraid to add more, and she blinked and cocked her head to the side. I opened my mouth, but nothing came out.

She lowered her voice and asked me to explain. I told her as much as I could without worrying her senseless, or landing me in worse trouble. All I said was that I went straight to the burger joint, Isabell and I were inside for an hour at most, and by the time we left, the tires were slashed. The truth, technically. I just left out the note and the window parts, for her own good.

"Landon is going to call me this morning. He thinks his cousin can cut me a deal on tires. I'm not sure if our insurance covers this kind of thing, but I'm prepared to pay for it myself," I assured her.

Meanwhile, Mom's face was blank. I couldn't read it. Since prompting me to explain, she hadn't spoken a single word. She was staring past my shoulder like a zombie, and it was freaking me out.

"Are you mad?" I cringed, rubbing my hands together.

Mom just let out a deep breath, and filled her coffee mug. "It's too early for this. Grab your dad's keys. You'll have to drive me to work this morning."

I responded immediately, ready to be at her beck and call until this was all smoothed over. Once we were outside and the truck was started, the porch light flipped on, and Dad came outside. He was already dressed in jeans and a white t-shirt. I rolled down the window to talk to him, a lump forming in my throat.

"What are you doing in my truck? Where's your car, Jeanie?"

I started to explain, but it was harder than I expected. "It, um, had to be towed last night. I should be able to get it back today, I'm just —"

"You *what*?"

"It wasn't my fault, but I'm real sorry. I parked under a light post, Isabell and I only went to get a milkshake, and only a half hour later the tires were—"

Just like Mom, Dad sighed deeply. "Hop out of the car, August."

"It's okay, Dad. I can drive her." I heard the desperation leak through my own voice, but couldn't help it. I was desperate to create some kind of treaty. "You get ready for work and by the time I'm back—"

"Do you think you still have driving privileges after you got your mother's car towed?"

"Daniel," Mom started, trying to coax him.

"I'll drive your mother to work," he repeated, addressing me. "She can fill me in."

Looking to my mom, she nodded. "Listen to your father."

Her voice sounded more tired than it usually does in the morning, and I didn't want to argue. With a big exhale of my own, I followed orders and hopped out of the car. On any normal day, my mom would chastise me for giving her attitude with a 'huff' like that. Today, she didn't have the energy, and that made me feel even worse.

Dad slid in to the driver's seat as I plopped myself down on the front porch steps. I lifted a hand to wave as they backed out, but neither of them saw.

Great, I thought. *Not even five in the morning and I'm already a disappointment.*

If other days of summer passed in horrible agony, this one was much, much worse. I was still in punishment purgatory, without even a text message or phone call from either of my parents. After dropping off Mom, Dad had come home to pack his lunch, and didn't bother to peek in on me in my room. In a Mississippi second, he was back out the door. Talk about isolation. This blew.

My only saving grace so far was that my parents hadn't taken my phone, at least not yet. I was able to have a few text exchanges with both Landon and Isabell. He promised to keep me posted on the car, which gave me hope. If I could have it parked back in the driveway before either of them returned from work, maybe I'd be in the clear.

By two in the afternoon, I still didn't have a definitive update from Landon, just the promise to keep me updated. When Isabell called me that afternoon, she had a big freak out. Tyler had finally made his move. She was squealing nine ways to Sunday over their upcoming date. He suggested they go for ice cream tomorrow, and he offered to pick her up from work. It would be sweet and simple: perfect for the two of them.

I tried to act surprised over the news, but soon caved and told her I knew the whole time. She was pleasantly surprised over that aspect of it, and liked that everyone knew but her.

As much as I wanted to fill her in on what exactly had happened with Landon, we ran out of time. It was probably for the best, though. After only one message from him today, the edginess was creeping in. I was starting to wonder if he regretted our almost-kiss. The thought still made my pulse race, but every time it did, I felt a little more stupid.

I plopped on to the couch in utter hopelessness. With the sound of tires skidding up our gravel driveway, my heart sank. I recognized the sound of the diesel engine. Any hope of miraculously solving the car issue today jumped completely out the window. Peering outside, only Mom emerged from Dad's truck.

Retreating to my room, I closed the door and sat on the edge of my bed. I couldn't resist sending another message to Landon.

Any update on my mom's car?

Maybe he'd respond before I sat down to dinner with my parents in the next two hours. I wasn't sure if I could handle a stiff meal of frowns and stern looks. Good news would be prime right about now.

Tapping my foot, I stared at the screen, willing it to respond. Nothing pinged through. My stomach started to twist as I thudded my head back on my bed, wishing I'd never pressed send.

It was static silence on his end.

Sixteen

Dad arrived home from work just as Mom finished up on our chicken Parmesan, then disappearing into his room without a word. Since I didn't hear a car pull up over the sound of Mom's cooking music, I peeked out to the driveway. I was half-relieved, half-worried to see his work truck. At the very least, it was a temporary fix.

Sitting down for dinner the three of us, Dad's first words to me were about the car. "Is there any update?" he asked as he scooped his first bite of food. It wasn't a specific question, but we all knew what he was referring to.

"Not yet," I replied through a mouthful of chicken. Hopefully the sound of my chewing muffled my lack of confidence in the repair. "Was the park okay with you taking a car?"

"For a few days, yes. They'll need it around the park next week with the Fourth of July coming up."

I swallowed the bite I had been slowly chomping, so I could speak with more force. "I tried for an update today and got nothing. I'm on it, though."

"Good. Thank you, Auggie," Mom said as she nodded in approval.

"We appreciate that," Dad agreed. "But we do still have to punish you."

"You know," I started, poking at my food, "it wasn't really my fault. And I have the cash to pay for it in full myself. I didn't total it, I wasn't recklessly driving, I parked in a well-lit area, and still—"

"Still," Dad interjected, "there has to be consequences. We don't have the money to allow this type of thing to happen."

I resisted an eye roll, knowing it couldn't possibly help my case. Last thing I needed was a lecture on my attitude. These next few days, it would be essential to perform my best behavior. Until they decided on a punishment, I had to be the model child.

Of course, as soon as I started to formulate a list of chores I could help with, my mom cleared her throat. With a look of concern, she creased her brow at me.

"We had hoped the problem would be resolved by the time we got home today, or that we could pick it up after work. Since it isn't, we have agreed that there will be no phone, and no friends, for the next four days."

The moment of truth I'd been waiting for: the punishment. It hit a little harder coming from Mom. She rarely is the one to hand down a sentence.

"Four days?" I dropped my fork on to my glass plate. "Can today at least count toward that? I was here alone all day. And, like I've said, I didn't even do anything wrong!"

"We were going to make it a week. Four days seems generous," Dad said.

"But Isabell leaves for vacation next week. She'll be gone for three weeks. I won't have anything to do the *whole* time she's gone. Isn't that punishment enough? Are you really going to extend my summer of nothingness by forcing me to stay here alone for the next four days?"

"We'll take your phone, too."

"Do you really think this punishment fits the crime?" I stood up, annoyed that this stupid tire-slashing-window-smashing jerk kept costing me.

Realizing they weren't going to change their minds, I asked through gritted teeth to be excused. It took all my strength not to throw my dish in the sink when I piled it up. Storming through the dining room, my boot clunked on the hardwood floor like the punctuation to my anger. Once I made it to my door, my hand gripped the knob tightly, begging to slam it shut.

"Phone, August," Dad called out, stopping me mid-close.

I blew out a loud breath and grabbed my phone from my nightstand. After limping five steps back to the table, I flipped right around to return to my room and shut myself in.

Leaning against the door, I listened for footsteps. All I heard were muffled whispers. A few minutes passed, and I heaved another sigh as I collapsed on to my bed.

A small ping dinged on my floor—my shush-kabob. I dove for it and slid it under the rug, flinching at the door. All hell would break loose if my parents were to discover my secret smartphone.

When nothing happened, I breathed a sigh of relief. Luck must finally be on my side. With a celebratory fist pump, I turned off all the sounds and vibrations to keep it secret. I fired off a message to Isabell, filling her in on my situation.

Crap, still nothing from Landon? And grounded? What will you do about Whiskey Creek? She wrote back.

Oh, trust me. I'll find a way.

Do you ever wake up in the morning and sense that things are about to spiral? Like if you stay in bed, things can't get worse?

My Wednesday started off a little like that. I was in utter misery. How could getting out of bed make anything better? My parents were out the door, leaving me on my own. I couldn't even go on a morning run thanks to my sprained ankle and stupid boot. Instead, I felt ready to go with nothing to do. One can only click through cheesy midday game shows for so long before going crazy.

Isabell and Tyler were supposed to have their date today, giving me one small token to look forward to. All afternoon, I waited on pins and needles for updates. I figured they'd be together until four or five, but when she called my house at 2:30, I was a bit surprised.

"Hi," she greeted, her voice low.

"What's wrong? Are you with Ty?"

She sighed. "No. He hasn't showed up. At this point he's a half hour late. I texted him, no reply. You know, of all people, I pegged him as *least* likely to stand me up. But, here he is, leaving me high and dry. Now I'm feeling super lame, like I've just been exposed for the massive crush I have on him. I just—oh, wait, he texted me."

"What did he say?" I paced, shuffling in fast circles around the dining room table.

She groaned. "He said, 'I thought I texted you. So sorry. It isn't going to work out.'"

"Were those his exact words?"

"Yes."

"Crap," I mumbled, my mind racing over the details of my own conversation with Tyler. "It doesn't make any sense. Do you think it's a misunderstanding?"

"What is there to misunderstand? He said *it isn't going to work.* He must have changed his mind." Isabell let out another long breath. "Whatever. Maybe it's for the best. He's starting college in like two months. I knew he didn't want to date a high school girl."

"But Isabell, I—"

"Thanks for taking my call, August. I know you're technically grounded, but is there any way we can hang?"

"I'll ask my mom. She should be home soon."

"Maybe I'll call her, too. She can't say no to both of us," Isabell pointed out, forcing a laugh.

I joined her, just happy to hear a little light back in her voice. "That's very true."

When Mom got home an hour later, I was posted up on the couch in anticipation. The pointed look she shot my way told me Isabell had already called her. With a hand on her hip, she narrowed her eyes like she suspected I was up to no good.

"Did you put Isabell up to that?"

"Believe it or not, it was all her idea," I pursed my lips to stop myself from begging right away. "Please! Can she just stop by really quick? She shouldn't be punished with me, forced to mend her broken heart all on her own."

"You," Mom wagged a finger at me with a brown paper bag in her hand. "I already told her yes. She will be here soon. She *will* be gone before your dad gets back. He doesn't find out about this. It's a girl thing. Got it, missy?"

My eyes widened, and I leapt over the back of the couch to crush her into a hug. "Thank you, thank you, *thank you*! Only one day and I'm going crazy here." A car pulled up the driveway, and I started to hobble toward the door.

"Wait," Mom beckoned, extending the brown paper bag out to me. "Cinnamon rolls."

I grinned from ear to ear, grateful that she was taking it exceptionally easy on me today of all days. As I stepped outside, Isabell slumped her shoulders.

"Apple tree?" I suggested, feeling a bit deflated myself once again.

"Apple tree." She nodded, moving close enough to link her arm with mine.

We love the apple tree when we have big things to discuss. Our first conversation under the there was about which tea to serve at our imaginary tea party. A few years later, we were talking about our first crushes.

Sitting under a shady tree with your best friend is such an underrated joy. It was like the understory protected us from outsiders, keeping all our secrets locked away. Even though it's in direct view of my house, it feels like our own world, and no one can touch us there.

Once we were situated, I unrolled the brown bag and set it down between us. "Mom brought cinnamon rolls," I explained.

Isabell raised an eyebrow, but smiled. "Next time I'm grounded, can I be grounded here?"

We ate the cinnamon rolls in silence, taking in the peace and quiet of my forested backyard. From my seat, I soon found myself studying the kitchen window. Listening to the faint sound of pots and pans clanging, I saw my mom shuffling around. In some capacity, she was always at work. She only stopped to watch evening game shows and to enjoy a meal with the family. I wondered how she did it, the constant cooking and baking and tending to what needs tended.

Looking down at the cinnamon roll in my hand, I knew it was how she comforted.

"I'm sorry about Tyler," I finally said, just as Isabell rested her chin on her knee. "Do you think it was just a misunderstanding?"

"I *wish*. But his responses were really weird. It felt like he was breaking up with me. But we aren't together. It just sucks."

"Why do we put up with those two, Isabell? One minute they're flirty and the next they're patting us on the back."

"No word from Landon, either?" she asked, her eyes full of mutual misery.

"Let's just say that the crickets outside my window last night weren't the only ones chirping. You said it best Iz, this sucks. If it weren't for this stupid treasure, would we even be hanging out with them this much?"

"Probably not," she grumbled. "I guess that's another reason."

"Another reason for what?"

She wiped her hands together. "August, I'm not going to Whiskey Creek tomorrow night. And, I'm taking myself out of the running for good," she admitted, holding up a hand to stop me from interrupting her. "Look, I've had my fun. I have. But it's different now. Those mean notes? Auggie, they freak me out! What if these people try to take the gold from us after we find it? I'm sure finders-keepers-losers-weepers doesn't apply here. And the ghost? That ghost probably cursed it. Odette, right? If we did find the treasure, I wouldn't want any part of it. I don't want to be connected to this thing at all."

Isabell fanned herself and took a deep breath in between her rambles. I knew she wasn't done, so I sat in waiting.

"You know what else? I hate to say it. But, I really, *really* don't want to see Ty."

Her words hit me like a ton of bricks. I leaned back against the tree, thudding my head. "You just gave me a lot to unpack."

"Sorry."

"Crap. If you're not going, then I don't want to go, either."

"You'll be fine," she rolled her eyes before lowering her voice, "if you can manage to sneak out. Can it wait until you're free? Are you still planning on going even though you're on house arrest?"

I shrugged and pinched my fingers as if to say, 'a little.'

She tried not to smile. "I had a feeling."

I looked down. "I don't know though, Iz. I haven't really heard much from Landon since, you know, he kissed me on the cheek, or whatever. Not so much as a text. Well, one text, but it hardly counts."

"Your phone is taken though."

"Yes, but I have my shush-kabob. I've messaged him. And still, nothing. I'm in serious trouble over this car thing and he isn't doing much to help me out or even check in. Is it a terrible idea to hang out with him by myself?"

"Do you still like him?"

I tilted my head up at the apple tree branches. *Just another secret to lock away.*

"Yeah, I do," I mumbled like a little kid caught red-handed. "But I can't ever tell if he likes me. One minute, yeah. The next minute, no. How long am I supposed to hang on to that?"

"I guess some one-on-one time might get you your answer."

"What if I lash out at him and blow it? I swear, Iz, I might burst at any second."

"Hm, I guess just take some deep breaths?" she suggested, but it didn't exactly ease my concern. "If going to Whiskey Creek does nothing but get you one step closer to buying a car, then it's still a win, right?"

She was right. Maybe I had to suck it up and get it done. I opted to shift the topic.

"But Iz, are you done for good? Or do you just need a minute to think about it all?" My stomach twisted in a knot, the back of my neck dripping with sweat. She played with her fingers in her lap and then looked up through the underbelly of the apple tree just as I had done moments before.

"I need a minute, or two. Or three. There's some messed up crap going on here that I'm not sure I'm down for. It worries me enough for the both of us," she told me, her eyes wide. "Be safe out there, okay?"

That night, as I stared at the ceiling in boredom, I thought a lot about my conversation with Isabell. What she said, how she said it, the look in her eyes when she said it. I turned to face out the window. Through my open curtains, I gazed upon the twinkles of the night sky. Curling my hands under my face, I nestled in, and let the stars comfort me in my time of doubt.

This whole time, I hadn't given the danger of this treasure hunt the time of day. It all seemed like a bunch of hogwash, or at the very least, something adults said to scare us off. But with the creepy notes, the angry ghost, the cop call, the slashed tires, and the warning from my dad, maybe Isabell was right.

Before I even teetered into the realm of giving up though, I stopped myself. All the constellations, they have their stories, their claim to infamy. Maybe this was mine.

I'd made it this far. Might as well push a little farther.

SEVENTEEN

If I woke up mid-spiral on Wednesday, my Thursday morning feeling could only be described as foreboding. I debated talking it out with Isabell, but decided against it. Without a doubt, she'd reassure me that there was no pressure to continue on. But I didn't want to hear that. So I forced off my blanket and pulled myself out of bed.

The ominous feeling didn't leave throughout the day, not completely anyway. I tried to busy myself by watching cartoons, but my mind was all over the place. There was no plan for the night, no word from Landon, and no update on my mom's car.

Taking matters into my own hands, I found the copy of the paper I signed for Buff and called the mechanic shop. They said there was an issue with the billing, and they'd call me back once it was sorted. It didn't make any sense to me, and my annoyance for the situation rose to an all-time high. Landon was part of the reason I was in this mess, and he said he'd take care of it. Where was he now? Avoiding me? Regretting me? The thought was driving me mad.

I was at a standstill. Scheming would have at least given me *something* to do, but *everything* was up in the air. Day three of full loneliness in this house (yet only day two of being grounded) was making my head hurt. After heating a can of soup for lunch, I was desperate for new ways to entertain myself. I started tiptoeing around the house, marking all the floorboard creaks with sticky notes.

Once mid-afternoon rolled around, I had resorted to picking at the sticky notes on the floor. Finally, though, I threw caution to the wind and whipped on my shush-kabob. So what if Landon had been ignoring my messages? I wanted to find this damned treasure, and I'd make our search happen.

Hi Landon. Remember me? August? Is there a plan for the night? Isabell is out. I sent to Landon.

His response was pretty quick considering it had been static silence for the last two days. *I'll pick u up at the end of your street. 11 on the dot. Bring a flashlight. No moon tonight. Delete the message.*

Ok. Any luck with putting a stop to the evil notes? I typed back.

No response. No car update.

Shoving the shush-kabob in my pocket, I laid back and clunked my boot loudly against the ground. It kind of hurt, and the floor groaned with me as I sat back up. The sore ankle, coupled with the creaky floor, reminded me of Odette's house, and Odette. If it bums me out to stay here all day by myself, I can't imagine how depressing it must be to live in her house. She's been there for close to a hundred years, probably without visitors. That must be terribly lonely.

Guilt started to creep in as I recalled the figure I had seen on the piano bench. Those green, glowing eyes and white dress had been haunting. Scary, but sad. As far as I knew, I was the only one to see it, or any other form of a ghost. Everyone seemed to assume it was a supernatural incident, but no one had confessed to seeing anything. In my mind, the ghost *had* to be Odette, though it can't be said with absolute certainty.

I got to thinking that maybe she almost tore her own house down not just to scare us away, but because she was scared. We were strangers, entering her home. Can we really blame her for setting off enough motion to stimulate the Richter scale?

Or maybe she's sick of being cooped up in there and wants to break free herself.

Goodness. Have I really reached the point of relating to a ghost more than to actual humans? Maybe I should tell that to Mom and Dad. It could re-enforce that I need a little social interaction to stay sane.

"Hey there, Auggie. How's Isabell doing today?"

From where I was resting on the floor, with my back to the door, I flinched at the clambering a few feet away. I hadn't even heard Mom come in, but she was carrying a few bags of groceries. In typical Jeanie fashion, she seemed to have a lot on her mind. She failed to notice the sticky notes that were peppering the main area of our house. She stepped on one, plucked it off, and tossed it in the trash without a second thought. I started to pick the rest of them up off the floor as I responded.

"I haven't really talked to her. No phone, remember? Do you need help?"

"Oh not with your boot, honey. I've got it!"

The evening came and went a little less painfully. Both my parents were both pretty tired from the day of work and turned in by half-past nine.

That left me in bed with my eyes wide open, staring at my ceiling in the dark. I pulled out my shush-kabob to message Isabell.

Landon is picking me up soon. PEP TALK PLS. What if it's weird?

I breathed a sigh of relief when the text bubble appeared right away.

Is THE August Moon doubting her involvement for the very first time? Groundbreaking news!!! Just think: CAR!!!!!

Before I could type, another message came through from her. *But, on the real, you don't have to do this if you don't want to. It's ok to back out if something doesn't feel right.*

My fingers hovered over the keyboard. Weird social tensions and looming threats were making me hesitant for the first time. I hated hesitancy. More often than not, I'm in things 100%. The lingering doubt stirred something unpleasant in my gut.

But I'm in too deep. Would stopping this thing really do me any good? With a little rush of adrenaline, I pull on my tan hiking pants and a long sleeve shirt. It wasn't cool by any means, but I'd rather be protected against poison oak or prickly plants. I also decided to ditch the boot for the night, opting for some tennis shoes instead. I'd probably pay for it tomorrow, but it was worth it for the stealth. I tied my hair in two long braids and tiptoed out the side door with my backpack at a quarter to eleven. Solo was sleeping in his kennel, so I moved with extra delicacy to not wake him.

At the end of my street, I sat on a rock to wait for Landon. I let out a loud breath and looked up at the night sky. All the stars were especially visible tonight, without the light of the moon to pollute the scene.

I'd been alone most of the day, most of the week. Despite sitting by myself in the dark, I didn't feel that way now. The crickets were chirping, and a car hummed by on the distant highway. Most of all, there was the company of a thousand stars in the sky above. I'm not sure what I think of mythology, but I like to think those are real people and creatures up there looking out for me.

Hell, it's in my blood. If I didn't feel a connection to the sky, I think I'd feel even more like I didn't belong. Here, I had a space.

A light caught the corner of my eye, and I stood anticipating Landon. I jogged to his car, momentarily forgetting the pain in my ankle before hopping on my good foot. In the backseat, I noticed he had a metal detector. When I opened the door, the first thing he asked was where my boot was.

"Didn't want it. It can't be nimble in that clunky thing," I told him as I strapped on my seatbelt.

"Maybe you shouldn't come."

His out-of-the-blue statement put me on edge, and earned him a baffled scoff. "What are you talking about?"

"Your foot. Obviously you're not well enough to be hiking. Who knows how far it will be."

"What's wrong with you?" It came out harsher than I meant, but I was thrown off by the sense he didn't want me here.

"Nothing's wrong."

The light of the dash illuminated his face, giving me a proper look at him. He was stoic, without the usual glint of mischief in his eyes. His brow was creased, as one hand gripped the steering wheel and the other rested on the gear shift.

"What is it?" I asked again, scanning his face for any clues. "I haven't heard much from you lately. Was the mission to stop the note sender unsuccessful? Did you get chased down an alley way? Cling to a precipice to avoid falling to your death?"

"I'm just tired, that's all. I went out to The Ranch last night."

"Oh." I paused. Before I could decide if my next question was a bad one, it came tumbling out of my mouth. "Who all was there?"

He shrugged, in that absentminded kind of way. "The usual folks. You saw everyone the other night. It was that crew."

I tried not to grimace, but I did cross my arms. "So, Stacey then."

He didn't respond right away, and fixated his eyes on the gear shift. He clenched his jaw before lifting his eyes to me, plastering on a smile. "I should have just said, I'm alright. Ready to go?"

"Guess so." I shrugged as he pulled a U-turn off my street. My stomach felt sick at the thought of him hanging out with Stacey last night, all the while ignoring me. "Are we picking up Tyler, or?"

"Isabell didn't tell you?"

"Tell me what?"

"I assumed she passed it along, but maybe not. Tyler got poison oak from our bushwhacking the other day. He said he's been throwing up and stuff, it's pretty bad. He can hardly get out of bed."

"What? He has poison oak? That bad? Gee, why didn't he just tell Isabell that instead of blowing her off?"

"Wait, he blew her off?"

"Pretty much stood her up. She's not coming either," I explained, even though I'd already mentioned it in my messages to him.

He clicked his tongue. "So . . . it's just the two of us?"

I nodded. "Looks like it."

Landon mumbled a simple grunt of acknowledgment as we hit the highway headed west to Whiskeytown. Compared to our other late night drives to the lake, this one felt a bit darker, and not just because it was a new moon. Landon was sitting a foot and a half away from me, but it might as well have been a thousand miles. *Why was he hanging out with Stacey last night? Why has he been ignoring me?*

The only silver-lining was that he wasn't frowning. He more or less seemed lost in his own head. My mom gets like that, where she has too much on her mind to be fully present in what's around here. I never know whether it's right to pull her back down or let her float away.

As I decided to let him float. It gave me time to think. That is, until he blew past the sign for Whiskey Creek Road.

"Hey, that was our—"

"Hm?" he interrupted, as if I startled him out of a daze.

"The turn, you passed it."

"Oh, oops."

While he flipped the car around, I stared out the front. I was sure that my face displayed my skepticism over this whole situation. Once we were back on course and twisting down the road to Whiskey Creek, I itched to probe his brain. We blew past the boat ramp, hitting all the potholes along the way, until he parked on the side of the road. We were right at the point where the creek drains into the lake.

"Landon," I started, sighing as he turned off his car.

"August?"

I stepped out of the car at the same time as him. "I can't take the stony silence. Something is bothering you, and it's not exhaustion. Does it have to do with Stacey? The notes? What is it?"

"Would you just let it go?" he asked in full exasperation, plucking his small backpack and metal detector from the backseat. I slung mine over my shoulder and hustled to catch up to him. On a typical outing, I'd question the metal detector and where he bought it and how much money it cost, but there were bigger fish to fry today.

"We're in the woods, in the dark, together. You don't think that earns me a little peace of mind over what's going through your head?"

"I think we should just keep quiet and walk the creek," he pleaded, gesturing in the general direction of the water. "Let the sound of the whooshing water wash everything away?"

I raised an eyebrow at him, but his back was to me. Maybe he really did regret the other night. Half of me wanted to push for clarity, but the other half worried I didn't want the answers.

He situated something on his head before flicking on a headlamp, and I grabbed my flashlight from my backpack pocket. Landon stepped off the road and into the bushes while I lingered a few steps behind, digging in my heels a bit. With a deep breath, I plunged in after him. At this point, what other choice did I have?

Whiskey Creek follows the road for a good while, meaning we could traverse upstream and scan the surrounding areas. It was fairly overgrown with brush and dense bushes, but the creek was low enough for us to walk on the bank. The riverbed was rocky, and made for a tricky traverse. Not even fifteen minutes after we started walking, my ankle felt the burn. Tailing an agile and pensive Landon was not an easy task for a busted ankle like mine.

I'd rather lick rust than admit I couldn't keep going. But as the pain increased, my dignity went down with it.

"Can you slow down at least a little? The ground is uneven and I'm not trying to fall in this creek at midnight," I asked, wanting to swallow my tongue.

He slowed down, but didn't say anything else. I frowned at his back. Maybe I didn't want to be that close to him if he was going to be so standoffish.

Again, as much as I was trying to hold it in, there were more questions that begged to be asked. "Why are you ignoring me?"

He scoffed. "*Me?*"

"Who else would I mean?"

"I'm not ignoring you."

"You're walking fast to get away from me. You've hardly talked to me, let alone looked at me."

"So now you're mad that I'm not looking at you enough?" he quipped back. His voice was calm, but his feet were picking up the pace.

"No, I'm not. I just don't really understand what I'm doing here," I said, stumbling as I fought to keep up with him. "Maybe I just shouldn't have come tonight."

When he didn't bother denying my suggestion, or show any regret for ignoring me, I felt like I had my answer.

"You know what, nevermind. Walk ahead. It's *fine*."

Again, he said nothing, but started walking faster. I threw my hands up in the air and looked around as if a studio audience was witnessing the events.

Why was I here? The cold shoulder sucked, but it also gave time for my anger to fester. I had been stuck at home, grounded, and he was off gallivanting at The Ranch? Partying, with Stacey? I suddenly felt like I was carrying a huge burden, forced to spend my days at home in solitary confinement, while Landon was *partying?*

"Here I thought we were all in this together," I mumbled under my breath.

Of course, he heard me, and it was the token that seemed to activate his voice board. He spun on his heel to face me. "*We* are all in this together? August, our team is falling apart. Isabell bailed, Tyler's bedridden, your foot is sprained, and me, I—" He blew out a deep breath, and ran his hand through his hair before dropping it to his side, where he slapped his leg.

"What? You what?" I spat out, heart beating fast in my chest.

"Can you please shine that light out of my eyes?"

With an eye roll I switched off my light. "You could shut off your headlamp too, you know," I snapped, but dove right back in to our previous conversation. "What, Landon?"

"I'm seriously regretting this entire thing." He pinched the bridge of his nose, while my stomach sank to my feet. The confusion set in too, like I was left out, like there was a missing piece to this puzzle that I didn't have. Perhaps it was just denial that he could be regretting *me*, but I was convinced there was more to it.

"I'm at a loss, Landon."

He rubbed his face some more and stared at the ground. "I never should have gotten involved. Or you. This thing's about to catch on fire, and I'm *not* going to be held responsible."

"Landon, we're so close. I can feel it. You said yourself, there really could be gold in Whiskey Creek, right? So if we could just—"

"No. There is no *we*. August, we can't be in this together, okay?"

Each word hit like a dagger. This whole summer was bleeding out, and I didn't know whether I should try to hold it together or let it crumble. I'd rather choke on rocks than let him see how much this was bothering me, so instead I let that so-called fire catch.

"For crying out loud, Landon. Do you really feel like you need to make it so clear that you don't like me?"

"That's not what I—"

"I've gotten the hint, okay? Instead of talking to me, you go to The Ranch to be with Stacey. Instead of helping me with the car, you refuse to clue me in. So I'm stuck at home, grounded, without my phone, no friends, and you just get to keep on like nothing happened."

My vision had adjusted to the darkness enough to notice his eyes widened.

"I didn't know you were grounded. Why didn't you say anything? How are you here?"

"I *told* you I was grounded! Do those texts *not* ring a bell?"

He shook his head, his frustration no longer palpable. "I'm confused. I thought your phone was taken?"

"It is. I have that old smartphone, remember? I've messaged you from it before. Geez, Landon. The point is that you just vanished out of thin air once everything happened that night." When he bit his lip, I swallowed the lump in my throat. "Plus, you know who slashed the tires! And you won't even tell me who did it or—"

"I can't tell you," he drawled like this was a painful conversation. "What part of that don't you understand? Why can't you simply trust me on that?"

I trusted him, but I still didn't understand the secrecy. Not a wink. "More and more, it seems like it's you who doesn't trust me. If this involves me, how can you exclude me from the circle?"

Landon started to explain his side, and I mine, and we went back and forth talking over each other. Our voices were rising in volume, picking up their cadence as we inched closer together. My arms were crossed while his were waving about in the air. I'd never had a fight like this before, it was like I couldn't sense anything else that was going on. I was trying so hard to get my point across, to talk louder than him so he would hear me.

A sound shot off close by, though, that outshone us both in volume. Landon dropped his metal detector in shock. I stiffened, and my heart pounded to the same beat as Landon's ragged breathing.

A loud boom, followed by crackles and fizzes.

"Is that what I think it was?"

Landon's face was turned up, scanning the sky. Then, the boom happened again. This time, we ducked and grabbed onto each other. A faint glow confirmed our mutual suspicion.

Fireworks. The big, Fourth of July finale kind. Illegal in California. Zero-tolerance during the hot, dry summer. Shooting one off is like dropping a match in a field of kindling and tinder. The hair stood up on the back of my neck when it dawned on me that we were in the thick of the dry fuels, with all the shrubs and trees and brittle grass.

"Holy mac," I covered my ears and jumped. The fireworks were continuously shooting off right overhead, meaning they *had* to be in the forest, off trail. *Goodness.* Only a pyromaniac would set them off *in the woods*. But who would be out here at this hour, let alone to shoot fire into the sky?

I sniffed, and something tinged the inside of my nose. I sniffed a few more times, like a dog on a scent. "Landon, do you smell smoke?"

"Shit. I do. It's close."

"What's close? The firework launch pad or a legit forest fire?" Landon didn't answer me right away, but my patience was low. "Well?"

He was staring off in the distance, his body aimed at the hill that followed the creek. I tried to see if he could see anything, but it was too dark to determine. Squinting my eyes at the hillside just made me feel like I was falling into the unknown, and I had the vertigo to prove it. My leg started to twitch with an undeniable need to run.

Another boom went off, and now that we knew was it was, it felt far too close for comfort.

"Shit. We have to go," Landon said, his voice breathy.

"We've been walking for a while, we could be a few miles away from the car by now."

"Then we have to hurry," he said like it was the most obvious thing in the world. He flipped his headlamp back on and moved to climb up the bank and through the brush. He was in action-mode, and I was helpless. My heart was beating at light speed as I thought about the possibility of fleeing from fire on foot with this wonky ankle.

"Where are you going?"

"Back to the road. If a fire did start, we don't want to be in this little gorge. A fire could whip through the river bank like a tunnel."

"Even if there's water in it?"

"With the brush on the sides, yeah, it's a burner kit. You can argue with me, or you can come with me. The road is flatter, it'll be easier to run and see from there. Are you coming?"

There was a crack up the hillside, in the direction he was headed. I shuddered, and he was part way up the bank staring back at me. "Come on, I'll help you up."

My head was spinning, and I thought I may pass out.

Breathless, I turned to the creek, and back to face him. "What about Whiskey Creek, and the treasure? What if it's here, Landon? We can't stop now, we're so close," I begged, gasping for air as I swiveled my head between my two courses of action. A voice in my head nagged to look a little longer for the treasure. In all likelihood this was a fire miles away, right? Still illegal, but not an immediate threat to our safety.

Right?

"This is a waste of time," he groaned. "Is the treasure really worth that much to you? You'd be willing to risk our safety for it? More than half a dozen of these rippers have been shot in the sky, we could be trapped back here. And you're thinking about the money?"

"I don't know! Stop yelling at me!" I shouted back, running my fingers through my hair several times over.

The fireworks were causing me some panic, and not because of the loud noises or the potential fire hazard. It was a visceral, visual display of how I'd been feeling on the inside. Lately, everything was slipping through my fingers. Any chance of having my own car. The option to go to college. My freedom. Money could fix a few of those problems. It could help Mom's shop, and it go toward a college fund or Grandma's bills.

But in terms of my freedom? Money can't buy that. These fireworks were like the universe slapping me down, right when things were about to get good. So close to the treasure, to the car, to the most epic summer of all-time, to the guy I've been falling for the last two years.

A lot had been right on track. I kept all those hopes and dreams bottled in, and in that process I became a pressure cooker on the brink of explosion.

"August!" Landon shouted again, catching my attention and stopping the wringing of my hands. "Someone probably called the cops by now to report the fireworks. The last thing we need right now is another run in with the police. Or a head-on collision with a forest fire. Are you coming or what?"

I pursed my lips, and blinked back the stinging in my eyes. Moving toward Landon, I took his hand for help up the small ledge. Just as we stepped back on to Whiskey Creek Road, a different sound cracked up the hill.

I recognized it right away. It was the sound of a tree falling. When my eyes scanned the darkness for any indication of the felled location, a golden glow erupted up the hill before shooting up tall and orange.

"Oh shiiiiiiiiit," Landon cursed, repeating the profanity under his breath a dozen times.

"We have to call 9-1-1, that's a fire, crap. I don't have my phone, can we use yours?"

"There's no time! We have to move, now!" He gave my arm a gentle tug as he started to jog, and I followed him. Despite what all the medical dramas on television taught me, the adrenaline did not stop the pain in my sprained ankle. What other choice did I have with a forest fire brewing just up the hill? We had to run.

We booked it down the road—a slight downhill grade—without speaking, just flying as fast as our feet would carry us. After several minutes of panting, it was Landon who spoke up first. To say he wasn't pleased would be the understatement of the century.

"I told you we needed to go, and you just stood there! What was that about?"

"I had a lot on my mind, alright?" I huffed. I was not at all in the mood to fight over this. It would be like beating a dead horse.

"I never thought you were superficial. Or irrational. Never. But that, that was ridiculous! You wanted to risk your safety, *our* safety, for the chance at some stupid cash prize?"

"It's not like that," I gritted my teeth, pushing my legs to pump faster down the road even though my foot was killing me.

"Oh, please, explain!" He challenged, his breathing heavy. "Because I don't understand what the hell that was."

"I told you, I had a lot on my mind and this is really stressing me out and it'd do me a *world* of good if the guy I'm *freaking in love with* would just . . . Stop. *Blaming*. Me." I couldn't help the way I snapped back at him, annunciating each syllable.

Whether he fell back to get away from me or just gave up on running altogether, I wasn't sure. But I knew we were getting close to the end. The road had turned back to pavement. I slowed down, to see what his deal was, but he was only a few steps behind.

"What did you just say?" he sputtered out as he stopped to lean forward on his knees.

"Can we keep going, please?" I urged him, my tone sharp.

This night just needed to end. I wanted to report it to the first responders. I wanted to fall apart in my bedroom. I wanted to go home and forget this night even happened. My humiliation was at an all-time high. Just as it became painfully clear that Landon doesn't like me, I go ahead and admit the feelings I've been stifling.

If there's a medal for bad timing, I think I just took gold. Ha. The irony.

He panted. "No, not until—not until you repeat what you just said."

I rubbed my hands on my face. "Really? So it's okay to put a pin in our fleeing the scene as long as it's on your terms?"

"It's not the same circumstance."

"I fail to see the difference." I started to walk back away down the road but my foot finally gave out on my and I tumbled to my knees. "Ow," I muttered under my breath.

"Shit, your foot. Is it okay? Why didn't you say anything?"

I blew out a loud breath and rolled my eyes, pushing myself back to my feet to face him. "There you go, blaming me again."

"I am *not* blaming you," he defended.

"Well your tone is accusatory," I snapped again, effectively drawing attention away from my horrible confession of love. Fighting with Landon—real fighting, not playful bickering—had to be up there as one of the top three worst things of all-time. My stomach was tearing itself apart. I couldn't bring myself to say anything to make it better.

Yet again, I wasn't sure *what* would make it better.

I didn't even try. Instead, I moved right along in fanning the fire.

He grunted in frustration. "You drive me *crazy*, August. I swear I don't know what to do about you half the time."

"Are you really saying you don't want anything to do with me?" I asked him, crossing my arms across my chest.

The words just hung in the air, like clothes on the line blowing in the wind on a cold, cold night. There was no time to think, or react, because a bright light rounded the corner. It was flashing red, and attached to a big vehicle moving very fast. Landon wrapped his arm around me and hustled us both off the road.

Headlights flashed at us, and the big engine skidded by us. The window was down, and someone called out. "You better be careful! More rigs are coming up the road. Where's the fire?"

"A mile or so down the road, up the hill," Landon shouted back.

The firefighter flicked a wave out the window as they rumbled on. More flashing flights were on their way, and the fire engines sped on. A few smaller trucks, and a cop car, stopped when they saw us.

I hung my head in my hands and slapped my cheeks. This had to be fake. Any second now, I'd wake up. How could this possibly get any worse?

"August?"

I froze.

"Dad?"

Correction: *now* how could it get any worse?

Eighteen

"Am I really seeing you here?" Dad asked, but something in his tone told me it would be wise not to answer. As he was dressed in his parks uniform, I assumed he had not expected to see me. I winced as he approached.

"Am I really seeing *you*?" I chuckled, but Dad didn't find it amusing. His mustache accentuated his frown, and together they cast a cloud of disappointment over me. I wished there was a rock I could hide under for eternity.

If your dad ever happens to find you down an untraveled back road, with a boy, where there's suspected illegal activity, call me for advice on what not *to say.*

"Aren't you supposed to be at home, grounded?"

Oh, *crap*. The grounding had become the least of my worries. I tilted my head up to the sky and closed my eyes, begging the stars to cut me a break.

"And where's your boot? August, you snuck out, with a boy, and you didn't even bring protection?"

"Dad," I whispered through a clenched jaw. Landon cleared his throat.

"Protection for your *foot*, Augustine," he said as he wiped a hand down his face, smoothing his mustache. "Lord help me. All kinds of protection." He started to mumble under his breath, narrowing his eyes between me and Landon.

"Daniel, if you've got things under control here, should we head up to search the woods?" It was one of the younger rangers.

A crew of four young rangers waited by one of the trucks, looking anywhere but at us. I crossed my arms and glared, envying their ability to escape this conversation. I guess I couldn't blame them. I wouldn't want to stick around and listen to my boss ramble about protection to his teenage daughter, either.

"Yes, go. Stay in pairs, I'll be there in a few."

I plopped myself on to a nearby log, feeling like I weighed an extra ton. Sending off the crew meant I was about to get reamed by my dad. "You should have let them stay, Dad. Nothing screams intimidation like scolding a rebellious seventeen-year-old."

"A sassy seventeen-year-old," he corrected. I could have sworn he almost cracked a grin: my glimmer of hope. But it disappeared, and I slouched. In the past, jokey-sarcasm has gotten me off the hook a little easier with my dad. This situation called for a dozen more sarcastic retorts. I kicked a pebble at my feet to plot my next move.

"Someone tell me what the hell is going on here," Dad said sternly. His park ranger voice was in full throttle. He never talked like this at home, and I dreaded what was to come.

Landon, bless his soul, spoke first, "Mr. Moon, first of all, I'm so sorry. We—"

Dad held up his hand. "I was referring to my daughter. Take a seat over there, Landon," he said, gesturing to the log. Landon followed the order like an obedient puppy and sat a few feet away from me. The truck with the rest of the rangers revved up the hill, leaving the three of us alone.

"I'm only going to ask this once," Dad started again, his voice a little calmer without his crew watching us, "did you, or did you not, set off fireworks in the middle of the damn forest? If it caused a fire, it has the potential to be construed as an arson charge, Augustine."

I blinked back at him, shaking my head. "Dad, of course not. It's stupid and risky. I don't even know where or how to get fireworks.

How could you think I'd do something like that?"

He gestured around at the wooded area. "Because you're here, in the exact spot I was called to investigate illegal fireworks! The city cops will be here any minute. You need to get your story straight before then."

"Fair point," I grumbled.

"We were walking along the creek, sir. A few days ago, we got a tip that there might be some gold in the creek, or buried in the mine up there. We wanted to see for ourselves," Landon explained, his voice breathless.

Dad turned to me, and raised an eyebrow. "Looking for gold? That sounds familiar."

"We're gold rush junkies, what can I say?" I shrugged.

"Augustine," Dad warned, his third use of my full name setting off a cringe, "is this about that Ruggles treasure again?"

"Do you know about the treasure, Mr. Moon?"

I shot Landon a quick glare, wishing he'd just sit there and mind his own business until this was over. If he was trying to help, this was still my dad, and my future punishment. His comments were rubbing salt in the wound.

"Oh yes, I'm familiar with it. Crossed paths with a very friendly gentleman by the name of Edgar in my own search a few decades ago. Do you know any Edgars, Landon?"

Edgar. The name came up recently, but when? My eyes flickered to Landon, who bowed his head.

Dad continued his lecture, "Your alibi is that you were searching for gold in the creek, at this hour? It's half-past midnight. Why couldn't this be a daytime outing? Did you bring anything to search for gold? The half-empty backpacks and the hiking boots are incriminating. You both look like you ditched half your load in the woods. Like, say, a pallet of fireworks?"

"I brought a metal detector with me!" Landon cheered, rising to his feet as if this was the key to our salvation. "Wait. Where is it?" he asked, scanning the surrounding area.

"Did you leave it by the creek?" I asked, picking at a loose thread on my pants, unable to remove the snark from my voice. It wasn't anywhere in sight now, so the creek seemed the best bet.

"No, I wouldn't have . . . oh, wait. Yeah. I did. I must have dropped it when the first firework shot off. And then I forgot. *Damn*. Mr. Moon, that metal detector is expensive, can I go grab it?"

"Thinking about money in a time like this, Landon?" I tsked.

He turned to me. "Why didn't you say anything if you knew I left it there?"

I cocked my head to the side. "I didn't know. It was just a guess, I didn't know that you actually—"

"Both of you, no more talking. Landon, you cannot go get it. One of the guys will grab it for you, or escort you up there to grab it. But no one does anything until the cops arrive, alright?"

More lights flashed from around the bend in the road. "Excuse me. Stay right here," he instructed as he walked to meet the officer.

There I was. Sitting alone. With Landon. I crossed my legs and rested my chin on my hand in a slump. If I thought my freedom was dead before, I couldn't wait to see what this round of punishment would entail. Slashed tires were small potatoes compared to being accused of smuggling contraband. They'd slap our photos on the "Banned from National Parks" list.

Hm . . .

"Are you really not going to speak to me?" Landon whispered from his timeout spot a few feet away from mine.

I blew out a huff of annoyance, but said no words. I was not about to dignify him with a response if he didn't want anything to do with me.

"August, we're in some serious shit here. Don't you think we should work together to get out of this mess?"

I picked more furiously at the thread on my pants, curling my bottom lip into my mouth, biting it hard enough that it almost bled. He called me crazy, superficial, and irrational. Meanwhile, I admitted, out loud, to his face, that I'm in love him. If he wanted me to talk, there needed to be some serious apologizing.

"You're the toughest damned nut to crack. First Russell, now this? I don't get you."

"Russell?" I snapped, "Seriously, Russell? You're still on that?"

"What do you mean 'still?' You were with him this week, weren't you?"

I groaned and covered my face with my hands, "No, Landon. I was not. Grounded, remember? I've been home all freaking week until now."

"Wait, really? Then why were you messaging me from his phone?"

"What are you *talking* about?"

"I've been so confused. You ignored all my messages, but then texted me from Russell's phone? It was like you wanted to rub it in my face. And then you tell me . . ."

A lump knotted in my throat. *What do I do here? Change the subject? Flee the scene?* I was paralyzed.

"Did you really mean what you said? When we were running down the hill? I need to know."

My heart was thudding so fast, I thought it might break a rib. Thinking back to my confession of love, I tried to brush it off. "Does it matter?"

"Yes," he answered immediately, his voice sincere. "Yes, it matters. It changes everything."

Staring in to Landon's eyes, which were flaming through the darkness, I was too stunned to move. Or speak. The only thing I could do was face my lap again. I didn't think my stomach could cave in any further on itself, but it was wrenching. From the tone of his voice, I couldn't tell if he meant a good or bad change.

What if I admitted it was true, and that was the end of us? Should I go for it, and tell him I meant it? It was too hard to decide. My tongue was like taffy in my mouth. For the first time since the fireworks shot off, I was acutely aware of the sweat dripping down the side of my face.

"See? You can't even be honest with me. Why am I even trying?" he mumbled.

I whipped my head, opening my mouth to *really* give him a piece of my mind, but Dad walked back over. Landon and I both stood up at the same time.

"We'll see what the other rangers come up with when they scope the woods. The course of action for the night will goes as follows. Landon, you'll go with Officer Leed down to the creek bed. He'll assist you with searching for your metal detector and take your story of the night. While that's going on, August, you'll be speaking with Officer Jenkins before I take you home. Clear?"

I nodded once, and Landon thanked him for his help. Dad turned back to the two cops waiting on standby, leaving Landon and I alone for the last time. I stared at the ground, too upset to speak to him, but also wanting to test whether he was giving up on me. The silence was deafening, louder than any unexpected fireworks, and the weight threatened to crush my shoulders.

Finally, I mustered enough courage to turn to him. His face was aimed at the sky, and he was shaking his head. As much as I wanted to say something, I knew if I opened my mouth, I'd end up crying.

When Officer Leed called for him, he dropped his arms to his side and marched over without so much as a goodbye or a nod of the head in my direction. My face fell as he met with Officer Leed to walk up the road.

I tried to resist, but I couldn't help watching him go. I wished he would look back over his shoulder, and flash me a little smile. Then, maybe things could be okay.

But he kept right on walking, without a second glance.

In all, I stood around for an hour of interrogation and anticipation. While Officer Jenkins asked me detailed questions about the night, I was on edge, gazing up the dark hill periodically for Landon. After my interview was over, there was still no sign of Landon—much to my dismay and relief.

"Alright, kiddo. I'm taking you home," Dad finally said. His truck was still flashing with lights, parked on the shoulder of the road.

"What happened with the other rangers? Don't you need to stay? Did the firefighters get the fire? What about Landon, what's going to happen to him?"

As much as I felt like a fool for it, I had to ask about Landon. At eighteen, I worried he would be in more trouble than me. In a way, abandoning ship here felt like leaving a comrade behind on the battlefield. I didn't particularly want to see him, but that didn't mean I felt good about bailing.

"Slow down. The crew is alright up there. They have the firefighters and the cops for back-up. I'll be high-tailing it back here after I drop you home."

"I can wait here while you finish things up, Dad."

Dad simply shook his head and nodded again toward the truck. I knew better than to complain, and followed his lead, doing my best not to limp as I made my way to the car. Soon we were on our way out, the flashing sirens and bright headlights fading behind us as we wound down the road into darkness.

We passed Landon's car, and I tried to pry my eyes away from it. Even when I sensed Dad noticing my stare, I couldn't stop. It was about to be dried up of all things Landon, and was soaking up every last drop of him. Once it was out of view, I addressed my dad with a heavy sigh.

"Lay it on me, Dad. How long am I grounded for now? Until the end of next week?" His side eye made me reconsider. "Until the end of time?"

"Most likely the latter, though your mom will try to lessen the sentence. What were you thinking going out into the park this late? Do you have any idea how bad it looks that you were out there when the fireworks went off?"

"I swear, Dad, we had nothing to do with that at all."

He rubbed his cheek with a hand. "I believe that you have enough sense to not start a damn forest fire. You love that place too much to do it any damage. And you know how I feel about fireworks. I know it all, and I'm still scratching my head over what the hell happened. I don't know how far your story will go with the cops."

"So what happens next then?" My stomach was a whole mess of knots thinking that my time wasn't over with the police.

"If they need more information from you, they'll call the house. They have to conduct an investigation and gather some more evidence before they can clear your name. Hopefully your story matches up with Landon's, and they can rule you out straight away. If either of you are lying, they will break you down and they *will* get to the bottom of it. So if you have any information to offer, Augustine, you best do it soon."

I didn't have anything else to add, so we rode the rest of the way in tense silence. Dad was speeding like a mad man down the highway. His eyes were glazed over, but narrowed, so I decided not to add any sarcastic icebreakers to the table. Instead, I stared out the window, wishing I could find refuge among the stars. I watched the black lake peek in and out of sight, before it disappeared behind us.

Once we arrived home, Dad stayed in the car, and skid out the driveway before I reached the front steps. I hopped to the side door, hoping to make it to my room without disturbing Mom.

I heard the floorboards creak in my parents' room, and Mom emerged seconds later. She jumped and gasped, flipping on the hall light. Seeing me, she placed a hand over my heart.

"Auggie Jane, what on earth are you doing up?" she asked at first, then she squinted at my clothes from across the room. "Why are you dressed like that?" She glanced around the room, expecting something to give her a clue. "What is going on?"

"Mom, I'm so tired. Can we please talk about it in the morning?"

"No, we will talk now. What's going on, Augustine?"

"It was a mistake. I snuck out with Landon out to Whiskeytown, and while we were there, some idiot shot off fireworks. I guess now we're the 'prime suspects,'" I said with air quotes.

"Who would do such a thing?" She put a hand on her hip and used the other to wave in frustration.

"It's hard to say," I mumbled, though her question got me thinking. "Dad dropped me off, but he is zipping back. It's a mess, Mom. The police interrogated me, and Landon and I had a huge fight," my voice started to crack. "I'm really sorry that I snuck out. Otherwise none of this would have even happened."

"You snuck out?" Mom gently patted her forehead like she was knocking some sense into herself. "Oh dear goodness, that had slipped from my mind in the midst of all this other nonsense. Honey, come here."

She held out her arms and ushered me toward her. Once she wrapped her arms around my back, I rested my chin on her shoulder. As soon as she did, it was like the floodgates had been opened. A few tears streamed down my cheek, and then a few more, until there was a whole freaking river.

"It's all my fault," I mumbled through my sobs.

Mom rubbed circles on my back while I cried into her shoulder for a few minutes, and then she pulled away. "It'll all work out, okay?"

"How do you know that? It feels like everything is falling apart," I grumbled.

"It always works out. *Always.* You didn't do it. I know that. The truth will come out. Get some rest, okay honey? We will talk about the rest of it in the morning, with your father."

She spun me on my heel, leading me toward my room and closing the door behind me. I changed into an oversized t-shirt for sleep, feeling like a sloth. Slowly, gingerly, I glided into bed. I buried my face into my pillow, muffling the sound of my crying as I drifted off to sleep.

NINETEEN

The next morning, my parents grounded me until further notice. They seemed to agree on the punishment before they had time to discuss it. Much to my surprise, they did allow me to have my phone again. When Dad held my phone out to me, I hesitated. Was this real? He sighed, and next to him, my mom nodded him on.

"You have your mother to thank for this. She says leaving you here alone all day without a phone is too harsh. So no friends or outings, but, here," he urged me to take the phone.

"Thank you," I settled on saying. As eager as I was to text Isabell, the phone felt heavy in my hands. "What happened last night when you went back, Dad?"

"Not much. I'm heading back now," he said as he packed his work bag. Mom, on the other hand, took the morning off to stay home with me.

I opened my mouth to ask what came of Landon, but thought twice of it, and sighed.

Dad didn't look up as he sifted through papers, but he still answered my unspoken question with a twitch of his mustache. "The boy is fine, they didn't take him into custody or anything yet. No grounds for it. He got that metal detector back. I'll see what the officers had to say about their findings and update you as soon as I know more."

The word 'yet' did not escape me, and my stomach tightened.

"Do me a favor today, August, and call the mechanic about your mother's car. Never in my life has a mechanic taken all week to replace a set of tires," he mumbled under his breath. "I'll see you girls tonight," Dad said. He situated his hat on his head and kissed my mother on the cheek before heading out the door.

I was too depressed to engage in any morning chit-chat. I moped to my room, closing the door and locking it for extra privacy. Mom kick-started the vacuum in the other room, and I knew she'd clean all day to distract herself. I didn't mind. It was better than silence.

Taking a seat at the foot of my bed, I turned my phone over in my hands. My finger hovered over the power key until I decided against turning it on. I wanted to wallow for a bit longer in my own world, so I collapsed back on to my pillows and yanked my mom's homemade quilt up to my chin. With my boot secured around my ankle, I closed my eyes.

It was a deep sleep. I know this because I woke up to Mom pounding on my door and it startled me enough that I almost rolled out of bed.

"What?" I yelled back, my voice hoarse as my eyelids struggled to peel open.

"Oh, you *are* in there. Why didn't you answer sooner?"

"I was asleep," I croaked again, rolling on to my side to face away from the door.

"Can you open up, please?" Mom asked, and though she used polite words, her tone was curt and impatient. I imagined she was out there with one hand on her hip, the other hanging by her side.

Fighting wasn't on my agenda today. I heaved myself off the bed and mumbled a sorry under my breath as I unlocked the door. When she flung it open, I was rubbing my puffy and crusty eyes.

"Thank you," she said as tugged down her shirt. But she didn't really sound that grateful, and it plunged me deeper into my own crappy mood. Mom usually is the bright and shiny one of the three of us. She can be a bit neurotic at times, but is always kind and warm. Today was different. Her lips were pulled in a straight line, and her eyebrows were creased.

In an effort to boost her spirits, I tried to make light conversation, even though nothing in me felt light at all. "Get some good cleaning done?"

She pushed a frizzy strand of hair off her forehead with the back of her hand. "I tried. But the café called. Mindy—remember Mindy, one of the baristas?—well, her son starting puking at daycare, so she needs to take off. I'm heading in to help for the last few hours."

"Oh, alright." Despite myself, I felt a bit disappointed she was leaving. It wasn't like I wanted to sit around and chat all day, but it was nice knowing someone else was existing freely in the house.

"Will you be okay here by yourself? I do hate to leave you alone today, Auggie. A lot has happened the last few days. I worry about you," she said, frowning. She was tired, and in a foul mood herself, but she was scrutinizing me. I wondered why. Was she trying to assess my well-being? Make me feel worse?

"I'll be fine," I forced a smile, keeping my voice upbeat to reassure her. "I've done it a million times before."

But it didn't seem to make her feel better. In fact, she just sighed and frowned deeper. "Keep your ears out for the phone, please. We don't want to miss the mechanic or the cops, if either happen to call. And empty the dishwasher for me while I'm gone."

"Okay."

"Door open or closed?" she asked, stepping out.

"Closed."

I heard her racing around the house, gathering her items and talking to herself as she rushed out the door. Not a minute later, the sound of Dad's engine growled to life, and Mom peeled out of the driveway. Listening intently, I stayed motionless until the truck's grizzle faded away.

It was perfectly quiet. This morning I had wanted peace. Now, I wished my mom had stayed to spend the day creating a ruckus all around the house. On a normal day, her constant clanking around is enough drive me up a wall. But on rare days such as this, I liked the reminder that someone else was here and human.

People are better than no people, even if people can be loud or in your business. The loneliness was much, much worse. An empty house was just an echo-chamber for my thoughts.

I blew out a deep, long breath, and reached down to the floor for my phone. For the first time in several days, I turned it on. My whole body ached, and right now I wanted nothing more than to talk to my best friend.

Once my phone lit up, it vibrated for almost five straight minutes. Never in my life had I received so many messages at once. It was bizarre, considering I only text three people. The final name to buzz on my screen, to be expected, was Isabell.

Clicking her name, I saw that she sent multiple texts each day this week, sharing her random thoughts and anecdotes from work. My phone buzzed again, with another from her.

I hope you liked all my cute little updates! Miss you, buddy!!!

I fired back to her using a million exclamation points and told her she had to call me as soon as possible. Returning to my inbox, the two remaining names were Tyler . . . and Landon. Seeing his name on screen dropped a bomb in my stomach.

My immediate reaction was to read his messages next, but I paused before clicking his name. I needed another moment to build up the courage. Did he send them today? Yesterday? Three days ago? I couldn't look yet. Thinking of reading his words made my hands tremble.

I opted for Tyler's message first.

August, you've gotta help me out. Does Isabell hate me now?

"Putting out fires all over the place," I mumbled to myself, contemplating how to respond. In light of the poison oak revelation, I did feel a *smidge* sorry for him. On the other hand, I was irritated that he didn't *tell* Isabell his situation. She would have understood, and instead, he caused my best friend very unnecessary heartache.

Putting a pin in my response to Ty, I returned to my inbox. I felt the blood drain from my face. Five messages remained. *Five.* All from Landon.

Tuesday morning: *Hey August :) been thinking about last night a lot*

Then, two hours later: *Right, yeah. It was probably a mistake. Won't happen again. Sorry.*

Again, two hours later: *It's better we stay friends. Much better.*

Another, close to ten at night: *Hm. Are we still on for thurs?*

Finally, the last message. From Wednesday morning: *Guess I'm going by myself.*

I read his messages over a dozen times, my eyes blazing. My thoughts raced at a thousand miles a minute, playing devil's advocate and arguing back and forth. Did this mean *something*?

No one sends that many texts in a row—especially not someone with Landon's confidence. It's common knowledge that double-texting is overkill. But three, four, or five messages without a response? Virtually unheard of.

Why would he send so many? With each message, it was like he took a step back. Was he was trying for a do-over? Was he nervous? Does he like me? Does he not? Do those questions even matter with the context of last night? There had been no messages since then.

Staring at the screen, it dawned on me that he was right about one thing: I had not told him I was grounded. I thought about the way I lashed out at him for not remembering, and the guilt started to trickle in.

But, shouldn't he have assumed I was grounded? We *talked* about it. Why else would I message him from a separate device? Did he have zero investigative skills? Just like that, I shifted back to frustration.

Then again, he didn't give me any update on the car in those messages, which was the other half of our argument. In frustration, I tossed my phone. It sprung off the corner of my bed and flipped to the floor with a small thud. Having the phone back was supposed to help the isolation, but why do I feel so much worse?

Taking matters into my own hands, I stormed out of my room to the house phone dock. I dialed the number for the mechanic and someone answered on the second ring.

"Yello," a young man's voice greeted.

"Hi. My name is August Moon. I'm calling to check on my mom's car. There's a lot of worry over the car and I'd just love to put the whole thing behind me, forever, please."

"August. Right. Gimme one moment, I'm gonna put ya on hold, kay?"

On hold, I blew out a low breath as my blood pumped faster. Less than a minute later, the guy picked the line back up.

"August, thanks for waiting. Good news, the car is ready!"

"Great!"

"Better news is, someone footed the bill for you."

"Wait, really?" If we had been face to face, he would have seen my wide-eyed blinking. "Are you messing with me? Are you sure you have the name right? It's August Moon."

"Yeah, really! Isn't that great?"

"Window and all? I mean, you repaired the window, and the tires?"

"Uh, yeah," he laughed. "Of course! Swing by this afternoon to pick it up. You'll be squared to go!"

"Wow, thank you. Is Buff in today?"

"Nah, he had some fam business to take care of."

"Oh, okay. Thank you, I'll be down this afternoon," I told him.

My feet felt a little lighter, despite the chunky boot. Skipping back to my room, I was elated to text Mom and Dad the good news. I passed the rest of my morning by doing the chores Mom assigned. In better spirits, I pulled a little extra weight with one load of my laundry and another one of towels. Anything to sweeten the day so my parents wouldn't be as sour.

Turned out the productivity was just a temporary fix. Once the early afternoon hit, the heaviness settled back in my bones. My phone finally rang with a call from Isabell, and at this point in the day, I was hesitant to answer. Not because I wasn't happy to talk to Isabell, but because it meant talking about the things weighing me down. Distractions are a good thing, I think, but they make the return to reality a little more jarring.

"What's wrong? Your voice sounds weird," she answered immediately.

I knew there'd be no hiding from Isabell. My voice struggled not to crack, thinking about all I had to tell her. "I went out to Whiskey Creek last night. With Landon."

"Want me to stop by?"

"Yes," I mumbled, "but it has to be quick. I don't want to push my luck with my mom right now."

"I'll be there in ten."

Grateful was an understatement. Everyone deserves a best friend like Isabell—a ride or die who will never think twice about being by your side. Some people in life stick around for the highlight reel, and watch from a distance as you fall. Then, there are people like Isabell. When crap hits the fan, they jump in to action. She arrived nine minutes later, and found me waiting under the apple tree with Solo's head in my lap.

"Tell me everything," Isabell said before she even sat down.

So that's just what I did. I told her about the weird texts I finally saw today, and the tense drive with Landon up to Whiskeytown. I explained all the details: the fighting, the fireworks, my dad, the cops. I told her how my dad had searched for the treasure himself, had a bad run-in with a guy named Edgar, and everything in between. My L-word confession. To Isabell, I spared no detail.

"Can you believe all that or what?" I chuckled, but I really didn't find it all that funny. Isabell was staring at the grass, her eyes blank. I didn't push her for a response. I sighed in relief as a warm breeze flowed beneath the tree, gently lifting some of my worry away.

After a moment she grunted and stood with her hands balled by her side.

"Do you want me to go beat him up? Because I will, August. I'll go and I'll ..."

I started to laugh—a small sputter at first, but it freaked out my dog. Solo pulled his head off my lap and sat upright. Isabell crossed her arms, but I was not a mocking her loyalty. I snorted, and she loosened up and sat back down. Soon, we were both howling, and for no particular reason.

"I'm sorry," I choked out between chuckles. "This whole situation is just insane. I needed a little unhealthy laughter."

"Me too," Isabell said, wiping away a tear. "But what are you going to do about Landon?"

Ripping up a few pieces of grass, I shrugged. "Nothing. I think it's over."

"I still can't believe you told him. And he said nothing back?" she clicked her tongue and shook her head. "How is it we've now been scorned twice by these boys? First, they string us along all year. Then, they don't even ask us to prom. Which, of course, we were never mad about. Now, this? I feel like we've been toyed and toiled and I'm ready to come at them with the vengeance of a thousand geese."

I coughed to suppress another laughter fit. "A thousand geese?"

"Don't get me started, Auggie. "You were there a few years ago when that flock charged at me," she said, pointing and narrowing her eyes.

"Oh, I *remember*." I shook my head at the memory, and cleared my throat. "Speaking of Ty though, Iz. There's something else you should know."

"What?" she asked. She was fixated on the tree trunk, scratching off thin pieces of bark.

"I figured out why Ty bailed."

"Stood me up, you mean." She made a face as she picked at some bark.

"He has poison oak," I told her simply.

"So?"

"That's what I said at first. But it's real bad. Landon said he can't get out of bed. He's been puking up a storm."

"Aw, what? Poor thing." She frowned, now looking up from her bark.

"The question now is what are you going to do about Ty?"

"I'm thinking I should probably respond to his messages. I've been ignoring them just a tad," she confessed sheepishly.

"Do you think you'd give him another chance?"

She shrugged. "I've been thinking about that too, Auggie. Maybe it's best that we don't date, you know? He's starting college this fall. I'm not sure about dating a college guy. And as I've said before, I doubt he wants to date a high school girl."

"Uh-huh," I nodded along, skepticism seeping into my voice. It was hard to tell what her true feelings were. Was she trying to convince herself it was for the best? Or did she really believe it? I didn't want to press her on it.

"The *real* question here," she grinned widely, repeating my phrase, "is are you really done looking for the treasure?"

At that, Solo jumped to his feet and trotted off. I took the moment to lean back against the narrow trunk of the apple tree and extended my legs out in front of me. Crossing my arms behind my head, I tilted my head to gaze through the branches of the tree. The tree was so packed with branches and leaves and budding apples that you couldn't see much of the blue sky. The branches were too knobby, the leaves too plentiful.

However, a few specks of blue could be seen here and there, but only when my sight aligned just enough to make out a crack of the bright sky.

I let my head swing side to side, continuing to search for those small gaps in the tree. Each time I shifted my head, I could see patches of the sky through different slots. Tilting to the left and right, I watched blue patches disappear and reappear over and over. It was very interesting, and though I'd done this before, now it was giving me perspective.

Sitting beneath the tree, I know the sky is above me. *Duh*, that's obvious. But from where I was seated, I could only see fragments of it in jagged, impermanent pieces. If I were to scoot away from the trunk six or so feet, and lay down in the grass, I'd be able to see the whole picture of the sky.

As Isabell's question hung in the air, she waited patiently while I shuffled with the breeze. I scooted away from the tree and the shade, into the sun. As I laid in the grass, I squinted at the sky as a whole.

"Maybe I need to take a step back, for a bit," I answered her finally.

"Until you're ungrounded?"

"Well, yes. There's that. But what I meant is that I'm too close. I'm on the inside. My perspective is tainted. I'm too easily swayed, to see what I want to see. I guess I need some kind of detox."

She crawled on her hands and knees to lay next to me in the grass. "That's fair."

I hummed in agreement, folding my hands on my stomach. My eyes latched on to a lone cloud drifting through the sky.

"All *is* fair in love and war."

TWENTY

Before Isabell left, we talked more about what could go wrong with this whole firework incident. For my part, I worried about Landon, and whether he faced more serious charges as an adult. For her part, Isabell assured me that if I had to go to jail, she would bring me a basket of muffins once a week.

Of course, all would have to wait until she returned from the road trip with her parents. Since she only worked the first session of summer camp, she was able to head out with her parents for three weeks of July. It sounded like fun, but selfishly I dreaded how bored I would be without her. The timing was terrible. It was the worst week of my life, and my best friend was about to leave town. *Great.*

Thirty minutes of hanging out with Isabell did wonders to brighten my mood. If I played my cards right, maybe I could convince Mom and Dad to let her spend the night this week. The very notion had me lighter on my feet.

That is, until the phone rang.

"Moon residence," I answered, scanning the bookshelf for a notepad and pen.

"Hi, is Mr. Moon there?" a man's voice asked.

"No, he's not. This is his daughter, August. May I take a message?"

"Hello, Miss August. This is Officer Jenkins, we spoke last night at the scene of the fireworks. Remember me?"

"Oh," I cleared my throat, "of course, sir. How can I help you?"

"As you know, we are dealing with a serious offense here. Fireworks are illegal in the state of California, and we are gathering evidence for an arson charge on top of that. Fires are no joke, and those who deliberately intend to cause harm will be brought to justice."

"Yes, of course. I agree." I nodded, hoping the shake in my voice didn't incriminate me. If he was trying to scare me, it was working. This felt like a preliminary interrogation.

"I'm glad to hear it. If you can come down to the station straight away, we'd like to ask you some questions."

"You see, Officer, I'm more than willing to cooperate. But, I'm here alone, and I really think my parents should know about this. They're working, but I know they can find time to take me in."

"Sure. When do you think they can manage the time?"

My face was hot, daring to drip with sweat. I swallowed the lump in my throat and wracked my brain for a coherent response. "Um, it's Friday today? Perhaps on Monday? Both my parents are busiest on the weekend, sir," I told him.

"Very well. Come down anytime Monday. We'll be expecting you. Take care."

The line went dead. I slumped onto a dining table chair, and my gut sank to my feet. The pick-me-up from Isabell's visit was now clouded by a new sense of dread—a world of trouble beyond the house arrest.

Mom pulled in ten minutes after I hung up with Officer Jenkins. I tried to snap out of my daze, so I relayed the good news about the car again.

That turned out to be a mistake. Immediately, her usual warmth returned, and I didn't have it in me to crush her spirits. Her only child, called down to the police station? It would wreck her all over again. Besides, she was so relieved about the car that she offered to make lasagna, our special meal, for dinner.

The two of us drove to the mechanic right there and then, which gave me a minor distraction from my all-consuming misery. Once we arrived, I kept my eyes open for Buff. I owed him *big* time. But there was no sign of him. I settled on asking someone to pass on my massive thank you.

With the car issue solved, a lot of the tension in our house diffused. When I heard Dad's work truck pull in, I watched him from the window. Seeing Mom's car, he nodded and knocked on the hood. His appearance was grey—baggy eyes, frowning mustache, two days of hat hair—and I knew I was to blame for his stress. I shrunk back and posted up on the sofa with my knees tucked in to my chest.

Thankfully, Mom's lasagna helped his case. As soon as he stepped into the house after work, he closed his eyes and took in a deep breath. When he opened his eyes, he smiled at us both, and let out a satisfied 'ah' sound.

As much as I was dying to ask about the fire, I stifled my curiosity to give Dad the lead. If he didn't want to talk about it, then I knew better than to dig too deep in my questioning. It was for the best to keep quiet. Any talk of the fire could easily transition to negativity —like informing them of the call from Officer Jenkins—and I wasn't about to spoil the meal that put everyone in a better mood.

Dad did offer one tidbit. "All's fine with the fire," he told me, without any more explanation. He wouldn't look me in the eye as he said it, and I wondered if there was more to this story than he was cluing me in on. Either that, or he couldn't look at me because I was a profound disappointment. Both scenarios made me feel like crap.

Mom chimed in, but whether it was for my sake or for hers, I didn't know. "Daniel, honey, what about Landon?"

"What about him?" Dad grumbled. He never had a problem with Landon before. But something about me and Landon alone in the woods put Landon at the top of Dad's list of unmentionables.

"Did you hear any news on what came of him? Is he fine, at home?" Mom pried.

"As far as I know, they let him go on the same pretense as August."

That was the end of it. But then Dad hummed. "That reminds me. Did the station call today?"

I fixated on my plate, poking at my food enough to wreck the perfect bite I had cut. "You see, Dad, the thing is—"

"They did call?" Mom interrupted, stopping her fork midway to her mouth. "Why didn't you say anything sooner?"

"They did, I'm sorry. Everyone was in such a good mood about the car, and I wanted to ride that wave as long as possible," I tried.

"Do they want you to go down to the station?"

I sighed. "Yes. They asked about Monday."

Mom was frantic, slicing up her entire plate of food like she was a surgeon trying to stop someone from bleeding out. Dad remained calm, eating his food at the same pace. He simply nodded. "Okay. I can take you. I have Monday off."

"Thanks," I mumbled. The table grew quiet, with nothing but the sound of utensils and the occasional sigh from Mom. My appetite was lost after realizing we resumed our earlier tension with disturbing ease.

After dinner, I sat in the backyard and toss the ball for Solo. Outside, I felt like I could actually breathe again. I stayed on the porch step long after the sun set—until the night sky flickered. The memory of yesterday crept in, and though I found comfort sitting under the moon and stars, I shivered and retreated to my room.

Despite being alone in the house most of the day, it didn't really want to sit with Mom and Dad. The air was too stiff. Knowing they were on the couch flipping between the news and evening game shows was enough to quell any feelings of physical loneliness.

It's weird—loneliness. Sometimes I think I need people around me to feel less isolated. Having company defeats solitude in the literal sense. If you're with people, you're no longer alone.

But what bothers me the most is the figurative loneliness: when you're around people, and still feel like no one sees, hears, or understands you. It's like there's no escape, and I'm trapped somewhere that I don't fit in. And I don't have the freedom to get out of town yet, the freedom to find where I belong.

I unlocked my phone, hoping to find a text from Isabell. When I opened my inbox, there wasn't anything new, and my eyes fell on Landon's name. I didn't think. I clicked his name, and typed.

Got mom's car back today. I guess I wanted to say thank you for helping.

I hesitated to follow through. After last night, the thought of reaching out to him first made me cringe. Except, there was a mushy part of my brain that figured it would be rude not to thank him, especially if he had any part in cutting the mechanic bill to zero.

Right thing or not, my thumb was indecisive over the send key. Would I look desperate? Like I was dying to talk to him? Did he deserve a thank you after everything he said to me last night? Ignoring my confession? It made my blood boil, but in the end, I decided to press send.

I waited and waited. With each passing second, I felt more and more like a fool. He didn't bother to respond—not to me, anyway. A couple hours later, Tyler texted our group in his sweet, oblivious kind of way.

Hi guys! How was the creek hunt last night? I was bummed I couldn't make it.

Poor guy. Tyler was so far out of the loop that he was practically in another galaxy.

Isabell: *Are u feeling better today Ty?*

Tyler: *Much. Thanks! Were u there Iz?*

Though I was watching the messages roll in on my shush-kabob, I stayed quiet. I refused to join the chat before Landon. He was quick to respond, and at that I scoffed out loud to my empty room. I swallowed my pride enough to send him a thank you, and he couldn't even acknowledge my message?

Landon: *It was shit out there dude. Whole thing's a sham. Consider me out.*

Tyler: *What?! What happened?*

Landon: *Hardly matters. I don't want any part in it.*

Tyler: *If you don't, then I sure as hell don't! What's with the sudden change? Was there another note? What happened?*

As I debated throwing the shush-kabob across the room, a message pinged in from Isabell.

Isabell: *So . . . what I'm hearing . . . is you guys lose . . . by forfeit? Time to prep those razors.*

It would be her final message, and I snickered at the little jab. She effectively claimed our place in the winner's circle. Even if we didn't find the treasure, even if we abandoned ship too, we still had this small pull over them. It felt pretty good to be the last ones standing, grand prize or not.

Tyler: *I'm not so sure about THAT.*

Landon: *You really mean to say you're continuing on after this?*

I knew that one was aimed at me—a challenge, of sorts. But it didn't bother me. In fact, I felt pretty good about the way Isabell responded, and the fact that I never joined in. He may have left me hanging before, but I suspected this feeling—of not knowing my stance—would drive him a little crazier than any unrequited thank you message.

Twenty-One

"That was horrible," I muttered to Dad, coughing in disgust as I strapped on my seatbelt.

"It wasn't so bad. I'm proud of how you handled yourself in there, hon." His mustache arched to form a genuine smile for the first time in days. If my mood was better, maybe I would have felt a little relief.

"Dad, it was a *humongous* waste of time. Nothing happened. They didn't clear my name. They asked for my story. Again. And reminded for the hundredth time how serious this is. Which, might I add, felt a *bit* offensive. Murderers walk through those doors, and sit in that same chair. I'm only seventeen, and I didn't do anything wrong. So why slap me with the lecture on criminal offense if there are serial killers that do far worse?"

His mustache turned serious again. "August," he warned.

"I'm *just* saying," I grumbled, but Dad was unfazed.

"Your job today was to cooperate with the police, and you did. By going in to the station, you demonstrated a willingness to assist with the investigation however possible. It's a step toward proving your innocence."

"But they said it could still be weeks until they find out anything else."

"Law enforcement has a lot on their plate. The process for these things can be time consuming."

I couldn't resist a snippy comment, and made a face. "Are you sure it's not just a low priority, given murderers on the street and all?"

Dad turned to me at a red light, his brow raised. "Why do I get the sense you have a distorted view of how many murders happen here?"

"*So* not the point, Dad. All I'm saying is they have bigger fish to fry, so I don't get why they're blowing time interrogating an innocent teenager. The Fourth is in a few days. It's not like they're making an example out of me because their 'investigation' is going to last weeks. Long past the Fourth. If they wanted me to be the poster child for the war on fireworks, they'd wrap things up already."

Dad adjusted in his seat. Clicking his tongue, he said, "I see you've given this ample thought."

Well, *duh*. All weekend, I ran over the details of that night in my head. Something wasn't sitting right with me. I conjured up a million explanations for what happened in the forest, and needed someone to confide in.

"Of course I did. I'm committed to getting the hell out of this thing. I'll tell you what, I care a lot more than the cops."

"Augustine," Dad said, his voice now sounding tired.

"It's true. I could solve this thing faster than them," I claimed, laying the groundwork to segue in to my theories.

"You may want to think twice before insulting law enforcement, young lady."

"Dad, think about it. Why treat *me* like the bad guy? With the way the fire started, and where Landon's metal detector was in the creek, there's just no way we could have set off fireworks and started the blaze."

He shook his head, keeping his eyes on the road. "You were so respectful at the station. Now, the cynicism? What has gotten in to you?"

His question wasn't meant to be answered. When a parent asks 'what has gotten in to you,' it's usually their way of saying you're acting out of line. I, however, felt like I was very much *in* line.

In any case, I had suspicions on what went down in the woods that night. The car ride with Dad was supposed to be the perfect time to share. Instead, he lacked all interest in my ramblings, and we rode most of the drive home in silence.

I was grateful Dad joined me down at the police station. But another type feeling gnawed at me—the inkling that I may be in this all alone.

It took a few days, but after a bit of delicate deliberation, I managed to convince Mom and Dad to let Isabell come over. They agreed that she couldn't spend the night. Isabell was leaving for the next three weeks, and whether or not I was grounded during her absence made no difference. I wouldn't have anything to do without her. It was nice of them, but at the same time, still harsh.

Once my parents went to bed, Isabel and I grabbed a few blankets and moved out to my backyard. The moon had grown a bit brighter since last Thursday, when Landon and I ventured to Whiskey Creek. I hardly gave a second thought to the fact the stars weren't as clear when Isabell started to talk.

"It kind of sucks that I have to leave."

"Yeah," I agreed, "but at least you'll be visiting colleges. I doubt my trip with my mom will still happen. You'll have to take notes for me."

"You know I will! Pics or it didn't happen," she said matter-of-factly. "Any word from Landon this week?"

"Nope. Tyler?"

"Nothing substantial. A few messages. All small talk. It's nothing. I'd rather not talk than talk about nothing, you know?"

In my periphery, I noticed her shrug. The crickets were chirping in the distance, a whole choir of them. Down the street, a dog was howling, like a coyote or a fox had entered the yard. Laying on the ground as creatures around us came to life was one of the only places I enjoyed the company lurking in the background.

"Hey, Iz?"

"Hm?"

"I know summer is only half over. Well, with how much trouble I'm in, my summer is probably all the way over. But whatever. Do you think it's been good?"

"How are you defining 'good' here, August?"

I grinned a little at her skepticism, but it soon faded. "You know, grand adventures. Exciting events. One for the books. What do you think?"

"Memorable, yes. It's been an adventure. And don't get me wrong, I've loved hanging out with you, but I don't think it's a summer I'd relive over and over. Tonight was great. Watching movies, eating popcorn, drinking soda. That's my kind of summer."

Even though it wasn't a dig at me, it stung a little. My drive—aside from a desire for a car, ironically—had been for an unforgettable summer. Somewhere along the way, it slipped my mind that the permanence of an everlasting memory was not always a good thing. Memories can be good and bad. In creating them, I had focused more on the final destination of the treasure than on whether the journey was actually enjoyable.

Worst of all, my best friend maybe suffered because of it.

"I'm sorry, Iz," I told her quietly after a minute had passed.

"Don't be," she said immediately. "I'm fine. It's been crazy, and a little freaky, but there's no one else I'd rather escape from a true haunted house with."

I chuckled. "I'm glad. It kind of slipped my mind that *that* really happened. Doesn't it feel like years have passed since then?"

"It was what, two weeks ago?"

"Wow," I blinked, "time is weird. It's slipping through my fingers, Iz, I swear."

It felt good to get it off my chest, especially because I didn't realize the thought had been weighing me down so much. Isabell seemed like she was going to say something, but stopped. She hesitated few more times before she spoke up.

"Auggie, just because it's our last summer before we turn eighteen, that doesn't mean our lives are over. It's really like they're just beginning."

"I guess you're right. Maybe I'm having some sort of quarter-life-crisis over here. Nothing interesting has happened to me. Sometimes it feels like that's a product of this place. I don't know. Every day I'm more and more ready to leave and start living for myself rather than on the terms of everyone else."

"Can you have a quarter-life-crisis before you're legally an adult?" she asked. I turned to raise my eyebrows at her, and she scrunched her nose. "Sorry. If it helps, you do a lot on your terms. You have this summer, anyway."

"I guess. But it's still under the scrutiny of being the only child my parents have to look out for. It's hard to get away with anything."

"It's really hard. Obviously, I've had Brett living at home most of my life. But after he moved out for college—as you know—it was hard for me as the only kid at home. I can't imagine how it's been for you your whole life."

I tilted my head back to check the house lights. They were all off, but I lowered my voice regardless. "It's not anything personal against my parents. The smallest missteps feel like a bigger deal when there aren't any other kids to worry them."

Isabell put her hands behind her head. "I hear you, but college will be better. More freedom."

"Ah, freedom," we swooned in unison.

"Only one more year between us and independence."

"Oh boy. Auggie, if this is how your summer went *without* all the independence you want, I fear for you after you get it." She laughed, and I did too.

We made a list of all the things we should do before graduating next year. The items were much more Isabell's speed—like going to midnight movie premieres, and attending as many football games as we can—but I was okay with that. As far as I was concerned, it was a fair compromise. Doing things my way, we failed at a treasure hunt and almost lost our sanity.

Once our brains spun out of ideas, Isabell took off and I crawled inside for bed. But I couldn't fall asleep just yet. I turned onto my side and eyed the moon out my open window. In the distance, I heard a coyote wail, and soon after the entire pack was howling. A cool breeze blew in, swaying the open curtains. Perhaps it was just my imagination, but it seemed to whip in and around me, as if attempting to lure me into the night.

I sat up on the edge of my bed, feeling the gentle tug of its swirl before it siphoned back out the window. Checking my clock, it was just a minute after midnight, making it officially Wednesday. I stepped over to the window and leaned on my elbows, my face against the screen as I listened carefully.

Leaves ruffled, and a bit farther off the coyotes barked. They paused, and at the same time, a slight shiver ran down my spine. For however brief a moment, as the air stood still and the silence of the night echoed, I could have sworn that in the far distance, the wind howled like the cry of a woman.

Twenty-Two

Three weeks had passed since our group collectively gave up on searching for the Ruggles treasure. Three *long* weeks. All the drama put me in a funk. When you're on the brink of something spectacular and the rug is yanked out from under you, it's pretty difficult *not* to fall down.

To make matters worse, Isabell was on her family trip, which left me high and dry. Okay, I guess it's not the *worst* thing—she's having fun, after all. She is spending a week in British Columbia for a reunion, and then another week and a half in Southern California for a wedding and college visits. It's all fine and dandy, but it would be better if she was here. Or, if I was there.

Or if Landon and I had spoken since our blow out. But I tried not to think about that too much.

One day, seemingly out of the blue, Mom suggested that I drive her to work, so I could use her car to do whatever I wanted. At first, I thought her offer was a joke. When I realized she was serious, I didn't question her on it. Instead, I took the keys.

She must have taken some level of pity on me with all my sulking. It was unintentional, I just couldn't help my misery. I wanted to wallow. Stuck at home alone all day without access to a car, in a house with sub-par air conditioning? Cruel and unusual punishment. For that, I thanked the skies for Mom's graciousness with her car. With all my time to think, I now had a few orders of business to take care of.

The first task was more investigative—more business than personal, one might say. The Old Shasta museum. I skipped up the steps and pattered into the building. Inside, I scanned the half a dozen faces in the room for one in particular. If the police and my parents weren't going to do anything, I had to take matters into my hands.

I must have looked like a woman on a mission, because someone came up to me right away. "Welcome to the museum! Have you been in before?"

"Yes, I have."

"Can I help you with something?"

Her question caught my attention, and I looked over to see her smiling at me with round cheeks. I nodded slowly. "Actually, yes. Is Dave working today?"

"He is, yes. He's right over there." She pointed over to a case, where a grey-haired, bifocal-wearing man was talking to a father-son duo.

I shook my head. "I mean the younger Dave. Is he working today?"

The woman tilted her head at me and pursed her lips. "We only have one Dave, as far as I know. And that's him."

"The old guy?"

The woman coughed and frowned at me. "The gentleman helping the little boy and his dad, yes. That's Dave. What business do you have with him?"

"You're sure there's not another Dave who works here?"

"Seeing as I'm in charge of all our stafff scheduling, I'd say yes, I'm sure." She crossed her arms, flashing me a fake smile. It hardly fazed me. My head was buzzing.

"Okay. That's interesting. Hm."

"Is that all?" she asked as she moved to open the front door for me to exit.

"Oh, um, yeah. That's it. Thank you." I nodded emphatically, glancing to her name tag. "You're Marissa?"

"Uh-huh."

"Thanks, Marissa. You have no idea how you just saved me," I told her. Her eyebrows raised, and her smile widened.

"Oh. Sure, sure! And you are?"

"August, August Moon."

"August. Well, it's a pleasure!"

I jogged out the door and back down the steps to my car.

I slid into the front seat and started the car, but before I took off, I rested my hands on the steering wheel. After a moment, I let my forehead fall between my hands. My intuition had been right. Something was very wrong here. I yanked out my phone, and without a second thought, I typed a new message to Landon.

Big discovery. Turns out Dave from the park isn't who we thought. Some soon-to-be-unlucky asshat is gonna pay.

I hit send immediately. Even though it kind of sucked, it felt too important to keep to myself. Sometimes, you have to put your differences aside to do the right thing, and that's just what I was trying to do.

My discovery at the museum shot me with a new surge of adrenaline. I wanted to figure all my crap out and put everything to rest. For the first time it weeks, it felt like things were moving in my favor. And in a stroke of almost perfect fortune, it also happened to be July 23rd. A day early, but that didn't matter. This visit was already long overdue. I just hoped it would be well received.

Stepping out of the car, the seer from the 116 degree heat wave dared to fry my skin on sight. I squinted up at the big, rickety old house, the sun reflecting bright from the faded, light wood. I paused, listening carefully for any truth behind the rumors. I had spent a fair time wondering about this house, especially after the cries I heard from my window a few weeks back.

But nothing. The silence was so pure it was ringing.

Right as I was about to turn around and give up, a sound startled me.

A loud, creaky groan echoed through the vacant home. It sounded like a whale, struggling through a lonesome heartbreak, to the point of scaring a flock of birds. They squawked as they fled from a nearby blackberry bush. When the throaty rumble stopped, it was quiet again. *Deathly* quiet.

Isabell would certainly be against this, and maybe she would be right. But, today, it was something I had to do. Swallowing the lump in my throat, I waltzed right up the front steps of Odette Dupont's house. I paused mid-reach for the handle, and knocked on the door.

A deep, subtle growl rattled the deck before fading back into a cry. My heart raced, and my eyes flickered between all the front windows, but I held my ground. If she wouldn't let me in, I would enter on my own. Again. This time, didn't pause as I reached for the handle.

Locked. How could I forget? Boot-free now, I maneuvered easily over to the unlatched window on the side of the deck. For the second time, I slid it open.

"Odette?" I called as I hoisted myself over the sill. Despite the sunny day, inside the house was pretty dark. Velvet curtains were draped across all the windows—something I had not noticed on our group excursion—and the air was cold and heavy.

I waded through the main floor, entering the formal dining area and then peeking into the living room. The house emitted another deep groan, and I felt like I was below deck on the Titanic as it struggled to stay afloat.

With nothing to see, I made my way over to the stairs. Stepping over the hole made by Landon, I didn't pause to look at it, or dwell on the fact I hadn't talked to Landon in weeks. It was a shitty thing to think about. I'd rather just get on my way.

At the top of the stairs, I noticed a lone window at the end of the hall. It was uncovered, and radiating light down the otherwise dark floor. As I wandered closer, it seemed less and less like sunlight. It was brighter, and white, and I had to hold up a hand to shield my eyes. A faint, high-pitched sound emanated from beyond the window, like a gentle wind chime. Scratch that—an eerie wind chime.

My eyes were finally adjusting, so I dared another inch forward. The white light snapped back into oblivion. I leaned in—thinking the window led outside—but there was nothing to be seen in the black abyss, save for a small, glowing orb.

A sudden screech threatened to break my eardrums and the fluorescent ball shot at me, breaking through the upper windowpane and tumbling into the hallway. I dove out of the way just in time, falling against the hall wall. Holding my breath, I watched as the twinkle began to take shape.

What the hell is going on?

I sat crouched in my position on the floor. Deep in my chest, I knew—this was my demise. The day that I pushed fate too far, and disturbed a haunted house for the third time. Why was I so stupid? To come here alone? Was I begging to be cursed by the supernatural, or dragged down into the underworld?

This was it. The end. I imagined Isabell standing over my grave with that sad I-told-you-so look. My father's mustache, turned down. My mother's eyes, dabbed with a handkerchief. Meanwhile, I'd roll over in shame.

Less than ten feet away laid a sort of human figure with a soft yellow aura. It was wearing a long dress, curled into a fetal position.

"Um," I coughed. The figure sat up abruptly, which startled us both.

"What do you want!" her voice rang. It was different than I expected, like a star sparkling.

"Are you Odette?"

She threw her hands in the air as she sat up. "You who barges into my home, uninvited and intrusive, does not even know *my* name? As the sole resident? That is rather rude and unbecoming."

"That's fair," I reasoned. "I'm sorry."

Her shoulders slouched, but then her radiance intensified, blinding me.

"What do you require from me? Do you wish to steal from me?" When she spoke, I felt the heat of her words.

"No, of course not."

"Berate me for information?"

"No, ma'am." I shook my head several times.

"Then good luck killing me."

She was swift, her long blond hair glowing behind her as she glided through the wall. I swiveled my head around the corridor, as if I was searching for some kind of answer.

I tiptoed to the door of the room she had just entered, debating my next move. *What do I say?*

Leaning in, I whispered, "Odette?"

She burst through the wall once more. "Leave me alone!"

At that, Odette floated like an angry cloud down the stairs. Again, against my better judgment, I slinked after her. She was in the sitting room, where Landon, Tyler, Isabell, and I set up our sleeping bags a month ago. Her gleaming figure was slumped over an arm chair like a cat that is perpetually disturbed while trying to nap.

I stood in the doorway, feet frozen in place. She shouted, "Tell me, young girl. *Why* are you here?"

It dawned on me just how strange this situation was. *Was I dreaming?* She was either a ghost or a freaky figment of my imagination. Perhaps she wasn't real, but I kept on. Though she never confirmed it, I did believe her to be Odette. And I knew I was overstaying my welcome. *Long* overstaying, probably.

"I'm sorry, Odette. For barging in here like I own the place."

"You think that because I am but a spirit that I do not possess feelings? Or rights? For shame!" she tsked. She dropped her head into the crook of her elbow.

"I know, you do. That's actually why I came by," I started. Odette sat up and narrowed her eyes at me. It sent a cold shiver down my spine, but I continued, "Today is July 23rd. I guess I'm a day early, but it was the night of the 23rd that John was kidnapped from his cell. On the 24th, he was hung, right?"

"Have you no manners? To speak with such ill-will on my John's untimely parting from our world?" she shrieked. Fire ignited in her eyes as she slammed a fist on the couch.

Serious conversations about death were not in my realm of expertise. I may make the occasional dark comment, but that's different. Standing in front of Odette, I felt awkward about my lack of understanding. I lowered my voice, "You're right. I'm sorry."

She closed her eyes, and I sighed. Resting against the door frame, I let the quiet hang for a moment. Then, I added, "Given that today is almost the anniversary of his death, I thought you might feel a bit lonely."

Odette grunted, "You are but a young girl. What could you know of this feeling I have? To speak so out of turn, to someone who is *clearly* your elder. Have you no manners? You must not."

"Again, I'm sorry." I held my hands up, backing away a few steps. "It's just that I also spend a lot of time sitting alone in an empty house. It really sucks, you know?"

As I peeled out of the room, I kept my eyes on Odette. Slowly but surely, she began to soften. Instead of buzzing with a vibrant glow, her aura dimmed to a light grey. She slumped further over the arm rest and put her head in her hands.

"Lonely." Odette chuckled. "Perhaps lonely is indeed a fitting description. But what would a young girl like you know about the loneliness that I bear? Do you truly believe what we feel is on equal terms?"

I sighed. "I'm not here to debate who has it worse. I'd never compare my isolation to the painful loss of the man that you loved," I tried to reason. The last thing I wanted to do was anger Odette *again*—thought that may be a lost cause. Whatever I said, it was never quite right. But she had chastised my poor manners, so I was giving it my best shot.

When she said nothing else, I took a chance and went on. "Have you ever heard the phrase misery loves company, Odette?"

She shook her head no, so I explained, "It means that when you feel like crap, it feels good to be around other people who feel like crap. I guess I thought by coming here, we would both be with someone who knew what it was like to be lonely. But I can see now it was a mistake, and I'm sorry for wasting your time and intruding on your space. I'm going to go."

I turned on my heel to leave, hanging my hat on the loss. It was embarrassing enough to confess out loud how I felt, let alone to a ghost that hated me. In some ways, confessing to an unbiased entity was like the release of a pressure valve. At least I'd take that with me.

I wasn't sure how I convinced myself this was a good idea in the first place.

As my fingers fell from the door frame, her voice called out, "Wait."

I paused for just a second, because her voice was so soft I wasn't convinced I heard her right. I stop mid-stride.

After a moment, I turned back around for another read. But I saw that she was sitting up a bit straighter, playing with the frill of a pillow. It was so tattered that I wondered if it was the oldest pillow in existence.

"I do suppose that there is no reason why we should not share a pot of tea, is there?"

I rubbed my hands together. "I don't wanna sound rude here again Odette, but can a ghost drink tea?"

Odette raised a single eyebrow. "Are you questioning my abilities as a partition? Have you no understanding of the concept of teatime? If I cannot drink the tea, I can still enjoy companionship over a piping pot of French tea had imported decades ago."

"Again, no offense Odette, but my parents taught me not to take goods from strangers. Especially if they're not willing to drink the tea themselves."

She crossed her arms across her chest and cocked her head to the side. "And my mother and father taught me that it is impolite and unbecoming to barge into the home of strangers, uninvited and unannounced."

"Fair enough." I laughed, and the corner of Odette's mouth twitched. "So how do we get this pot boiling in here?"

Odette rose from the couch and floated right through the wall, into what I can only assume was the kitchen. Not sure if I should follow her, I stood stiff in the sitting room entryway. I looked around as if I would find some kind of clue about what to do next. She hollered at me, and I scampered into the kitchen to offer my help.

Although Odette was French, she told me that she preferred the English way of making tea. Coffee was too much for her she said, and the tea give her much more peace. Her exact words were, "coffee is for the living, tea is for the dead."

The phrase didn't make much sense to me, but I let it be. I'd rather have a cup of tea than coffee anyway. And Odette had a really fancy tea set that made me feel like I was living out the ultimate imaginary tea party of my childhood. The China was white with beautiful pink flowers painted on, and a gold streak lined the opening and the spigot. I didn't notice the gold until we sat down in the sitting room together.

"Whoa. I love the gold on there," I told her as she poured our drinks.

Odette rolled her eyes and gestured for me to grab a cup, "Of *course* you are fond of the gold. You are a treasure hunter, are you not?"

After picking up my dainty cup, I was stumped. Did we mention the treasure while we were in the house? I couldn't remember.

"I—what do you mean?"

"That boy you were with," Odette started. She gestured toward the door, her French accent especially apparent as she frowned.

"You mean Landon?"

"*Oui.* He is a Jones, is he not?"

I set my tea down on the coffee table before I even had a sip. I squinted at her. "Well, yeah, he is. But how did you know that?"

"Oh, darling. Upon living in this town for more than a century, I have learned a few tricks about the people, their motives, and their *desires.*"

I wasn't really sure what I was hearing here. I tried to laugh. "Their desires? What? The people? Does that mean you knew Landon's family?"

"But of course! That Landon looks much like Frank, if I recall properly."

"Frank?"

"Frank, FJ, the night bandit. He was known by many names, and that boy you were with in the ballroom bears a striking appearance to FJ."

"You think Landon is related to him?" I asked her, my hands rubbing on top of my knees.

"Oui oui. I believe. Though I cannot say for certain," she said matter-of-factly. Her eyes were fixed on me.

My mind raced with a million questions about Landon, and the Jones family, and what the Jones' knew about treasure hunting. But as I was on thin ice with Odette, I did not want to push her too far on any particular topic.

"Guess we both have a thing for treasure hunters, then." I shrugged to Odette, reaching for my cup. Caressing it in my hands, I stared at the spiraling steam.

"Ah, so you *are* fond of that boy," Odette's voice sang. When I looked up at her, jaw dropped, she was grinning.

I huffed and stuttered, a feeble attempt to defend myself. "I do. Or, I used to. Or something. Whatever. It's history now."

Odette hummed traced the rim of her cup with her pointer finger. "It is a shame, I say. He is a rather handsome young man."

All this talk of Landon, my fingers itched to check my phone for a message from him. Instead, I steered us toward a subject change.

"From what I've seen in pictures and read in articles, John was known for good looks, too," I started. Her face fell, and as she stared past me at the wall, I worried I had said the wrong thing again. "Can you tell me about him?"

"Tell you what?" Her head whipped back to me, and her tone was accusatory.

"You know, was he funny? Did he tell lots of stories? What did you like about him?" I asked her, slurping my first sip.

She nodded her head like she understood, and turned her gaze over to the curtain-covered grand window. "He was not a funny man. Nor was he well-liked. I might say, he enjoyed how little people respected him. He was obsessed with treasure, much like a pirate, and he drank like one, too."

"That's what you liked about him?"

"Oh, don't be silly, child. Of course not. I am a Frenchwoman, after all. Romance is the way to my heart. So when I was walking around town with a few other ladies, and John made a sort of *feral* sound. Dear. I was *not* impressed," she paused to frown and shake her head. "Perhaps, I might have glowered at him, for his eyes widened. By the time I retreated to the end of the street, he had trotted the whole length of town to catch me and offer a small bouquet of the loveliest flowers." Just like that, Odette's grimace had disappeared.

"So did he ask you out or something?"

"Such courting was done a bit differently then, but indeed the pioneer women from the late 1800s had a bit more freedom than others. But I was not quite so easily persuaded, though his charm was much like a magic spell. For the next week, I saw him in town, as I walked the row with the other ladies.

"John, from what I could tell, was *not* a kind man. I studied him from afar, to determine how he discoursed with others. His expression was often very serious. Arms crossed, and brow deeply creased. But, when he'd observe me walking down the street, it all vanished. His cheeks, I recall, would fill with a gentle rosiness, to which I'd reward him with a small wave. He'd tip his hat, and shortly after come find me walking around town. John was never unkind to me, not once. It was a week of bliss. John, I knew, wished to marry me—and I him—but my father was set to leave for one month on a business venture, and we knew it best to wait for his return."

"Did you and John get married?"

Odette raised her eyes to the ceiling, before looking at me. "No, dear," she shook her head, "we did not."

I felt timid, but I asked anyway, "What happened?"

"The week of courtship took place in May, of 1892."

It clicked, and I nodded in understanding. "You met him right before the stagecoach robbery?"

"Yes. That is correct. A few days passed, and I had not laid eyes on my John around town. I thought, perhaps, he had abandoned me, that he had never really loved me. What is a woman to think, when the man she loves disappears without a simple farewell? One day, he arrived on my doorstep and begged me to take him in. He offered no explanation, and pleaded that I house him in secret. That if anyone were to know about his location, he could die. It frightened me deeply, but I'd rather live in risk than lose my dearest love."

"Did you know that he robbed the stagecoach? That someone died?"

"Once I agreed to house him until my father's return, he confessed to all. I would have learned of it in the local papers had he not. His behavior was odd while he stayed. He'd venture out late at night, for hours sometimes, and return once I had fallen asleep. The floorboards would creak as he stumbled in. Perhaps he was intoxicated. He loved his whiskey—though all men here did, of course."

"Wow, Odette. This is crazy," I said, blowing out a low breath. No one in the world knew this information about John Ruggles, yet here I was, listening to basically a first-hand account of him. Was this all a dream? "But, wait, was he found in Woodland?"

"Ah, oui. Your memory is quite good. After three weeks, he fled. It was no longer safe for either of us, he said. He promised to return for me. I did not expect his to return to be with the sheriff. I visited him in jail, along with the long line of women bringing gifts to him and his brother. But soon after, they were hung. And that is the end."

"If that isn't the most tragic love story I've ever heard . . ."

"You forget Romeo and Juliet," Odette reminded me, wagging a finger.

"No, I just think this is more tragic. Geez, I'm sorry, Odette."

Her golden aura was back now, and she stared me dead in the eyes. It didn't strike fear into my heart like before, but it was a little unsettling. She was unmoving, like a doll eyeing you eerily from a bookshelf. Shifting in my seat, I sniffed and rubbed my nose just to have something to do. That's when I smelled it.

"What is that?" I asked her.

"What is what?"

"That smell," I answered as I crinkled my nose. Setting down my cup of tea, I scanned the area around my chair. It was pretty dark, but I was able to see with the faint streams of light that were stemming from outside. "I don't see anything in here. Can I open the curtains?"

Odette gestured toward the curtain as she sat back and crossed her legs. I walked over and pulled the heavy, velvet curtains open. Dust caked on to my fingertips. Right away, I found the source of the smell, and I gasped. Though the window had a film of grime on it, the sight was clear as day.

"Oh no," I mumbled, staring at the dark, billowing cloud. "It's smoke."

TWENTY-THREE

"Smoke? What kind of smoke?" Odette floated over to where I stood by the window. Her hand covered her mouth as she asked, "Oh, dear. Is that a fire?"

"Looks like it," I frowned. I could feel my heartbeat in my temples. "I think that's my cue to go."

Odette wrung her hands together in front of her chest. With a little sigh, she reminded me, "A small fire bursts forth out here nearly every year or two, as far as I can recall. None of them have stirred much cause for true concern."

"That's true. It's probably nothing, but my parents will be worried if they aren't able to get ahold of me. There isn't that great of service here, you know."

"Service?"

"Nevermind," I told her as I peered back out the window. "What do you do when there's a fire?"

"Darling, I am a ghost, don't you recall? Do not waste your breath worrying of me. I have already passed. With a snap of the finger, I can be gone."

I squinted out the window, trying to determine the severity of the new blaze. Odette was right. Little brush fires usually aren't a big deal. They happen all the time. With all the undeveloped land here, a few hundred acres was really just the natural course of the forest.

"Well, since I'm still living, I better not take too many risks."

"Must you leave then?" Odette whimpered, and for a moment she seemed disappointed by my departure.

"Don't worry, Odette. I'll be back. I'm already in serious trouble with my parents, so I have to play my cards right. But I'll be back. Thanks for talking to me." I smiled, part of me wanting to hug her.

"I see. Alright, girl. Go on, go on. Make good on your promise, return at once."

I waved to her as I skipped backward out of the room. "Will you be okay here? You can always come with me," I pointed out.

"Puh!" she said as she turned her nose up. "No, *thank you*. I choose to stay."

"Okay, okay. Stay safe Odette, alright?"

"Of course, I *am* a ghost, am I not? You must go—and make haste, in case there is danger after all."

Odette could not touch me, but I felt an unexplained push behind me. I hustled to the front door and watched as the three padlocks unhinged at once. It swung open, and Odette gestured outside.

"Go," she urged. Next thing I knew, I was stumbling, falling face first onto the deck as the door slammed behind me. I thought we had made progress, but Odette certainly didn't hesitate to kick me out.

It's for your own good, a voice echoed from inside.

I sighed, and looking forward. In the yard, ash was falling like snow, and the air smelled like fresh barbecue. Standing, I dusted myself off and jogged over to the car with a pit in my stomach. Before I reached for the handle, a gust of wind whirled by me, and up in the sky I noticed embers kicking up and swirling around.

I gulped a lump in my throat and tried to ignore my rapid breathing. Fumbling in my pockets, I struggled to find my keys. With shaky hands, I climbed in to the driver's seat and started the engine. As I strapped on my seatbelt, I risked another look at Odette's house.

It looked the same, despite the growing smoke plume in the background. The windows were all blackened, save for one. Upstairs, a single window revealed a glowing orb. It was no longer yellow, or orange, or red. Instead, it was blue. A deep, cool blue.

I felt compelled to wave, and seemingly in response, the orb flickered, before going out entirely.

Heaviness set in throughout my body, but I finished buckling. A loud pop down the hill reminded me that time was limited, and I shot out of the driveway. High-tailing it out, I watched in horror as flames erupted clearly in to view.

The road was open, but the farther down the hill I got, the taller the flames were. Sweat dripped down my forehead as I white-knuckled the steering wheel. A section of the blaze hopped the road right in front of me, and I didn't have time to react. I shrieked as I plowed through—no clue if I was staying straight or veering off the road.

In that split second, my life flashed before my eyes. Of all the ways to die, burning alive in a car was not my top choice. My vision was splotchy, with specs of black and white and blue flashing before me. I must be dying, I must be . . .

Air struggled to fill my lungs, like I was suddenly choking. I had no idea what was happening, and just when I resigned that all was lost, the car emerged from the fire.

By some miracle, I stayed on course. My head whipped over my shoulder to see the road now clear, flames fanning on both sides of the road.

"Oh no, oh my . . . what the . . ." I coughed, still feeling out of breath. "What the hell?!" I screamed. Part of me wanted to stop and assess the damage, and make sure I was actually okay, but I had to keep going. There was no time to pause for any reason. Pushing damp strands of hair out of my eyes, I hit the pedal harder to speed out of the gulch.

At the bottom of the hill, I hit the highway, and still couldn't bring myself to stop. Farther to the west, cops were stopping traffic. I turned to head east back to my house. With the lake on my right, I finally managed to calm myself down a little. I watched the turquoise water glimmer, letting myself submerge in its serenity.

My ringing phone startled me out of a mild trance and put me right back on edge. Without checking who it was, I answered, "Hello?"

"Auger?"

The sound of his voice sent my heart pumping even harder. I was hit with a massive wave of nerves, but there was also a great sense of relief. "Landon," I whispered.

"Are you okay?"

I bit my lip so I wouldn't start sobbing, hoping to compose myself before I responded.

"Meet me in the parking lot of the Old Mill?" he suggested

Ten minutes later, I came into view of my meeting point with Landon. He was already there, which gifted me the ability to take a deep inhale and exhale all the air that had been trapped in my lungs. He was leaning against his car with his arms crossed, and as soon as I parked, he was rushing to open my door for me.

When he extended his hand to help me out of the car, his brow creased, it dawned on me that I had not seen him since that night up Whiskey Creek. Before I had time to dwell on what was running through his mind, he pulled me in to a bone-crushing hug.

Without Landon's embrace, my body would probably give out on me. My legs were limp noodles—either from the release of stress, or exhaustion. Or, the proximity to Landon. One of his arms was wound around my waist, while the other wove back in to my hair and caressed the back of my head.

I committed the moment to memory. The way he smelled like his usual pine and black licorice again. The way he gently nuzzled his nose into the crook of my neck. The way his fingers pressed into my side, clutching the fabric of my shirt and sending goosebumps down my spine.

"I missed you," he whispered in to my hair.

As if I could turn in to putty any more than I already had. My inability to stand on my own gave me all the more reason to hold him tighter.

Landon pulledaway, shifting his hands to my shoulders and dipping his head to look my straight in the eyes. "Are you okay?" he asked.

"I'm fine," I answered right away.

He cocked his head to the side. "August, what's going on?"

I pursed my lips, hoping it'd suppress a little cry. "Can we sit?" I breathed.

So we did. On the tailgate of his truck bed, I told him everything I could, starting with Odette and the house and driving through the fire. The words spun out of me like I was a spider weaving a speedy and messy web.

Not that I wanted to give him too much credit, but his listening skills deserved a gold star. I wasn't sure if I was making any sense. A lot of people might have grown impatient with my fast rambling. Landon didn't. He nodded along, like he understood my point just fine. It encouraged me to keep going and lay it all on the line.

By the time I finished, I let out a long breath. But it wasn't enough to relieve my anxiety. Without any warning, I burst in to tears. My emotions were running too wild. It was overwhelming— especially sitting beside Landon. I didn't even have the energy to censor my sobs, or wipe my tears, or think about how awkward Landon must feel. I just sat there with my arms limp my lap, ugly crying.

A few minutes passed before I took three deep sighs. Pulling my knees in to my chest, I tried to dry my cheeks with the bottom of my shirt. A piece of white cloth dangled in front of me, and I tentatively turned to Landon. Once I did, he nodded for me to take it. I grabbed it, and he rubbed a few circles on my back. It did wonders to soothe me, and I closed my eyes.

I sniffled, and dabbed my face to soak up the tears. "Do you just carry a hanky?"

"You never know when it'll come in handy." He shrugged. When I chuckled, he cracked a half-grin.

It felt nice to smile, so I sat up straighter and rolled my shoulders. All out of tears, I extended the napkin back to him. He shook his head, and I waved him off, "I'm done, really. Unless you don't want it. I think I just needed to get it out of my system."

Once he stuffed the hanky in his pocket, I rubbed my hands together as if wiping myself clean of the embarrassing cries.

"Are you okay?" he asked quietly.

"I will be. In the meantime, I feel like I'm going crazy. Talking to a ghost. Can you believe that? I shared a pot of tea with a ghost—the ghost we thought was mean and horrible, *made me a pot of tea*. I know, it sounds fake. But it's true, Landon, I swear."

Landon nodded carefully. "You've given me no reason not to believe you."

"Thanks," I sighed. A little gust of wind blew my hair, drying the remaining dampness from my cheeks. The air smelled faintly of smoke, and I chuckled incredulously.

"What?"

"How is it that twice this summer, I've been caught in the war path of a fire? Most people don't experience that once. I'm in a bit of disbelief over everything that has happened. I thought it would be a fun adventure, but—"

"But it was," Landon interjected, and I looked up at him. He was staring back at me with a fiery intensity in his golden-brown eyes. "It was for me, at least. And I have you to thank for that."

"Landon, thanks. You and I both know though that you pushed things along just as much as me."

"Well, I couldn't let you win *so* easily. It had to at least be a challenge."

"All's fair in love and war," I reminded him.

"Damn straight." Scratching the back of his neck, he asked, "Hey, August? You never answered. Do you think you're done looking for the treasure?"

I paused, but I already knew my answer. I'd stopped weeks ago, really, after our night up Whiskey Creek. Pursing my lips, I confessed, "I don't think it's worth it."

A silence fell between us, and it wasn't horribly awkward like I expected. Maybe it was my freakish sobbing, but an ice shelf had been thawed. Despite not talking for weeks, and trouble with the cops, and my cringey confession, sitting beside Landon felt like the most normal slice of my day. It eased my worries. It made me feel relaxed, like I could be myself.

I was glad the wall had been broken down between us. If there was anything I had learned in the last month, it was a healthy dose of perspective. Teaming up together mattered a lot more than harboring a grudge. We all need someone to lean on, whether it's a ghost or a teenage boy or a parent or a friend.

"True as that may be," Landon added, "I still have to say I'm sorry."

"Sorry? For what?"

He cleared his throat, "Well, for starters, that we never found it. And, for, um . . . for our fight when we were out at the river. We were supposed to be in it together, and I was kind of a jerk. Maybe I was hungry, and a little spooked."

"A little," I shrugged, playing it coy. "It's water under the bridge, Landon. It was a crisis, and we stayed *relatively* calm I'd say. People say a lot worse things in pressure cooker situations. And I played my part in it just as much."

He shrugged. "I guess. I've wanted to talk to you about it, but I haven't been able to."

"Why not?" I asked before I could stop myself. With all my might, I wished my voice didn't sound desperate.

"With the investigation, my attorney said I couldn't. Something about the information I was providing the cops, about the anonymous notes and what I knew."

"They asked you about the notes? Why wouldn't they ask me?"

Landon rolled his shoulders, looking to the sky. "I don't know."

"Huh," I hummed. It seemed weird to me that I was not once questioned about the notes. Granted, I did not bring them up myself, but I also failed to see how it was relevant.

"You know, the last month or whatever has sucked."

"Agreed."

"Like, really sucked."

"I know. Me too."

"I've been stressing the fuck out," he said with a chuckle, running a hand through his hair. "And, I made a decision. I just, I can't stay here anymore."

My heart thumped in my ears. It was so loud, I wondered if he could hear it. With a controlled breath out, I managed to ask, "What is that supposed to mean?"

"Call it getting out of town. Call it searching for another damn adventure. Call it running from your problems, but I can't stay here anymore. I guess I have you to thank for that, in a way."

"Me?" my voice was defensive, and a hand flew to my chest. "What did I do?"

Was it something I said? Was it because I told him how I felt? Or because I dragged him in to this mess? My mind raced with all the ways it was my fault.

"Nothing," he denied right away. "Nothing, you did nothing, I promise. I just want a fresh start after all this shit. My uncle lives up in the Trinity Alps. He said I could head up and stay with him for a while. Help out on his ranch. Learn the ropes. Enjoy the open air."

I sunk in my spot, a wave of disappointment crashing over my like a tsunami. Since Landon didn't want to go to college right away, I hadn't considered the notion of him leaving. It made me feel all the more stuck in this town.

Something clicked, and I gasped as I reached to clutch his arm. "But what if I told you about Dave? Remember? I texted you?"

"Oh, yeah. What was that about?"

"I went to the museum. The guy named Dave who works there? He's an old guy. Not a younger one like we saw. Bear with me, but I have a theory."

Landon perked up and leaned in with a furrowed brow. "Go on."

"We've clearly been followed, right? The notes, the shattered window, the whole thing," I started, and Landon nodded along. "So it's not out of the question they would have known we were at the park. My theory is that they trailed into the museum behind us, nabbed a uniform with a name tag, and posed as a park guide. In this case, posed as Dave."

"Posed as Dave, okay?" Landon scrunched his eyebrows together.

"If this false Dave was in fact in cahoots with these people stalking us, then he could have set us up."

"Wait, are you saying—"

"I'm saying I think we were framed."

Holding my breath, I watched Landon's reaction without blinking. His eyes were fixed on the dirt, his body frozen. After what felt like forever, I expected him to speak up and say I was wrong. Instead, he rose to his feet and stood in front of me. He reached for my hands and lifted me off the tailgate.

"August, you're a genius!" he finally said, picking me up and swirling me in a circle. Once he set me down, he wove his fingers into his hair, his jaw dropped and his eyes shining. I was glued in place, captivated by the excitement which he was looking at me. My blood seemed to dance through my veins, stomach fluttering and heart pumping overdrive.

What was he about to say? Or do?

"I have to go," he breathed.

"Wait, right now?" I whispered as he backed away.

"I'll call you later," he said, returning to stand in front of me. Placing his hands on either side of my face, without giving me a second to think or panic, he leaned down and kissed me.

Simple as that. Landon kissed me. I was kissing Landon. Holy mother of . . .

It was sudden, but very smooth. I didn't know what sensation to focus on most. His warm hands caressing my cheeks? The chapped texture of his lips, creating the perfect amount of friction between us?

Much too quick, he pulled away. In a feeble attempt to hide my immediate reaction, I curled my lips in to my mouth and held my hands over my chest. For his part, Landon was not shy in flashing me a crooked grin, one eyebrow quipping up ever so slightly.

"I'll call you," he whispered.

"Landon, I—" I was interrupted by a little peck on my forehead, and then he vanished. Without his hands, my cheeks still flamed. My eyes fixed on him as he trotted to his truck's front door.

Before he stepped in, he tossed me another gleaming smile. He was Landon, and he was happy. Confident. Effortlessly charming.

"August Moon," he nodded, "you may be my favorite person in the world."

As *if* my cheeks could flush anymore. I'd spend every penny to my name to buy a CD with those words recorded. I committed them to memory, but I wanted to hear them forever.

He spun out of the dirt lot, and though I wasn't sure if I could see me in the rearview, I mustered a small wave.

"Landon Jones..."

For the rest of the afternoon, I was buzzing. I paced around my house, double checking that my phone ring was on high volume. There was a tightness in my chest and a jitter in my stomach as I oscillated between anxiety and giddiness. The day had passed with such a dramatic sweep of emotions and I couldn't seem to hop off the rollercoaster.

I felt like I should focus more on the fake-Dave lead, but I obsessed over the details of my last interaction with Landon. *Our first kiss.* Each breath I took after sent a shiver down my spine. Then I'd get a flashback to Odette's, and driving through the fire, that I'd shudder more.

Finally, after what felt like years, my cell phone rang. My heart pounded wildly. Without looking who it was, I answered, "Hello?"

"Hi sweetie," Mom greeted. "Just checking in."

"I'm fine. Are you ready for me to pick you up?"

"Oh, no! Your father said he would pick me up. He's off early today so he can be on call tonight. Did you see that there is a fire out at the lake? Such a shame."

I rubbed one of my eyes before squeezing my hand in to a fist. "I did. Yes."

"Are you okay? You don't sound quite right."

"Yes. Yes. I'm fine."

"Auggie," she warned.

"I am," I breathed, forcing my voice to sound less rigid, "really, I am. I just . . . I'll tell you when you get home. With Dad. Okay?"

She sighed, "Okay."

Once we hung up, my phone immediately rang again. This time, I grunted, thinking it was my mom calling to ask me to pull out some chicken to defrost.

"What?" I answered the phone with a snap.

"You good there, Auger?"

I sharply inhaled. "Landon. Hi."

"Hi," he teased. For a second, we didn't say anything.

"Any good news?" I managed to ask.

"We're free. You were right. They cleared our names. I'll bet they give you a call any time now."

"Holy crap. Seriously?"

"Seriously."

I collapsed on to the couch, putting a hand to my forehead. "Thank *heavens*. Landon, whoa, it's over? It's all over?"

"For us, yeah. They just got access to security footage at the park, and confirmed that a guy stole a uniform and impersonated an employee. Hopefully they track down and arrest the guy by the end of the week."

When I let out a deep exhale, I felt like I was releasing all the pent-up, bad energy stored in my body. My muscles relaxed and stirred toward delirious joy. Sitting up, I chuckled. "I can't believe it."

"I can. You were right not to trust that pseudo-Dave. You know, I was the one who was too blinded by some superficial urge for the treasure," he said with a click of the tongue.

"Yeah, you know, with that treasure obsession you'd make a great pirate," I joked, thinking of Odette and what she said about John.

"Shut up. You know if I were a pirate, you'd be my first mate."
When I paused, he muttered a few curse words under his breath. He
tried to backpedal, but I busted up laughing. "Oh, uh, I didn't mean
it like that," he defended. "August, *please* say you know that's not
how I meant it."

"Fine, fine, I know that's not how you meant it. I can't say the
same about your subconscious though," I chided. He chuckled, and
I let my laughter die out to save him a small amount of his dignity.
"I guess they'll get the people that were sending us those notes
then?"

"Looks like it. We can rest easy for the first time in awhile, huh?"

"No more bashed in windows?"

"Hell, I hope so."

"By the way," I started, "if you had anything to do with the bill
being dropped, I just—"

"I'd do anything for you, August," he interrupted in earnest. My
cheeks flushed with heat and I didn't bother fighting my smile. "I
had some old debts to settle. And it felt like the least I could do for
you. I still feel responsible. I'm glad it's done with and over."

I wanted to ask about the slashing and the bashing, but thought
better of it. If those people were being locked away with pseudo-
Dan, and Landon did his part in offering that information to the
cops, then maybe that was all I needed to know. It was water under
the bridge now, and things were finally looking up.

And, perhaps more than anything, I wanted to start fresh with
Landon. To do that, I couldn't ruffle any feathers. I had to bury the
hatchet. I opted for a subject change instead, to keep us cheery.

"You know what the best news is?"

"What?"

I found myself smiling as I rubbed my hands together. "Now, you
don't have to leave. Since they cleared your name, you can stay."

His answer was not immediate, and the silence rang in my ears.
When he sighed, something in my gut twisted.

"August."

"What?"

"I'm still leaving."

"What?" I repeated, feeling myself blink much more than normal.

"I still want a fresh start. I want some space from the drama here."

"The drama?" I nearly coughed out.

"It has nothing to do with you. I promise. There's other shit, and . . ." he trailed off, leaving me wondering if it *was* because of me. "To be honest, you kind of gave me the courage to go."

"I did?"

"Yeah. I mean, we had a pretty badass summer. I kind of want to chase a new adventure, you know?"

Hanging my head, I nodded. "I do know."

I did get it—probably better than most. All summer, I'd been pushing for an adventure, wishing for independence. Maybe I would have done things differently if I realized I was contagious to Landon.

The more I thought about it, the more I realized it was a lie.

I wouldn't have done anything differently.

TWENTY-FOUR

In the two weeks before senior year started, a lot happened in my little world. Landon and I were dismissed as suspects for the contraband charge. Isabell and Ty started a let's-see-what-happens fling before he left for college. My mom let me actually work for her at the bakery, and get paid for it.

And, Odette's house had been demolished in the fire—the day after I last set foot in the house. It was destroyed on the same day John died in 1892.

On the news, her great-niece had made an appearance. The woman, named Jane, was ninety years old. Knowing her first name was my middle name, I felt my connection to Odette soften even more.

When the news anchor asked how she felt about the destruction of the home, her spirit remained lively.

"Oh, that old thing?" She laughed on my television. "You know, years ago, the community wanted me to tear the house down, and I refused. Now that it is gone, my feelings have changed."

"How did the fire change that view?" the anchor asked, nearly shoving the mic in the old lady's face.

"My Auntie Odette never traveled. Never! Can you believe it? In all her years, I never once saw her leave. It was as if she were confined to the walls of the home. The more she aged, the sadder it became to

me. I can't explain it. Dare I say, she was . . . protective of it," Jane tapped a finger on her wrinkled chin. *"Like she was guarding a most treasured secret.*

She smiled rather slyly. "But anywho. I have no doubt her spirit lived on in that home. She was so attached to that dear place. Now, my only hope, is that she is free."

After watching the segment, I wished to venture out to the ruins of Odette's house. Perhaps she was still there, awaiting my return. I had promised here I would. Shouldn't I at least try?

It wasn't the only thing I was debating. Landon was moving forward with his plan to skip town. One day, I went over to his house and kept him company while he fixed up his truck. I hoped to talk to him about the treasure, and our summer, and whether things were for better or worse now—whether our friendship was different because of the kiss and my open confession. But he never said anything about it. And I didn't know how to start a deep conversation with him. I hadn't a clue where we stood.

It didn't help that in the final two weeks before his untimely departure, nothing happened between us. In fact, I only saw him three times—once, with our whole group. I began to think the kiss was a fluke, an act of passion that didn't have much to do with his feelings for me. It drove me mad to wonder, and I didn't have the guts to out and ask him anything. Besides, let's say we were to start a relationship. It seemed ridiculous to get in to anything when his move gave us an expiration date. Watching Isabell and Ty start something, knowing they would soon be apart, I realized I didn't want that for me and Landon. If we didn't start now, there was a still a solid chance for a future start date.

Right? I hope I'm right on that one.

He sent me periodic updates and pictures over text, describing the mini-trailer set up he was creating in the bed of his truck. Every day, he seemed to be packed more than the last, and I wondered what I could say to convince him to stay. But he set his departure date for three day before my senior year started. Once his date was decided, I realized I didn't have it in me to try to stop him from going. It was his life, and his freedom, and he should do what he wants.

I would do the same.

On the other hand, I saw my best friend every single day. Once she was back from her road trip, we were basically inseparable, aside from the time she spent with Tyler.

The four of us only hung out together one time before Isabell and I started senior year and Landon and Tyler went their own ways. Maybe we would have done more as a group, but Isabell and Tyler seemed to be cozying up quite a bit. Though Landon and I flashed a thumbs up behind their backs while they were holding hands, it did put something of a wall between us. Our two best friends were together. Watching the happy couple nailed a flashing neon sign on the wall that read: *This could be you and Landon!*

But, for the most part, I was okay. It was back to me and Isabell against the world, our normal world. Our lives had died down quite a lot, compared to how the summer started. In reality, those last days were really as summer was intended. Staying up late, lounging by the pool, drinking cans of soda.

Aside from the budding relationship, something was different with the four of us now. Through our trials, it was like we had developed a deeper understanding of each other. We all carried around small, dark tokens from our experiences. But at least now, we could find comfort in one another, and know that in those precious few days at the end of the summer, we had exactly what we wanted.

Well, for me especially. I had good news to share with Isabell that I chose not to share with the boys. I called her on the last day of summer, two days after Landon left.

"Come over to my house, as soon as possible," I told her, hanging up before she could respond. Dutiful as ever, Isabell parked in my driveway less than five minutes later. I was already sitting on the front porch step, waiting for her, and from my seat I could see her dropped jaw.

With a massive smile, I skipped to her car and opened the door.

"Shut up! This isn't real. What? Auggie are you serious? What? How? When? How? How did this happen? Is this yours? You got a car?! WHAT?!" she stuttered. She had one hand over her mouth as she stared at the brand new, little black car gleaming in my driveway.

"Yep, all mine!" I beamed, grabbing her arm to yank her out of the car. "Come look!"

She wobbled over to it, touching it like it was fire. "It's so pretty," she cooed. "Did your parents change their mind?"

I pursed my lips, staring at my innocent, beautiful best friend in her state of shock.

"Something like that," I told her.

She squealed and jumped to hug me, and we both laughed and hopped around.

"Well can we take it for a spin or what?" she asked. With an eye roll, I smiled and held up the keys. She clapped her hands and climbed in the passenger seat.

"Where to?" I asked.

"The stars," she joked. I knew she was referencing the movie we had watched last night rather than the piece of jewelry around my neck. Nonetheless, I reached up to turn it over in my fingers. "Or, maybe, we go get a burger."

"Aye, aye," I cheered, backing out of my driveway. I had my best friend by side and a grip on my own steering wheel.

It had its ups and downs, but it was—without a doubt—the best summer of my life. And the best, I knew, was yet to come.

TWENTY-FIVE

That first day of summer is supposed to be one of peak freedom, of endless possibilities. But as I slipped into my jean shorts and favorite black t-shirt on the first day of senior year, I wasn't sad summer was over. Senior year was a different kind of start—it was the beginning of my transition out of here. I didn't want to make a big deal about it, but I could feel Mom's excitement bubbling through the cracks of my closed door.

Before stepping out into what would surely be an overly zealous hug from my mother, I laced up my shoes, which were a little scuffed with charcoal. I brushed the soot off my hand before clasping on my new favorite necklace. I pressed it in to my skin, and bent down to pull the shoebox out from under my bed. My heart pounded as I lifted the lid. I'd peeked in this box every day for the last ten days, but the glimmering pieces still stirred the same thrill in me. Today, a knock at the door stopped me in my tracks.

"Augustine," Dad called.

I shoved the box back into hiding and rose to my feet. Letting out a quick breath, I turned back to look at my book shelf, and the China set I now had on display. It seemed to give me the small bit of strength I needed to face the barrage of photographs awaiting me on the other side of my door.

"Oh, honey!" Mom squealed as I emerged.

"Jeanie, we said we wouldn't crowd her, remember?" Dad teased, giving me a small wink.

Mom didn't waste any time before she tsked him, "Hush! It's not every day that your only child starts her very last year of high school. This is the first day of lasts!" She clasped her hands over her heart. "We have to get a few 'first day of school' photos, don't we? Daniel, don't give me that look. It's tradition. We've done it every year since she was four."

"I'm not saying a word," Dad surrendered, gesturing like he was zipping his lips shut. "I'll even take a photo of the two of you together."

I rolled my eyes at my supposed ally. "Dad."

"Just one picture, Augustine," Mom fought. I resigned, knowing I had no other choice. After letting them get a few spots shots in, I insisted it was time for me to go.

"Drive safe, okay hon?" Dad smiled.

"I will," I shouted as I raced out the door. When I looked over my shoulder, Mom was snapping another photo of me at my car from the front porch. *My* car. Brand new. Pristine. The best bass in the stereo.

"I'm so proud of our little girl," Mom whispered to Dad, loud enough for me to hear. They waved and turned back inside, giving me a peaceful moment before I took off for school.

For the first time in my life, I turned the key to drive myself to school in my own car. As it purred to life, I inhaled a deep breath, the new car smell serving as a little dose of caffeine. Turning the dial to my go-to radio station, I backed out of the driveway and hit the highway to head in to school. Mine and Isabell's favorite song came on the radio, and I cranked it up. I faced the passenger seat with a wide smile, expecting to see my best friend beaming back at me, but she was not.

She wasn't there, of course. She was driving her own car to school.

Maybe it was for the best that we would be apart a little. If it was sad now, the separation anxiety of going our own ways for college next year would be complete crap. Spending thirty less minutes together *could* prepare us, I guess. Without my best friend by my side, I didn't jam along to the song like I usually would. At least, not at first.

Something felt weird. In all my wishing for this car, I hadn't thought about all the time I'd be missing with Isabell. For all four years of high school, we had driven together almost every single day. Now that we could drive ourselves, I was already nostalgic over the mornings and afternoons where we would catch up on the events of our days. I wouldn't get to hear about how her final days with Tyler were going. I'd have to wait until I got to *school* to be filled in. How lame was that?

I assumed the car would bring all the freedom I ever wanted. And it was a true, in a sense, but it sure came at a price. I spent what felt like half the summer grounded thanks to my quest for this car. Whether it was a sprained ankle, sneaking out for the night, ignoring vile notes, I charged on like a steam engine. It was the first and only summer that my big, grand plans didn't fade after that first day by the pool and its subsequent sunburn.

I still had that itch for freedom, as is normal for any seventeen-year-old starting their final year of high school, but thanks to the car, it was much more subdued.

A car honked next to me at the stoplight, causing me to jump out of my skin. I turned my head to glare at the culprit, only to see my bouncy best friend cracking up in the car next to me. Her window was rolled down, so I shook my head and did the same.

"I've never gotten you like that!" she croaked.

"I'll get you back, you know!" I yelled over the sound of both our stereos playing. "Wait, is that what I think it is?"

In response, Isabell reached for the volume and started to dance, belting the song at the top of her lungs. I followed her lead, and we rocked out together until the light turned green.

"See you in a minute, bestie!" Isabell howled at her window, flipping me a cheesy peace sign as she hit the pedal to the metal. I trailed after her, speeding the final mile.

The last time I was stood on campus, I had been both envying the seniors and dreading becoming them. Stepping out of my car, I realized I still felt a bit of that. Now I was them, or what they used to be, and I was still caught between that desire to grow up and live my own life, and a fear of that very thing. And there wasn't a class above me as a buffer between those worlds. They were on to bigger and better things, all of them. Landon, Ty, and everyone else.

Landon. Now that's a guy who has freedom. As I parked my car in the school parking lot, it hit me just how strange it was to know I wouldn't see him at school today. Or any other time soon, for that matter.

He was gone. Taken to the hills. Turning off my engine, I took a moment to rest my head on the steering wheel before embarking on the new school year.

THREE DAYS EARLIER

"So, today is the day?" I asked, snapping my fingers and rocking back and forth on my heels. We were standing in my front yard, next to his fully packed truck. He was on his way out of town, and my house was his last stop.

"It is," he nodded.

"Are you excited?"

He kicked the dirt beneath his feet, his white shoes blackened around the edges. Lifting his head, he smiled at me. "I am."

I squinted at his shoes, and then to the side of his truck. "Are those new tires?"

He turned to where I was looking and scratched the back of his head. "Oh, yeah."

"They're really nice. Lots of tread, sleek rims. When did you get those?"

"Um," he faced me with pursed lips, "a couple days ago. Why?"

"Hm. No reason, I guess. They just look expensive."

"They were."

My tongue begged to ask how he got the money to pay for them, but forced the question back down. Maybe it was none of my business. Maybe I didn't have a right to be suspicious. "Okay," I said instead.

He chuckled. "Okay."

With a deep breath, I stuffed my hands in my back pockets. My fingers picked at the folded-in-half envelope, tracing the circular object through the paper.

"Well," I started, but I was unsure of how to proceed. A million things felt left unsaid, buried beneath the surface. Part of me wanted to tell him—more than anyone else, including Isabell—what I knew. The secret I'd buried so deep and tossed out the key for.

Shaking my head, I crossed my arms over my chest.

Not the right time, August. Not yet.

Meanwhile, Landon was beaming. "I have something for you."

"What? Landon, you didn't need to—"

He grinned, in that way that made all the girls in the hall stop what they were doing to stare, and reached in to the back of his truck.

"Here," he said, extending a small white box out to me.

My heart pounded in my temples, but I steadied my hand before gently grabbing it. It was tied with a red ribbon, and when I unlaced and flipped open the lid, my eyes widened.

"Landon . . . I . . ."

"Do you like it?"

"Like it? I don't even know what to say."

"Auger, speechless? I hope that means you like it."

"I love it, Landon. Where did you even find this?"

Landon ruffled his hair. "Well, um, I had it made, for you. I know you like stars. I feel like you said one time it is a way to immortalize people and their stories? So, um, I kind of wanted you to have a little star to remember me by, too. And, well, a little piece of treasure."

Words continued to befuddle me as I stared at the little round necklace. The pendant was gold, and etched with two black stars.

"A little treasure? You're not saying this is real gold, are you?

"I am."

"Landon, I can't believe you did this. Where did you . . . How did you . . . Ah. This has to be one of the nicest things anyone has ever done for me."

"I have connections. Promise you won't forget me while I'm gone?" he asked, his eyebrows raised in uncertainty as he extended his pinky out to me. How he thought I could ever forget him was beyond me, but I played along, sticking out my own pinky.

"As long as you promise to never forget me."

He locked his pinky with mine right away. "Easiest promise I ever made."

Staring into his eyes siphoned all the oxygen from my lungs, and his gaze flickered all across my face.

"August, you should know. What you said to me the night at Whiskey Creek, I—"

"Landon, please," I strained, our pinkies still latched.

"I . . . love you."

"You *what*?"

"I do," he confirmed simply, like it was the most obvious statement of fact. "I love you, August Moon. And I know my timing sucks, like really sucks, but I couldn't leave if I didn't say it. I had to get at least one secret off my chest."

My head was spinning, and I sputtered out the only thing I could to diffuse the uncontainable excitement bubbling through my body. "What else aren't you telling me then, Landon?" I challenged, but a smile broke out across my lips.

He tossed my pinky and quipped a crooked grin. "Hey Auger," he said with his hands up, "all's fair in love and war, right?"

I shook my head, and he stepped closer to me. Bowing his head, he kissed me for only the second time ever. I gripped his hands, which were clutching my face. Once he pulled away, he rested his forehead to mine.

It was quick—much too quick, again. With that, I knew, that it was a goodbye.

"Do you really have to go?" I whispered in between breaths.

Weaving a hand into my hair, and sliding the other down to my waist, he wrapped me in a tight hug. He was hovering dangerously close to the envelope in my back pocket, and I debated for the umpteenth time whether to give it to him. As much a tried to work up the courage, I couldn't bring myself to do it.

Landon *loves* me. *Me.* Handing him the letter had potential to ruin everything, and I refused to spoil this perfect moment.

The letter would have to wait.

As we pulled apart, he scoffed. "Come on, August. It may be goodbye now, but trust me. This isn't over."

"If you say so," I teased, smiling despite the wrench in my gut. I hated feeling like this was the last I'd be seeing of him.

I escorted him over to his truck, my arms feeling twenty pounds heavier as they opened his door for him. He hopped in, and I caught a glimpse of a familiar handkerchief sitting in the cup holder of his car. It was the one he let me borrow. I failed to realize before, but it was the same one I nabbed from Odette's house the night of the haunting. It was a little odd, but not worth commenting on. I'd rather get through this goodbye, try not to cry, and get on my way.

But it sucked. As Landon would say, it *really* sucked.

"Bye, Auger." He waved out his open window as he kicked his car to life.

After his car disappeared down the driveway, I exhaled all the pent up air in my chest. Plucking the envelope out of my back pocket, I tracked back inside to my room. I slid out the shoebox from under my bed.

Cross-legged on the ground, I tore open the loosely sealed envelope, and gingerly freed the gold coin from within. I flipped it over in my fingers a few times, the shine calming me as I took three deep breaths. Tucking it back in the envelope with its letter, I studied Landon's name on the front before storing it safely in the box with the rest of the goods.

After that, I stood and moved to the bathroom. Facing the mirror, I looked myself in the eyes, wondering for the millionth time this week whether I liked what I saw. With a roll of my shoulders, I disregarded the thought. I flipped my hair to one side and clasped on the new necklace. Once it was on, I leaned in close to examine the two little stars.

Of all the stars in this universe, the story of these two were my favorite. And I hoped with all my might that Landon was right.

We were still unfinished.

THE END

ACKNOWLEDGMENTS

My first published book. This is surreal! I don't really know what to say here, but I'll do my best.

When I first decided not to return to grad school in the spring of 2021, I was hesitant. Not go to school? Pursue starting my own publishing business? Write books? Live out my childhood dream? Surrender to a bit of financial uncertainty? It's been a crazy year since I made that decision, and I'm very fortunate to be surrounded by people that have done nothing but build me up.

First of all, my best friend and supportive partner, Alec. Some people might freak out when their girlfriend decides to drop everything and write books at home all day, but not Alec. He has cheered me on, boosted my spirits in times of doubt, and smiled at me across the room countless times now. As this first person to read this book, he graciously helped me by pointing out the typos I missed—even though I did not make that easy for him! For that, I am eternally grateful!

My parents, Jim and Susan, who understood my decision to go down this path. They've read so many stories and writings of mine since I was a kid, and having parents that encouraged this pursuit has been such a fortunate experience. My sister Jamie and brother Chase, too. Talking with them about publishing and books and sharing the cover with them has been so fun. My grandparents,

Mary, Jerry, and Donna. I joke that they are my honorary marketing agents because they brag about my books to whoever will listen!

Really, I just can't believe this is out in the world now! Thank YOU, dear reader. It means more than I can express that you chose to read my book. Of all the things you could be doing, you read this. My book. By choice! That's pretty remarkable.

Thank you!

About Author

M.P. Heller grew up in the foothills of Northern California, filling up notebooks with stories and writing chapters of books on her phone late into the night. She has always been a fan of young adult novels, and books that center around human relationships.

When not writing and scribbling down notes, M.P. loves to walk down to the ocean, do crosssword puzzles, re-watch her favorite TV shows over and over, and go camping. She can often be found sitting outside a coffee shop with her laptop, crafting her next book with the help of a strong latte.

ALTERNATE ENDING

Interested in how things could have gone differently for August and crew?

How would things have been different if the fire that destroyed Odette's house actually destroyed whole neighborhoods? Would August's perspective have changed? Would the group need the treasure more than ever?

Luckily, I have five chapters of an alternate ending! And they're yours for the taking. You can head to the site below and access the *original* ending this very book!

Here it is!

https://www.subscribepage.com/augustmoonaltend

By signing up, you will also receive updates on future book releases of mine. Joining my newsletter means access to behind the scenes content, free short stories here and there, and first-hand info on all story ideas, titles, and book covers! I only send an email every two weeks.

Made in the USA
Las Vegas, NV
27 March 2022

46376570R00155